The Monster

He gaped . . . his heart began to pound. He had seen sharks in the waters off Messina, as a boy. He had seen them on TV. They bore no relation to the monster on the film . . .

Above a cowering scuba diver loomed an enormous shadow, blending into a mammoth mouth studded with gray-white teeth. It looked like the garage door to his mansion on the Knolls.

A chill began in his gut, spread to his legs and arms, weakening him. *Johnny was on the ocean, and the shark could still be there.*

The monster on the film could smash a boat like his son's to powder, razor his boy in half with a flick of the tail, guillotine him with a fin, grind his flesh to pulp and his brain to water.

"Jesus . . ." he gasped.

JAWS 2

JAWS 2

A novel by Hank Searls.

Based on the screenplay by Howard Sackler and Dorothy Tristan.

BANTAM BOOKS • TORONTO • NEW YORK • LONDON

JAWS 2
A Bantam Book / April 1978
2nd printing
3rd printing
4th printing
5th printing
6th printing
7th printing
8th printing
9th printing

ISBN 0-553-11708-4

Published simultaneously in the United States and Canada

Bantam Books are published by Bantam Books, Inc. Its trademark, consisting of the words "Bantam Books" and the portrayal of a bantam, is registered in the United States Patent Office and in other countries. Marca Registrada. Bantam Books, Inc., 666 Fifth Avenue, New York, New York 10019.

PRINTED IN THE UNITED STATES OF AMERICA

JAWS 2

PART ONE

1

A flattened, blood-red sun rose dead ahead.

The white Hatteras powerboat, *Miss Carriage* out of Sag Harbor, slithered around Montauk Point. She emerged from Long Island Sound and rose to the swell of open ocean. The two half-suited Scuba divers high on her flying bridge took wider stances.

The taller of the two, an obstetrician from Astoria General on Long Island, flicked off the running lights. The shorter was a Manhattan attorney for Union Carbide. The two had little in common except an interest in diving, diminishing as they aged, and a partnership in the boat. They almost never met except on summer weekends.

Years ago the doctor had decided that his little partner was a Jewish pinko, and simply accepted it. The lawyer sensed bigotry but ignored it. Friends or not, each had some $30,000 in the boat, and there was the security of a known companion. Each was sure that the other was a steadier diver than himself.

Every year, the physician dreaded the first few scallop dives of spring. Equipment always felt strange at first. The water would be cold and cloudy. And here, off Amity Township, lurked a ghost.

The beast was dead. The doctor had all but forgotten the stories in the *Long Island Press*. The Manhattan lawyer seldom thought of the pictures the *Times*. But a secret half-tone specter swam in the subconscious of each.

The doctor was suddenly cold. He glanced at the recording fathometer tracing the depth. They were searching for a clump of bottom-rocks they knew, but the graph on the instrument was still flat as the trace of a terminal patient in Intensive Care. The doctor pictured mud below, and silt.

He shivered and swung down the flying-bridge ladder. He tugged his neoprene upper-suit from behind a tank-rack in the cockpit, and squirmed into it. He had put on weight.

Even after he smoothed it on, he was still shivering. He stepped into the cabin. He had not got his sealegs yet. Crossing to the stainless galley stove behind the service bar, he lurched into a rattan barstool and knocked it over. He swore softly and set it up. Then he moved behind the counter and took two cups from a rack. He poured a double slug of Old Grandad into his cup and a single into his partner's, then filled the cups with coffee from the stove. He started out, remembered that it was impossible to carry two cups up the ladder to the flying bridge, and sat down at the lower steering-station to sip the stronger one below.

The groundswell, which was making him queasy, told him that they were paralleling the beach too closely offshore. He gazed for a moment, through binoculars, out the starboard window. The gray summer cottages of Napeague, Amagansett, East Hampton and Sagaponack slumbered less than half a mile away. In them, early tenants would be awakening to the gut-growl of the boat's twin Chryslers. A child poked along the tide-flats, teased to run by a huge woolly dog. The doctor found a strange comfort in the cottages and decided after all not to ask his partner to move further out.

The sound of the engines suddenly diminished to a quiet chortle. Obviously, the first trace of the fathometer had sprung to life.

The doctor slipped down from the lower helmsman's seat. He hesitated, then slugged down the drink he had intended for the man topside. He went forward and dangled a stainless Danforth anchor until he felt the bottom some 30 feet below. As his partner backed slowly, he paid off chain and line. Finally he snubbed the line on a bow-cleat, and signaled his partner that the hook was properly set.

Sidling aft along the narrow deck outboard of the cabin, he glanced at the shoreline. All the shoulder-to-shoulder communities lining Long Island dunes had always looked the same to him, but he was pretty sure he had anchored on the doorstep of Amity.

The Great White swam south, 20 feet below the surface, leaving Block Island to her right. She came left, dead on course for Montauk Point.

She was gravid with young in both uteri and her hunger was overwhelming. She had fed last night off Nantucket on a school of cod and all night long she had held course southwest along the coast of Rhode Island. She had swept into Newport Bay and found nothing, banked gracefully like a cargo plane, and resumed her track south. Her six-foot high tail propelled her bulk with stiff, purposeful power.

Before her, an invisible cone of fear swept the sea clean, from bottom to surface. For a full mile ahead the ocean was emptying of life. Seals, porpoises, whales, squid, all fled. All had sensors—electromagnetic, aural, vibratory, or psychic—which were heralding her coming. As she passed, the Atlantic refilled in her wake.

Man would have ignored such sensors, if he still

had them, in favor of intelligence. But man was not her normal prey.

To overcome the clairvoyance of her quarry, she was ordinarily swifter than whatever animal she pursued. Her food included almost any creature of worthwhile size that swam, floated, or crawled in the ocean. But she had become so large, near term, that her speed was down.

She grew more ravenous with every mile that passed.

Halfway down the anchor-line the doctor paused. His panting, amplified in his regulator, was earsplitting. He was sure his partner, descending in a green flowering of bubbles 10 feet below him, could hear every gasp. Clinging to the half-inch rope, he tried to relax.

Hyperventilation in the first dive was normal. But if he could not slow his breathing he would be out of air and forced to surface in ten or fifteen minutes. There was pride involved. Despite his size and greater metabolic requirements, his tank always outlasted the smaller man's. He could not understand the apprehension that was making him pant.

When his respiration eased, his ears began to ache. He jammed his mask tightly against his face, wheezed air through his nose, and cleared his Eustachian tubes.

He resumed his descent. Visibility was better than he had expected—15 feet or more—but he had already lost his partner. When he reached the bottom, he followed the anchor line along the sand until it became chain. Fifteen feet further he found the lawyer in a cloud of silt, trying to bury the Danforth against the outgoing tide. He assisted in this and finally they had the anchor-flukes buried.

The lawyer glanced at his wrist compass,

jerked his thumb toward the north, and began to swim back along the track they had taken, searching for the clump of rocks. The doctor followed, cruising five feet above the bottom and off his partner's left hip. He began to feel at home again. His heart had stopped hammering. His three-shot breakfast was working through his system, calming him wonderfully.

Swimming along, he glanced at his partner and found himself smiling. The little attorney was burdened with all the equipment that money could buy. His mask was prescription-ground so that he needed no glasses. He wore a pressure-equalizing vest. This was its maiden voyage, and he kept climbing and descending as he tried to regulate it.

On the lawyer's left wrist was the compass, and on his right an underwater watch to give him bottom time. From his neck dangled a Nikonos underwater camera. They had used it last year and found the light below too weak, so now it had a strobe.

Strapped to the lawyer's left calf was a Buck diving knife; on his right leg was an aluminum scallop-iron for their prey.

He looked, thought the doctor, like Dustin Hoffman in *The Graduate*, hiding from the festivities at the bottom of his parents' swimming pool.

Dawn had begun to shimmer faintly down to her as she passed Montauk. Her eyes were black, flat, and unblinking, giving her an air of profound wisdom. Her pupils were mirror-polished inside, so she had excellent vision even in this dim light. But she continued to navigate as before, blindly and mindlessly as a computer would, using the electroreceptor *ampullae* which covered her head to sense the orientation of the earth's magnetic field.

Two years before, not far from here, she had been hit by a male not much smaller than she. Grasping her dorsal in his jaws, he had somehow borne her, despite her superior strength, to the muddy bottom. There, passive and supine, she had received both of his yard-long, salami-shaped claspers into her twin vents.

Her back, though her skin was composed of thousands of tiny teeth itself, was still scarred from his grip.

Even before her pregnancy she had outweighed her passing mate and any creature in the seas except for some cetaceans and her own harmless relatives, the basking and whale-shark.

At 30 feet and almost two tons, she was longer than a killer whale and heavier by half.

Now, near term, her girth was enormous. In her left uterus squirmed three young. In her right lived five, three females and two males. The smallest was a little over three feet long and weighed only 22 pounds. He was, nevertheless, a fully functional being. He had survived *in utero* for almost two years, eating thousands of unfertilized eggs and, with his remaining brother and sisters, some 30 weaker siblings.

He himself was not out of danger yet, especially from his sisters, who were uniformly larger than males. If the mother hunted successfully for the next few weeks, her egg production would satisfy his siblings and he would probably live.

If he successfully fought off his sisters, he would be born at the top of the oceanic feeding triangle.

Already, he feared no kind but his own.

The lawyer slowed and the doctor almost overran him. His partner was pointing to the left. The doctor turned his head. He saw a shape, tinged darker green than the pale water through which they swam. It was not the clump of rocks they had dived last year. It was abrupt, angular, man-made.

Excitedly, his partner swam toward it. The doctor followed. The stern of a wrecked fishing boat, bigger and heavier than their own, loomed from the murk. Green shards of light played on her barnacle-covered transom. She was an immensely rugged old craft. The growth on her twisted planks told them that she had been here for some time.

The doctor spotted a heavy hawser lying along the sand. It led below the half-buried quarter of the hulk. He pulled himself along it, jerked at the line, could not move it. He rounded the stern to see where it led on the other side. The lawyer porpoised along beside him, trying to adjust his buoyancy.

The doctor found the other end of the rope. Secured to it by a giant shackle, a 55-gallon iron drum bumped restlessly against the hull. It was crushed and dented, but the remains of yellow paint showed that it had once been meant as a float.

The current swept it suddenly against the hulk with a mournful clang. The Old Grandad left the doctor's veins in a rush. He was very cold.

The lawyer had swum aft. He was rubbing at the seagrass whiskers growing on the stern. He suddenly yanked his scallop-iron from its scabbard and chiseled loose a half-dozen barnacles, loosening a mist of mud. When the water cleared, the doctor could read, in faint orange letters, the name *Orca*, home port *Narragansatt*. The name chorded some deep memory. He looked at his partner.

Behind the lawyer's face-plate, enlarged by the prescription lenses, he saw his companion's gray eyes crinkle in thought. Suddenly the lawyer jammed a fist into a palm, remembering something. Excitedly, he began to grunt, their signal for something out of the ordinary. He waved toward the orange letters. Then he took both hands, fingers clawed like teeth, and swept them through the motion of huge jaws closing.

He pointed again at the name on the shattered stern. The doctor understood.

The half-forgotten news story of a shark-fisherman, a tank-town police chief, and some oceanographic expert or other, read long ago in the *Long Island Press*, surfaced in his mind.

He discovered that he did not like it here. They were after scallop, not wrecks, and anything of souvenir value must have been salvaged by other divers long ago. He found, in fact, that he was no longer even interested in the scallops. His breath was rasping again and his heart hammering, and he felt the first indications of low tank pressure.

He pointed to the surface, but his companion shook his head, tapped the camera, and drew him to a position by the stern. He planted him under the overhang of the sternboards. Then the lawyer backed off, camera-to-faceplate.

The doctor pointed obediently at the letters on the transom, smiling idiotically around his mouthpiece. His partner, trying to stand erect on the bottom, seemed to take forever.

The doctor had suddenly to urinate. The strange apprehension he had felt all morning gripped his bladder and squeezed it tight. When he could wait no longer he simply voided into his wet-suit pants. The warmth of it was good along his side, but did not help the chill in his gut.

He heard the *clunk* of the steel barrel against the hulk, and felt it through his glove where he held to the plank. He could hear his own hoarse gasping and his companion's breath as well.

The strobe light fired, turning everything momentarily white. All at once he heard a sound like a subway train, fast approaching from his rear. His partner, dancing on sand as he tried to balance in the current, wound his camera, then stopped. He stared at something approaching from above and behind the doctor. His mouthpiece fell from his face.

The doctor, startled, began to turn but instinctively hunkered down instead, clinging to a broken plank. His eyes were riveted on his companion. A great bubble soared from his partner's mouth. The lawyer threw up an arm to protect himself. The camera strap fouled and the strobe fired again, illuminating everything and making the doctor feel naked.

The green surface light faded. An enormous bulk, descending like a gliding jet, swept by, a foot above the doctor's head, blotting out the dancing sunlight. It seemed to pass forever. The last of the shape became a tail, towering taller than himself. It swished once, almost sweeping him loose and blotting his view of his partner in a cloud of bottom-silt and mud.

There was silence. The barrel clanged.

The doctor clung to the splintered plank, peering into the settling murk. He could hear only his own tortured breathing. He was terrified at the loudness of it, and of his bubbles, beckoning whatever it was back to the spot. But he could not quiet the panting, and he could not budge from the stern.

One of his partner's diving fins bounced past, heading to sea on the tidal current. He could have reached out and touched it. He made no move.

It was fear that finally drove him from shelter. He became more frightened of dying where he was with an empty tank than of discovery. Tentatively, he moved a few feet from the stern and waited. Nothing happened. In a burst of courage, he kicked off.

He remembered to rise no faster than his bubbles,

remembered to kick slowly and steadily without panic—for whatever it was would be attuned to panic—remembered, as the depths turned from dark green to shimmering jade, to breathe and breathe again, so that the expanding air in his lungs would not burst them—though the noise of his breathing terrified him. He remembered, when he surfaced into golden sunlight, to shift his mouth from regulator to snorkel. He remembered to drop his weight belt for easier swimming. And he remembered, for a while, to kick with a careful, pedaling motion so as not to splash the surface with his fins.

He eased his head from the water. The Hatteras slapped at anchor hardly a hundred feet away. His fear diminished. A rush of joy that it was he who had survived, a flow of ecstasy almost sexual, warmed his veins.

Carefully, he slithered toward the boat. He hardly broke the water. Once he stopped and glided, gazing straight down. He saw nothing but shafts of emerald light lancing the depths below.

He raised his head. A thousand yards beyond the boat slept the houses by the dunes. Two tiny figures raced along the tide line. It seemed an eternity since he had seen them from the cabin, but it was the same child, same woolly dog. He could hear the dog barking.

He shivered suddenly. Deep in his soul he felt another onrush of terror. He quickened the beat of his fins. One of them plopped loudly, and then the other, but he had less than 30 feet to go. He could no longer stand the dragging pace.

With 20 feet to go, he was sprinting, thrashing recklessly, breathing in enormous chest-searing gulps.

All at once, 10 feet from the boat, he felt a bump and a firm, decisive grasp on his left femur, some three inches above his knee. It was surprising, but not at all violent. His first thought was that his partner had somehow survived, caught up with him from below, and plucked his thigh for attention. He dipped his mask, looking down.

He was amazed to see half a human leg, swathed in neoprene, tumbling into the depths. He observed that, though fully detached from the upper femur at the *superpatellar bursa*, it exhibited little bleeding from its own portion of the femoral artery, though a cloud of blood from somewhere else was forming quickly. Whoever had amputated had performed neatly: the skin along the incision was scalpel-clean.

He was filled with sudden lassitude. He floated, fascinated by the leg spinning into the depths. He had the sense of something vast moving below the limb, out of his zone of visibility, but he was strangely giddy and somehow did not care. The leg rose as if bumped, and disappeared.

His left side was weak. He wondered if he had had a heart attack or even a stroke. He was getting too old to dive. He might even sell his share in the boat. He began feebly to swim again.

He heard the faint subway roar. He did not care. He stopped moving. He was too tired to fight his sleepiness, though the boat was only three strokes away. He would doze awhile like a basking seal, and swim the last few feet later.

Then he was borne aloft. He sensed that his ribs, lungs, spleen, kidneys, bowels, duodenum, were being squeezed firmly together as if in a giant hydraulic press.

He felt no pain at all.

2

Chief Martin Brody of the Amity police sat at his desk and watched the clock on the wall. It jerked to noon, croaked for an instant, and subsided. A light on his desk phone began to flash. He glared across the office at Polly Pendergast, dominating the switchboard.

She was supposed to *hold* lunch hour calls, damn it. She was too old or too obstinate to remember anything, and absolutely unfireable. He stared her down, refusing to reach for the phone.

"Who is it?" he demanded finally.

"Nate Starbuck," she announced. "Parking."

"Shit," he breathed. She disliked profanity, and pursed her lips. Good. She slid open a drawer and drew out her lunch bag. For what she called her lunchy-munchy, she selected first a cream-cheese-and-jelly sandwich. His stomach turned.

She always ate at her desk, brought an extra sandwich for him, and hoped that he would be delayed so that she would not have to eat alone.

To frustrate her, he continued to ignore the phone. "Tell him," he said, "I'll drop by on the way home for lunch."

It suddenly struck him that he had not had a parking complaint in over a year. "*Parking*? Things must be looking up."

He took his hat and book of traffic tickets and

started for the door. She looked up at him adoringly. He grabbed the sandwich from her hand, turned away, and pretended to wolf it down. She shrieked and he returned it. He patted her flabby cheek and emerged from Town Hall into bright spring sunshine.

He slid behind the wheel of Car #1, turned on the radio, changed his mind and flipped it off. It was just like Polly to come up with something else to turn him around when he was homeward bound. Senile, like the town she served.

But the town was being reborn. There was no rebirth in sight for Polly.

He drove down Main, almost deserted, toward Water. Two years ago there would have been cars lining both sides of the street, even this early in June. But today, though it was Saturday, there were not half a dozen vehicles slanted into the meter spots. The meters themselves had been plugged and emasculated last year, in a futile effort to placate downtown merchants who thought, or hoped, that 10¢ an hour parking was the root of their troubles.

As he approached the center of town his spirits were buoyed by the construction he saw there. Chase Manhattan had bought out Amity Bank and Trust, and the facade of the new branch, still very Cape Cod, was getting a white coat of paint. What was more, they were building a drive-in teller window, on Saturday overtime, and there were contractors' trucks scattered all over the bank parking lot.

He parked in the red zone in front of Martha's Dresses. Martha's husband Roger was crawling among the manikins at skirt height. He saw Brody, leered, reached up and patted a dummy. He was priming the platform for a new coat of paint.

Three doors south, a new neon sign, "Amity Hardware," leaned against the building front, waiting to be craned into place for Albert Morris.

Brody stepped into the dim coolness of Starbuck's Pharmacy. Even Starbuck's seemed to be coming back to life. Nate had come very close to bankruptcy during The Trouble, as Amity called it. He had laid off his own nephew, who had handled photo processing in the rear, and fired the delivery boy and the girl behind the old-fashioned fountain. For over a year Nate had developed film between prescriptions, refused to deliver, and let his scrawny wife Lena, as grim and taciturn as he, jerk the sodas behind the marble counter.

Now, Brody observed, at least he had hired a new fountain girl: Jackie Angelo, the 15-year-old daughter of one of his own patrolmen. She was a great improvement on Lena. She was becoming, he observed, another—younger—Gina Lollobrigida. She had sky-blue North Italian eyes, and black hair. She seldom smiled. When she did, her eyes danced, her nose crinkled, and her hand flew to her mouth to hide the most blatant braces in town. She winked at Brody as he passed, rolled up her eyes in resignation, and pointed to the prescription counter.

Starbuck, lank survivor of a line of Bedford whaler-merchants, was standing behind the prescription window typing out a label. The typewriter was a Woodstock which, Brody was sure, was worth more as an antique than Nate's whole store. Starbuck was fantastic, right off a Norman Rockwell cover, green celluloid visor and all. And despite what seemed to be a minor renaissance in his business, he remained as sour as ever.

"Morning, Nathanial," murmured Brody, without enthusiasm.

Starbuck did not look up. He drew the label across a sponge and plastered it carefully onto a bottle. He put the vial on the counter. "Your wife phoned yesterday. Her thyroid pills."

"What's the parking problem?"

Starbuck jerked a thumb toward his side door and spat: "Casino del Mar." He pronounced it distastefully, with the accent on the *Cas*, as if to show his scorn for foreign names. "Next to my delivery truck. Saw Peterson park it. He's in the bank." He stared at Brody. "On a Saturday."

"You think he's trying to rob it?"

"Shouldn't wonder, but not with a gun. Bank don't open for *me* on Saturday."

"Maybe you don't owe them enough money."

Starbuck's eyes went cold. "Don't everybody? Except," he added significantly, "them as sold their property?"

"I *shouldn't* have sold?" Brody snorted.

Starbuck shrugged. "Good business to sell. Wish I'd had beach."

"A crummy hundred feet, Nate? Just about *everybody* sold. Christ, how much you think I got for it?"

"None of my business."

"No," agreed Brody. "Look, Peterson *couldn't* park in the bank's lot. It's full of trucks. Yours is empty, what difference does it make?"

Starbuck's lips grew thinner. "Township ordinance, ain't it? *Pharmacy* customers only?" He shrugged. "Course, you might be afraid to ticket him. Hadn't thought of that."

Brody spun on his heel and strode through the side door. Peterson's Monaco, with New Jersey plates and "Casino del Mar" gilded discretely on the doors, was parked next to Starbuck's delivery van. He glanced up at the wall of the building. No out for him there. The sign "PHARMACY CUSTOMERS ONLY: Violators Will Be Towed Away," had been freshly repainted, with the number of the municipal ordinance below. It was Starbuck's contribution to the general face-lifting, he assumed, and it would probably stop at that.

He was starting to write the ticket when he saw Peterson, a slight, intense man built like a bantamweight, approaching. Peterson flashed him a grin.

"My God, is Amity *that* broke?"

"Look, Pete, go in and buy something from the old bastard? A piece of bubble gum, or something?"

Peterson thanked him and entered the store. Brody put his citation book away and went back to Car #1. He surveyed the street again.

It was really looking pretty good. The man he had sent inside was saving the town, and idiots like Starbuck didn't even seem to know it.

He'd forgotten Ellen's pills, but it was too nice a day to face Starbuck twice.

He climbed in and drove home to lunch.

"Sean," sighed Ellen, "are you going to finish your succotash or not?"

Brody sipped his beer, tilted back his chair, and observed his younger son's plate across the table. Eleven peas, in shotgun offense, were lined up in the shadow of their own goalposts. Eleven corn kernels, the Jets, opposed them in a 4-3-3-1 formation. Obviously, Buffalo was in deep trouble. But not for long.

Fascinated, Brody watched O.J. Simpson slice off tackle, propelled by a single tine of Sean's fork. The deep safety seemed about to get him when the point, flashing from nowhere, impaled him. O.J. sped for the edge of the dish.

"Way to go," murmured Brody, finishing his beer.

Ellen was not amused. "If he's through, I'd like to wash his plate."

"Come on, Ellen," said Brody. "You see that block? Fastest fork in the East."

She whisked the dish away, over Sean's protests. "Don't forget Mike," she reminded Brody.

He hadn't forgotten, just put it off until after lunch. Mike had conned his mother into serving on the Amity Boat Club Junior Race Committee. She had busted her tail to arrange next Sunday's junior regatta. He had got his younger brother all steamed up about crewing for him. And then Mike had apparently quit cold. The boat looked like hell, his rigging needed tuning, he had a rip in his mainsail, and he hadn't run the course to Cape North light since late last summer.

Heavily, Brody stood up. Sean stood too. Brody eased his belt. So did Sean. Brody squatted suddenly, eye level to his son. "Hey, how about we go surfing? Maybe a little swim tonight, off the Casino?"

Sean grinned. He was missing a tooth. Even the hole was beautiful. "No way," said the little boy, pretending a bite. Suddenly, impulsively, he kissed Brody and scampered out the kitchen door.

At least, thought Brody, there's that. Reluctantly, he climbed the stairs.

Ellen Brody began to pull on a rubber dishwashing glove. Then she remembered that it had a split in the forefinger and pulled it off disgustedly.

She poured Joy into the sink and followed it with scalding water from a leaky faucet, splattering her blouse. She cursed, keeping it quiet so that she would not scare Sean away, for she knew he was at the laundry room workbench painting the tiller from his brother's boat, in accordance with some heavy contract having to do with the regatta. If he heard her washing the dishes, he would be halfway to Amity Beach by the time she wanted him to dry them.

She immersed her bare hands in the water and

flinched. Brody was supposed to have brought home another pair of gloves from Amity Hardware yesterday. He didn't give a damn if her hands turned to a washerwoman's.

As a matter of fact, she wouldn't even need the gloves if he'd fixed the dishwashing machine instead of spending last Sunday rigging the stupid boat with Mike and Sean, and now summer was here and she'd lose him for three months to the g.d. town.

Not that that mattered: she already seemed to have lost him to her sons.

"Sean?" she called.

Dead silence. But the creaking of the screen door told her that she'd not gone unheard.

"Hostess Ding-Dong?" she called, sneakily. There were none, but all was fair in love and war. And it was his week to help with the dishes.

Sean entered, unsuspecting. "Hi," he smiled. There was a spot of white paint on his nose. She wiped it off and handed him a dish towel, firmly.

"Hi, there. How's the boat?"

He looked at the towel as if he'd never seen one. "We got Ding-Dongs?"

"You ate them all last night, remember?"

"You said—"

"I was thinking out loud. I didn't know there was anybody out there, nobody answered." She handed him a plate. "Don't drop it," she warned. "I mean it."

He scowled. "Mike says I got to finish painting the tiller, or I can't crew on the regat—"

"*After* the dishes."

"Aw, Mom . . . *Dad*!"

"He's up talking to Mike." Now, *wipe*, you little goldbrick, she added to herself, or I'll strangle you with the towel.

He began to wipe, slowly. "I'll never get the boat done, and he won't let me crew!"

"Sean," she said seriously. "Now I want you to listen, and I want you to remember."

He looked up at her. His lower lip was out, his eyes were hostile, he was the picture of a spoiled, pampered brat. His father would hardly have recognized him. "Yeah?"

"If you don't help me, today, and for the rest of the week, there will *be* no junior regatta."

"How come?"

"Because you ain't gonna have no *race* committee chairman! Chair*person*. How do you like *them* apples?"

"Aw, mom!"

"I mean it."

He wiped a little longer, then smiled. "He wouldn't *let* you quit."

"Dad? What do you *mean*, he wouldn't *let* me quit? You want to try me?"

Sean considered her through his china blue eyes. He decided not to press the argument. "No."

"OK," she subsided.

Still steaming inside, she finished washing the dishes. *Let* her quit? What did they think she was, a slave?

The trouble was, they were probably right.

Brody stood at Mike's desk by the bedroom window. He leafed through *Skin Diver Magazine* while he gave his angry son, lying on his bed, time to cool off.

Helping him buy the boat, then, hadn't done the trick . . .

The magazine was the top issue of a pile a foot high. Brody stopped at a two-page ad from U.S. Divers, full color, center spread. A macho diver, who wore a husky moustache, dripped with seawater and gleaming new equipment. A model, who looked as if her rubber suit had been sprayed onto her, gazed at him wet-eyed with lust. *The bastards,* he thought. *Money-grabbing bastards . . .*

"What are you going to do, burn them?" complained Mike, addressing the ceiling. "It's not *porn*!"

He regarded his older son. Mike looked tired. He had skipped lunch, not only today, but yesterday too. The hunger strike revolved around the printed form that his friend Andy had picked up at the Aqua Sport Diving Center, and given to Mike. Andy's father had signed his, and Andy was presumably deep into a Scuba-diving course. It would be a cold day in hell before Brody signed Mike's.

He tapped the pile of magazines. "No, Mike. I *wish* it was porn."

"You do? Okay, I can take care of *that.*" His voice was strangled. "Magazine rack at Starbuck's, Jackie won't even open them, they're so raunchy. Sure. I saved the money for the course, I can buy the *porn* instead."

"Take it easy, Mike."

His son rolled over, facing him. "Then, see dad, while Andy and Chip and Larry, you know, and everybody else in the crummy town is diving, I can, you know, lie up here with *Gallery* and . . ."

"Cool it!" Brody barked. "Look, if you want to swim, use Town Pool! Your baby brother's got more sense than you! And *he* was on the beach! You were in the *ocean*!"

"In the ocean," squeaked Mike. "For the last time! I can swim like an eel! I live on an island! And I'm not allowed to—"

"You can sail!"

"And *that* took like an Act of Congress! I'm tired of the dumb Laser—"

"You're the best sailor in town!"

"Look, I want to be the best Scuba-diver instead, OK? It's *my* life!"

"Cool it!" Brody's voice lashed across the room. He moved from the desk, overturning the chair. His son stared at him, shocked. Brody stepped to him, reached out. Mike flinched. *God, did he think he was going to get hit?* Brody felt his forehead. It was hot, maybe he had a fever.

"You think I'm *sick*?" quavered Mike. "Maybe I am. Sick of your hang-up. Sick of 'Spitzer'."

"Who's Spitzer?"

"Mark Spitzer." Mike was crying now. "Great Olympic . . . swimmer. 'Hey, Spitzer, come on down to the beach, you won't get wet . . .' 'Gimme a swimming lesson, Spitzer . . .' 'Spitzer, hey, move your towel, man, tide's coming in.' " He drew in a great shuddering sigh. "*I'm* frigging 'Spitzer'."

"Mike—" Brody began helplessly.

"I wished we lived in Omaha!" blurted his son.

"But we don't."

"Dad?"

Brody brushed his son's hair from his eyes. "Yeah?"

"The shark is dead."

Brody nodded. "The shark is dead."

He talked Mike into going down for a sandwich. Then he sat, flipping the magazine pages, until he realized he was not really looking at them.

He folded the form, slid it into his jacket pocket, and left the house.

3

The fat little girl was digging a hole to China in the sand. Next to her, the lean hard-muscled man she called "daddy"—but she was sure he was not really her father, or else how could she be so fat and stupid—seemed to be sleeping behind the mirrored sunglasses she hated.

He was not. "You see Uncle Brian lately?" he asked suddenly.

She looked into his face. It was turned a little toward her, but there was no way to tell if the eyes behind the mirrors were on hers.

Her mommy had told her not to answer such questions, but if she did not, he might get mad and take her back early.

"No," she lied. "Look, daddy, an ant fell in the hole!"

There was no ant, but she had to say something, and she wasn't supposed to talk about Uncle Brian, or Uncle Jerry, or Flip, or just about anybody else.

Her father turned over on his side and inspected the hole. "Ant?"

She reddened. "Well, there *was*. Daddy? There *was*!"

He grunted and turned back. "So what have you and mommy been doing? Same baby-sitter?"

A trap. She nodded. She did not feel like digging

anymore. She began to watch a flock of five pelicans, diving for fish very close to the beach.

"You watching lots of TV?" he asked.

He was a male model, working steadily, and she watched for him constantly, if she was alone with the sitter at night. Another trap.

"Look at the pelicans, daddy!"

He did not stir, only muttered that yes, he had seen them before, they were rare this far north, endangered, but coming back, Amity was famous for them.

She waited for the next question. She was following the leader of the flock, plummeting like a diving plane on TV. He smacked the water in a splatter of spray.

"She take you to the dentist, like I said?"

"Yes." She felt her teeth. "Yuk!"

An outright lie. She concentrated on the reappearance of the pelican, who had not yet risen from the depths. If she could just get him interested in the diving birds, he might forget about it. "Daddy! They're going to eat all the fish!"

"Everybody's got to live. Any cavities?"

Now she had done it. How could she know if she had cavities, when her mother, with her own help, had forgotten to take her? And now the money was probably spent.

"Daddy, the pelican didn't come *up*!"

"Maybe a fish ate *him*. Any cavities, honey?"

"No." Now she was truly concerned about the pelican. "How long can they stay under?"

"Beats me. A long time, I guess." He looked at his watch and her throat tightened. Not yet, not yet, it was just past noon . . .

He rolled over on his tummy. She relaxed. That was all it was, time to roll over. He had to brown evenly, like timing a piece of toast in the oven, in case he got a Jantzen commercial or something, which he might, he was so beautiful.

The pelican must have come up somewhere else, where she wasn't looking. She counted the birds skimming the surf line, then rising and diving again. Only four left. Another dropped for the surface. This time she stood, to better scan the water.

That one didn't come up either. "Daddy? *Daddy*!"

He was asleep, or pretending to be.

He wouldn't believe her anyway. He knew she told fibs all the time.

Angrily, she kicked sand into her hole to China. If there *had* been an ant, he was sure dead now.

Brody parked outside Amity Aqua Sports, Inc., which was housed in a huge green structure a half block from Town Dock, sandwiched between Amity Sea Food and Roy Schwartz' poolhall. The building had been a rope-walk in Amity's early days. After that, it had been a warehouse for nets, lobster pots, and marine supplies for the commercial fishing boats that had once been the town's only industry.

All winter long, Tom Andrews had sawed and hammered inside, doing the whole job of reconversion himself, and angering the local building trade.

Now the place glistened under dark green paint. Behind its new plate glass windows, around an old-fashioned copper diving helmet, were grouped scuba tanks, water skis, and wind-surfers, which Andrews hoped to popularize off the breezy sands of Amity.

Brody had met him only once. He was a Californian bucking the normal east-west tide of migration. He had applied for permission to install a burglar alarm facing Water Street. Brody had smiled: they hadn't had a break-in downtown in ten years. And any thief who caught a glimpse of the great, bearded proprietor, and knew he lived above his store, would have been an idiot to try.

Now, seeing the array of kid-tempting equipment, he decided that maybe Andrews had been right.

Brody entered the building. It still smelled of paint. He stopped and marveled at the stock. Big Mercury outboards lined half of one wall. The other half was taken up by a glittering red ski-boat that must have come in through the huge warehouse doors at the rear.

There were racks of hanging wetsuits, counters full of diving knives, underwater watches, spear-guns, and scallop irons. There was a display of chrome cleats, shackles, and pint-sized motorboat anchors. Whatever Andrews' plans, they expressed vast financial faith in the future of Amity. Brody liked him more and more.

Andrews had just sold a water-ski flag to a cheerful young couple Brody recognized as regular summer visitors. When they left, Andrews extended a hand the size of a catcher's mitt.

"Hi," he grinned. His eyes twinkled from between rolls of fat, but even the fat looked muscular. Brody decided that he weighed 300 pounds, including the beard, and that he had probably carried the ski-boat into the store in his arms. Next time he got a call to toss a drunken fisherman out of the Randy Bear, he might deputize Andrews.

"What can I do for you, chief?" the giant asked.

"Skip the 'chief,' Tom. Makes me feel like a navy lifer or something. And my whole department is just me and three other klutzes. 'Martin,' or just 'Brody,' OK?"

"Check. What's up?"

Brody produced Mike's form. The effect was

startling. Andrews rounded the counter, moving like an athlete. He flung an arm like a tree limb around Brody's shoulder and squeezed. He was beaming.

"Great! Just great! How'd he do it?"

"Mike?" Brody looked at him, shocked. "Didn't know you'd even met him. Look, I haven't signed the damn thing, I just wanted to talk to you about it."

Some of the exuberance left Andrews' face. He moved back behind the counter, sat at a work bench, and began to disassemble a diving regulator.

"Okay. The course for juniors is four weeks. They graduate with a full-fledged diving card. No dive shop will fill your tank without it, so it means something to them, like a driver's license."

He told Brody that the schedule was two hours Saturday and two hours Sunday. Basic testing of swimming ability, skin diving with a snorkel, basic introduction to Scuba equipment, buddy-breathing, emergency ascents.

"In the Town Pool?" Brody asked. His mouth was dry.

"Everything, so far."

"So far," repeated Brody.

"Then comes a written exam on theory." Andrews tapped a pile of texts on his workbench. "Permissable bottom-time, decompression curves, nitrogen effect in the bloodstream, 'rapture of the deep,' the bends. 100% is passing."

Brody felt hope. Mike, as he boasted, might swim like an eel, but he'd never concentrate long enough to pass the technical exam. OK, he'd sign. At least it would be off his own back.

He reached for the pen. Andrews' voice went on: "Then a final checkout. For the first class, it's tomorrow. In the water."

"Water?"

"Ocean."

His hand began to tremble. Stupid, stupid, stupid, what the hell was wrong with him? This man oozed competence.

Still, he could not sign, and he put down the pen. "How much . . . How much does it run?"

Andrews smiled. "For Mike, nothing."

"Come *on*, Tom!" As police chief, he was uncomfortable when offered a favor, although God knew at $600 a month they needed every cent they could save. "You can't do that."

The giant was reassembling the regulator. The screwdriver seemed lost in his hand. "Actually, I've done it already."

"What?"

Andrews blew into the mouthpiece, tossed the regulator into a box marked "Tested," and opened a file drawer. He pulled out a folder and extracted an exam. He slid it on the counter in front of Brody.

Mike's name was printed at the top, much more neatly than on any school paper he had ever brought home. Brody read a few of the questions: "State Boyle's Law . . ." "If a balloon occupies two cubic feet at sea level, how much cubic feet will it occupy at 60 feet?" "What is the percentage of nitrogen in the air?"

Across the top Andrews had scrawled *100%*. This, from a kid who couldn't pass Algebra I?

He felt a flash of anger. "Why does he want me to sign? He seems to have done all right without me!"

Andrews faced him, speaking softly: "I started the class last month. Twelve kids. Signed forms in their hands. All suited up and jumping with joy. And one kid in a bathing suit at the other end of the pool—Christ, it was cold. No wetsuit. But listening. Pretending he wasn't. After the class, he's standing around digging the ice out of his ears. He tells me you've got this hangup, and why. He's not allowed in the ocean, he can't get his diving card, but could he kind of listen in, at the pool? He's saved enough money if I want it . . ."

Andrews shrugged. "I figured, what the hell, I'm probably not liable if it's for free, and maybe he can talk you into it before the ocean dive, and he's looking at me with those big blue eyes . . ."

"OK," Brody said abruptly. "OK!"

He was angry, not at Andrews, or even Mike, but at himself, for forcing his son into this charade.

He'd blown it. People dove the Amity coast all summer long, and even in the winter. There were so many spear gunners that the fishermen complained. It was said that they'd almost cleared the bottom of scallops already. More divers seemed to arrive every year.

People swam and sailed and water-skied and surfed, and no one got a scratch.

The Amity shark was dead. Statistically, there'd never be another. Not in his lifetime, or probably Mike's either.

He thanked Andrews. He bought Mike a wetsuit, and Sean a jacknife to balance it. Finally he faced the form again. He took out his pen.

This time his hand shook hardly at all.

All afternoon Brody jiggled and stewed behind his desk. The wetsuit outside, on the rear seat of Car #1, was driving him nuts. It was hardly fair to let Mike suffer until quitting time, but there was no way of telling where he was. And Saturday afternoon was not the best time for the chief of police to take off.

So he tried to sweat it until 5, mending the normal rips in the fabric of Amity. Len Hendricks found Minnie Eldridge's Siamese, which had been missing for three days, trapped in an empty mailbag on the rear step of the post office. Roscoe Turner's daughter Lily was struck by a hit-run bicyclist, illegally riding on the sidewalk outside Martha's Dresses, and Dick Angelo had to use the department dune-buggy to take her to Amity Community Hospital, since the ambulance was being lubed at Norton's Esso. Lily's right calf was cut and she bled all over the front seat. They hadn't found the cyclist, whom she'd recognized but wouldn't identify. Probably a schoolmate. They'd find out if he tried to get his bike repaired.

Brody finally quit five minutes early. He was on his way home when he spotted Sean sprinting up Water Street in a dead run for home. He stopped and opened his door.

The little boy tumbled in. "Fish! Going home to get my pole! There's cod all over the harbor. *Big* ones!"

Brody glanced down Water Street. It was true. There were more people on Town Dock than he ever remembered seeing. Half of them had poles already, and the rest were queued in front of Hyman's Bait & Tackle, trying to rent more.

"Daddy! Let's *go*!" Sean was bouncing up and down.

"Fasten your belt."

Sean groaned and clicked the latch. "Use your *siren*!"

"No siren. And you have to eat dinner first."

"Mike didn't have to eat lunch!"

He had something there. "We'll see." He pulled away from the curb.

He glanced back at the dock in his mirror.

Strange. He had never heard of a cod run in Amity Harbor before.

He had intended to lecture Mike on evasion and dissembling and communication between father and son. But Mike had broken no family law by swimming in the Town Pool. And, watching TV, his face was so sad that Brody could not wait. Ellen, who seemed relieved that the no-ocean edict had passed, gift-wrapped the wetsuit in the kitchen.

Sean had departed for Town Dock, staggering under a pole three times longer than he. On his shoulder rode an old trout fisherman's basket. A gunnysack for his catch was jammed under his belt. He had a can of sardines for bait. His new knife was tied to a lanyard around his neck. Brody's old dry-casting hat, studded with rusty lures, was jammed so far down on his head that he could barely see.

Brody poured his evening belt and walked into the living room. Ellen bore the gift behind him. Mike turned away from the TV. "What gives?"

"We do," grinned Ellen.

"It's your birthday," explained Brody. His heart was pumping. "We've never told you, but you were born twice, like the President."

Mike took the box and began to open it. A year ago he would have torn into it like a dog at a rabbit hole. Now he carefully untied the ribbon, unfolded the Christmas wrapping, and froze.

"Aqua Sport," he breathed. "Aqua Sport? Dad?"

He took the top off the box. He did not remove the folded suit. He stroked it for a second. All at once he was in Brody's arms, face pressed tightly against his stubble. Sean kissed his father all the time, but it had been ten years since he felt his older son's cheek. Embarrassed, Mike pulled away.

"For tomorrow," Brody said softly.

"You signed it!" whispered Mike. "Thanks. Thanks a lot."

"Try it on," said Brody. The vision of his son at the bottom of the ocean in the suit had tightened his throat, and he loosened it with a long sip of scotch. "Let's see it on you."

Mike kissed his mother, dropped his pants, and squirmed in.

He was 15 years old, and the fuzz on his cheek was growing stiffer. He was going to be quite a man, his father thought.

But, like a little boy, he ate dinner in the wetsuit, just the same. And passing his room to go to bed that night, Brody glimpsed him inside, preening before the mirror.

For a happy kid, his eyes seemed strangely haunted. It must have been a trick of the light.

4

At seven a.m. the young engineer pushed his bright yellow ski-boat from Town Dock, climbed aboard, and took the wheel from his wife. He eased the throttle forward and came left to avoid a towering Hatteras cabin cruiser under Coast Guard tow. He saw that the red Amity Police Launch was safely unmanned, and poured on the coal.

His bow came up, his stern squatted, a nearby dinghy almost capsized, and they were bound for open ocean.

Only then did he breathe deeply. It was good to get away from the smell of cod, diesel, and creosote, and into the cool sea air.

"Skis checked?" he asked his tawny, long-limbed wife.

"Checked, commodore," she sighed. "Towline shackles OK, life vests aboard, warning flag stowed, horn, flares, and Very pistol—"

"Look," he yelled above the howl of their engine, "this isn't just crap. The engine quits, or something, you'll be glad we do this."

"First-aid packet," she chanted, "paddle, dock-bumbers, three ham sandwiches, one six-pack Schaefer, two cans Diet Rite, grass for four numbers, two spare spark plugs, extra gas—. My God, did you fill that can?"

He nodded. He was assistant head of quality control at Grumman Aircraft. He never forgot anything.

She began to rub Coppertone onto her forehead. "What'd I leave out, commodore?"

"Radio. Shinnecock coast guard."

She reached under the foredeck, drew out the microphone, and intoned: "Coast Guard Radio Shinnecock. This is *Overtime*. Radio check. Over."

Shinnecock Bay crackled back instantly. "Loud and clear, *Overtime*, good morning. Shinnecock out."

He relaxed, letting the boat leap across the dawn-flat water. Before the morning breeze arose, they would have skied an hour or two, anchored in a tiny cove he knew off Amity Neck, cracked a couple of beers and lit up.

He began to weave, drawing a rooster-tail across the mirrored water.

He had the best boat in the world, the best woman, and a two-week vacation. He liked Amity.

Another winter behind them.

It was good to be alive.

"If it was the fish," Sean wanted to know, "why aren't I sick, too?"

Brody looked down at his elder son, lying on the fake leather couch in the sunroom. Not a breath of air stirred the flimsy curtains beside the open windows, and he could hear the bell from St. Xavier on the Neck across Amity Sound. It provided him, as always, with a tiny tug of guilt to spice his Sunday.

"It was the fish, all right," groaned Mike. "It was your goddamned little minnow—"

"Mike," warned Brody, voice rising. "Knock it off!"

Mike tried to get up, but another cramp seized

him, and he lay back, shivering. "Why'd he have to catch the frigging thing? And why'd she have to cook it? For *breakfast*, for crying out loud! There wasn't enough there to eat, just enough to poison everybody!"

"It was a regular-sized fish! And it didn't! It didn't poison me, or dad, or mom!" Sean marched off, head high.

Ellen arrived, professional as always in the face of crisis, shaking down a thermometer. She poked it into Mike's mouth and began to feel his pulse. He mumbled something, mouth closed, his eyes pleading with his father's.

"Pulse is 80. That's high for him," Ellen said. "He wants to know what time it is."

Brody looked at his watch. "9:20. Christ!" He was due at the station house 20 minutes ago. It promised to be one of *those* Sundays, and a scorcher besides.

"9:20?" Mike sat up as if galvanized. The thermometer fell from his lips. "I got to be at Town Dock at ten! Suited up!"

Gently, Brody pushed him back and reinserted the thermometer. "You aren't going anywhere, Cousteau. Not out there, anyway, with cramps *already*."

Mike's eyes were stricken, but he left the thermometer in and lay back, shivering.

The phone rang. It was Len Hendricks, who took Polly's place at the dispatch desk on Sundays. "Chief?"

" 'Brody,' " sighed Brody. "Or 'Martin.' Or 'Marty.' Or 'pal,' even, I don't care."

"Sorry, chief. We got a problem."

"At 9:20, on a Sunday?"

"That's *it*. The 9:30 ferry's due in ten minutes."

"That's certainly true, Len."

"And there's a big enormous yacht blocking Town Dock."

His temple began to throb. "Tell them to move it, Len," he breathed. "Tell them to *move* the mother."

"Who?"

"Why, the owner. The captain. The crew!"

"That's our problem, chief. There is none."

A deep bellow sounded across Amity South. He looked out the window. The Amity Neck ferry churned toward him from Cape North, black with cars and on schedule for the first time in living memory.

"Len?"

"Yeah?"

"*You* want to be chief?"

"Come on!" muttered Len hopefully. "You kidding?"

Brody hung up. During The Trouble, everyone had wanted him to quit when he tried to close the beaches. He'd fought them off, from stubbornness, or pride, or, he liked to think, fear for the safety of swimmers. Even Ellen had wanted him to quit, and still did.

"What did Len say to *that*?" Ellen demanded. "*Does* he want to be chief?"

"I think he does," murmured Brody.

Hendricks was stupider than he'd thought.

The young engineer waited until his wife gave him the thumbs-up signal, checked that the warning flag in the stern was up and erect, and eased the throttle forward until the slack was out of the ski-line. He glanced ahead to clear their track and gave the boat full throttle.

She rose gracefully in his wake, like a mermaid from the deep, riding one ski, intent on form, not as relaxed as she had been at the end of last summer, for it was their first time out this year. But good, very good. By tomorrow she would have it right again, and if they could find someone to run the boat, they would be skiing tandem in a couple of days.

The water was still glassy, with the slightest suggestion of swell. She was weaving from one side of the wake to the other, overconfident as usual. Impishly he threw the wheel over, half-stopping the boat, slowing her, then jerking her ahead as he took off in a new direction. She survived that one, gyrating wildly, but he got her with the next one. She crashed in a sheet of spray. He wheeled to starboard, slowed, and dragged the line close to her. She gave him the finger and took the towbar. He had her set up again, and she was nodding, when he suddenly tensed.

A hundred yards behind her an enormous, lazy fin was beckoning. She did not see it, and while he stood frozen in horror, he saw it move, in a leisurely manner, up their trail.

His first thought was that it was a killer-whale, did orcas attack humans? Or a shark, no, too big for a sharkfin. Then he remembered the Amity shark, but it couldn't be, that shark was dead . . .

"Dee!" he screamed.

She smiled at him over the water and took a hand off the towbar, waving him ahead. The fin was coming up on her now, weaving across their dying wake. It was simply gigantic.

He jammed the throttle forward, way too fast, catching her off balance. She lost the smile, shaking her head in irritation. Her weight was too far forward, and for a moment he was afraid that she would pitch headfirst into the wake when she rose, but if he tried to help her and eased the throttle to take tension off the line, she might overcompensate.

Just leave it, he thought, and pray that she'd get up, once he had her *up* he could outrun any fish that swam . . .

She was squatting, half erect, and then pitching, and the fin was faster than he had estimated, but not that fast, dropping behind, perhaps fooled by her sudden acceleration, she was on the ski now, and rising . . .

"Weight back!" he shrieked, but of course, over the howl of the Merc she would hear nothing. "Get your ass *down*!"

She made it, took one hand off the bar, grinned, and signaled him OK with thumb and forefinger. She favored him with her most forgiving smile.

He stood erect, searching their wake for the fin. The thing must have dived, that was it, he had fooled it. Now, all he had to do was head for the beach: no fish like that would go into shallow water. She was capable, when he signaled her, of casting off and riding her ski onto dry sand, if he could get close enough.

He scanned the beach for a safe place. Where they were building the Casino there were people, and suddenly he wanted to be where there *were* people, but there was a more gentle slope of beach in front of an old, weatherbeaten cottage further from the town . . .

Gently, his eye on his wife, he began a sweeping curve toward the cottage. She was weaving again, jumping the wake each time, exuberantly. He signaled her to take it easy, simply to ski, finally slowed the boat so that she couldn't do it at all, and then saw the fin again, coming up fast astern.

He found that his hand was so wet he could hardly hold onto the throttle. But he eased it forward, again, and the fin disappeared. She began to weave once more, port to starboard, head back and golden hair flying, soaring higher each time she crossed the wake. "Dee," he croaked. "No, Dee, no!"

He remembered the radio. He lunged for it, but the boat, without his hand on the wheel, slewed sidewise, almost spilling her.

His mind raced. He could probably tug her off, if he tried, make a violent turn and a fast run up and yank her from the water . . .

He didn't dare. Whatever it was, orca or shark, if it was fast enough to keep up with the boat, it was fast enough to beat him back.

He looked aft. She was doing well now, maybe tiring enough to stop the horseshit, to simply ski until he had her safe: *that was it, Dee, that was it, honey. No more hotdogging, just ski, OK?*

He headed dead for the house on the beach. Two miles away, maybe less. Not all that far.

Suddenly he froze. Halfway between him and the beach was the fin. He couldn't understand it. He was making 20 knots easily: could the damn thing make 30? Could it compute a pursuit curve? "Holy shit," he moaned. He curved back out to sea. The fin disappeared.

He was an engineer. There had to be a way. He had it, suddenly. He would stop, put slack in the line, warn her of her danger, tow her again if necessary, slack the line, haul in more, and when she was close enough, drag her into the boat.

But not now. The fin reappeared, still a football field behind her, and he would have to wait until it disappeared before he stopped . . .

The throttle was against the stops already, but he found himself shoving anyway. Suddenly it came off in his hand. "No!" he wailed.

No slowing, now. No stopping, either. So much for hauling her in. He headed back for the house on the beach. He looked at his wife. "Don't!" he bellowed.

She had not tired, only been thinking, probably, in the cautious, lip-nibbling way she had. Now, tentatively, she was trying something. By the set of her body he guessed what it was.

He had learned to turn and ski backward. It had taken him three summers to do it, and she'd so far been unable to. Maybe her arms were too weak, or her back. She'd tried it last year, jealous that there was something he could do that she couldn't, and now she was trying it again.

"No, Dee, no!" he howled. She seemed to hear him, turned her head, almost fell. He shut up.

The fin was back in their wake. It was a hundred yards, perhaps a little more, astern of her. And coming up, surely coming up.

His wife teetered, made the move, and turned. By God, she had done it! She was skiing backward, and if she could just get turned around again . . .

The fin was gaining. Her body went suddenly rigid. She had seen it. Somehow she whipped around without falling. Now her face was a mask of horror. She was yelling, and wobbling . . . Steady, Dee, steady . . . Not far to the beach . . .

As if she heard him, she seemed to relax. Solidly, carefully, she skied out from the wake into smooth water. The fin disappeared. He chanced a look at the beach. Half a mile. A white speck on the weatherbeaten porch, a person, someone to care for her when she sliced to the beach if she collapsed from shock . . . And he'd be OK, without her drag, no fish in the sea could catch *Overtime* . . .

But when he looked back he knew that they had lost. The fin was closing fast. In seconds it was towering above her. Instinctively, he grabbed the flare pistol, jammed a cartridge into it, fired it into the air. It rose in a gentle arc, burning with a feeble orange light hardly noticeable against the glaring sky. He would need help, fast: *medical* help, even if the best happened and she survived the first attack.

Why hadn't he put the radio where he could reach it from the throttle?

"Dee!"

A leviathan snout broke water ten feet behind her. He could not credit its size. A hideous maw ringed with white opened behind her, twisted sideways, closed on her, shook her once, tossing her as it reared in a froth of blood and flesh and the long, tawny hair. And then she was gone.

He ripped at the ignition harness. The engine quit instantly, hurling him forward. He reloaded the flare pistol. The flare reappeared. "Come on, you bastard!" he shrieked.

The snout rose, heading for the boat. Lurching back, Very pistol at the ready, he stumbled and discharged it. For an awful instant he knew. He had fired straight into the spare gas tank.

His world went up in a dull orange boom.

A half-mile away, Minnie Eldridge, Amity's ancient postmistress, stopped her rocker. She spilled her Siamese off her lap and set aside the *Sunday Times.* She took off her glasses and peered seaward. Behind the gentle surf blossomed a dirty pall of smoke.

She hobbled inside to phone.

5

Hauling on lines from the dock, Brody and his patrolman Dick Angelo got the Hatteras 42 snugged closely enough to the quay to allow the ferry to make her slip.

"Coast guard dumped her," volunteered Yak-Yak Hyman from the bait shop. Last night's windfall of cod had made him positively garrulous. He'd even said good morning.

"Just *dumped* her?" demanded Brody. His temple began to throb again.

Yak-Yak simply looked at him. *That's right,* Brody thought. *You already told me that. Sorry, Yak-Yak.*

"Nobody aboard?" he asked.

The same look. *Right again, Yak-Yak. The one implies the other. Why repeat it?*

"Coast guard say when they'd be back?"

Yak-Yak shook his head. Not too much—you had to be quick to see it—but a little. Brody walked to Starbuck's Pharmacy and called Shinnecock Bay on the phone.

The coast guard, said Shinnecock duty officer, would not be back until evening. They'd noticed the yacht yesterday, anchored over the *Orca* wreck. No anchor light last night, a lobsterman had almost run her down. She'd have been a menace to navigation again today, if the afternoon fog drifted in. They'd stood by for an hour this morning, in case divers, if any, reappeared. They'd even sent their chopper on a search to see if they'd surfaced and been swept to sea.

They'd buoyed the site and were towing her away when they'd got an emergency call: a sailboat was sinking off the Hamptons. So they'd had to dump the yacht at the first harbor and split.

They'd just contacted one of the yacht-owner's wives, he was a doctor from Astoria, due home last night. She was on her way, they'd launch another search later, do everything they could, but Brody was the closest law enforcement officer. They'd been trying to reach him but his line was busy, he'd have to send down divers and handle the paperwork. OK, chief?

"Wait a minute," begged Brody. "The *Orca*'s a quarter-mile out! I *got* no divers! It's not my jurisdiction!"

"Look, we just got *another* call. Speedboat blew up, or something. It's Sunday, we only got one cutter, there'll be idiots out there in trouble all day long. You got a question, call the district commandant, OK?"

Now Brody's whole head was aching. He stepped back into sunlight. He looked toward Town Dock at the gleaming cruiser. On a fancy plastic sternboard, he read *Miss Carriage*, out of Sag Harbor. He had no feeling for boats, except revulsion, but it seemed a sad and sterile name for so expensive a yacht. And if the damn thing was from Sag Harbor, why hadn't the coast guard towed it home?

He climbed aboard. Divers had been here, for sure. There was a rack of tanks in the cockpit. He wondered what the attraction was at the wreck of the *Orca*. For four years amateurs had been picking over the carcass of Quint's old boat. What did they expect to find? Blood?

He scaled the ladder to the flying bridge. Nothing there except what you'd expect: a pair of sunglasses jammed behind the binnacle, a sweater slung on the wheel.

He swung below, entered the cabin. Wall-to-wall carpeting, stereo speakers, another steering location. In case it rained? A bottle of Old Grandad and two coffee cups sat on the service bar. There were binoculars in a varnished rack near the wheel. He stepped behind the counter to the galley stove. He felt the coffee pot. Cold. He picked up one of the cups. There was a trace of coffee in the bottom. He sniffed it. He smelled whisky. He smelled the other. It seemed even stronger.

Well, there was no law against drunken diving, so far as he knew.

Except the law of survival.

He glanced out the window at the dock. Down the length of it, heading for Andrews' *Aqua Queen*, staggered a sweating procession of teen-agers in wetsuits: Andy Nicholas, Chip Lennart, Larry Vaughan, the mayor's son. Leading the troup was the bearded giant. Brody tensed. Tagging last was Mike, looking very white. He got whiter when he saw his father. "No temperature," he explained quickly. "Mom said I could—"

Brody ignored him and caught up with Andrews at the *Aqua Queen*.

"Tom, what's your time worth?"

The township emergency fund was low, but Brody could fight it out for him later before the selectmen. He explained the situation, booze and all.

"Liquor," Andrews groaned. "Damn! Happens all the time. No charge, Brody. Let's go."

"Hey," Larry squealed. "What about—"

Andrews held up his hand. It was the size of Larry's head. Reeves shut up.

"Next Saturday, troops," Andrews growled. "Same time, same channel. Tanks back to the shop, OK?"

Everybody groaned, including Mike, but for some

reason the color was back in his cheeks. He drew his dad aside. "Dad, I felt fine."

He hadn't *looked* fine, until this moment, but it was all academic anyway. Brody followed Andrews aboard the *Aqua Queen*, and Dick Angelo tossed off their lines.

The fat man woke up again to a madhouse.

He was paying a hundred a week, a *hundred* for the cottage; it was Sunday, and the dog was barking and his son screaming on the beach.

A jungle, a stupid jungle by the sea . . .

He swung his feet over the side of the crummy bed and rubbed his head. His hair felt like straw. The inside of his mouth tasted of whisky, stale beer, Fritos, and the old lady's idea of a Saturday night special: knockwurst and sauerkraut.

He longed for their flat in Queens, and the soothing growl of the Main Street bus.

"Shut up!" he bellowed.

His wife rolled over like a dead whale in the surf. That would be the next thing, probably, a dead whale.

Pot-belly hanging over his pajamas, he charged out the kitchen door, over the scrubby sand, and down to the surf.

It was another seal. It was backed to the water, its tail wet by every lapping roller. King, their shabby sheepdog, was yelping at it mightily from 20 feet away. When he perceived reinforcements, he moved six inches closer.

The seal swung its soft brown eyes at him. "*Split*, you mother. Shut up, King!" He shoved his son roughly aside. "Pipe down! It's Sunday!"

He regarded the seal. The gentle eyes infuriated him.

He kicked its side as hard as he could, stubbing his bare toes. The seal only shook its head, showering him with water. He spotted a stick of driftwood, the size of a baseball bat. He picked it up and advanced.

The seal sighed, backed up, and turned. It flounced into shallow water, wheeled once reproachfully, then wallowed away into the surf.

He was breathing hard. Cardiac City: the old lady must want his Police League insurance.

"Next time," he told his son softly, "next time, tie up the dog. And come and wake me up. Real quiet."

"What are you going to do?"

"I'm going to *shoot* the son of a bitch!"

He clumped back across the sand. He had been sentenced to Amity for years, every summer, two weeks.

He had never in all the dreary summers seen a seal on the beach. There had been two yesterday, and this was the second today.

Brody tried to ignore the radio on Andrew's boat, concentrating on the bubbles he was trying to follow. He was standing on the helmsman's seat, to better see them, trying to steer with his foot and to work the throttle by tapping it with a toe. He must be careful, very careful, not to outrun the bubbles, because if he did they would be lost in the wake, and he was sure that if he had to turn the boat around he would screw up and lose track of the man below.

He hated every moment of it. He wondered how it was, skimming the murk on the bottom. He could hardly conceive of any man brave enough to enter such a hostile environment. When he himself swam, he couldn't even put his face down. He progressed, in the water, in a series of spasmodic spurts, feeling like an idiot and quivering like a fish on a hook.

He craned his neck, chilled for an instant when

he thought he had lost the path, then spotted a healthy upswelling of air, followed by a chain of smaller bubbles. He steered a little left, slowing.

They had left Amity Harbor to look for the buoy that the coast guard had left. It was supposed to be very close to the wreck of the *Orca*, and God knew he should be able to find *that*, so they had churned along, at high speed, south southeast from Amity breakwater light. Finally, to Brody's regret, Andrews turned over the wheel to him, and began to don his equipment.

He had snapped a tank into a backpack, unscrewed a handle on the tank-top, twisted a bright stainless fixture on that. This, he told Brody, was his regulator, key to underwater life. He grabbed the whole cumbersome mess, which looked as if it weighed a ton, and threw it over his head, ending up with the backpack neatly on and the shoulder straps over his shoulders. He drew tight the straps, stooped, ran his hands over his equipment in a last-minute check. Brody noticed that he wore two knives, one on each calf, and what looked like a navy pilot's inflatable life-vest. A heavy lead belt encircled his enormous gut.

Brody had found the buoy. It was orange, with USCG printed on it in black.

He did not like it here at all, with good reason, but he had swallowed his discomfort and cut the throttle. The rumbling engine behind him quieted.

"Just follow my bubbles," Andrews had ordered. "I'll start at the wreck and swim north, then east, then west, then south. Then out a little farther and the same thing again. Dig?"

He dug. He watched the big man draw on fins, gloves, spit in his mask, turn on his air and suck through his mouthpiece. Andrews peered into the water alongside, and then dropped in backwards.

His fins flashed in the sunlight once, and he was gone.

Brody thought of Mike plummeting to the bottom weighted with similar gear and his mouth went dry. But it was too late to do anything about that.

He was glad that next Saturday was a week away . . .

Daydreaming, he had lost the track. He ran to the side of the boat and searched the water desperately. *Christ, what had he done?* He put the engine in neutral, let the wheel go, and climbed onto the foredeck. A soft breeze had begun rippling the surface, and he could not distinguish the bubbles from the wavelets.

He looked at his watch. It was ridiculous, but he had forgotten to ask Andrews how long he could stay down. Fifteen minutes, half an hour, an hour? He had no idea. In fact, he hadn't even checked the time Andrews went, so he wouldn't know whether he'd been under too long anyway. Where the hell *was* he?

Andrews had left the radio on, and it had been crackling sporadically, breaking his concentration. Now Brody heard Shinnecock coast guard, loud and clear, talking to one of its cutters.

"What's your position, skipper?"

"Half a mile off South Amity Beach, bearing one three seven from Amity breakwater light. No visible debris."

Sounded near. He tried to concentrate on the water, but what was happening a half mile from Amity Beach?

"She reports the explosion was just past the surf line. Suggest you move inshore . . ."

"Roger, out."

God, the explosion was at *Amity*?

He glanced down the shoreline. He could see a

coast guard cutter off South Amity Beach, and the coast guard helicopter was thrashing down the shoreline, tail high.

Where was Andrews?

He heard a sound behind him and almost fell off the boat. He whirled, going for his gun.

The giant was standing on the rear diving platform, looking down at him. He held out a small black camera, with a very large strobe-light.

"Sorry," said Andrews. "Spooked?"

Brody took the camera. His hand was shaking. "Yeah."

"Bad vibes down there, too." He took off his mask and shook it off. "Funny . . ."

Brody saw that his deep-set eyes were troubled.

"I found the camera right away. Ten yards off the stern of the *Orca*."

"Nothing else?" His voice sounded hollow in his own ears.

Andrews shook his head. "They're gone, man. Booze, nitrogen narcosis, 'rapture of the deep,' down too long, maybe. One panics, maybe the other tries to help him, they're trying to buddy-breathe, a fin comes off, the tide sweeps them out, I don't know . . ."

Brody felt seasick. He wanted to get home.

"Worth another search?" he asked Andrews. "More divers, I mean?"

Andrews shrugged. "If they're on the bottom, they're long dead." He swept his hand seaward. "And if they're out *there*, they're dead, too. 60° water. Hypothermia. Eight hours max, wetsuit or not."

They contacted Shinnecock coast guard by radio. Brody reported the dive.

"Thanks, chief," Shinnecock crackled. "We got another problem for you . . ." The idiot who blew himself up, said Shinnecock, had been off South

Amity Beach, maybe towing a skier, maybe not, conflicting reports. Would Brody check it out?

"Oh, God," moaned Brody. "OK, OK."

He hung up the microphone. He looked at his watch. Barely eleven o'clock. His headache had spread to his neck.

They churned past Amity bell-buoy and back to Town Dock. Andrews, who seemed to know everything, had inspected the camera, announced that two pictures had been shot, and carefully removed the film.

Brody dropped it at Starbuck's Pharmacy.

He was no detective. The coasties had had no right to stick him with the yacht.

But there might be a clue on the film to what happened.

For the next of kin.

6

He pulled the department dune buggy to the rear of Minnie's house. The Casino del Mar had built a chain-link fence between Minnie's and the 100-foot strip he used to own, but had sold to the Casino almost two years before.

He moved along the flagstone walk to her kitchen door, between the miraculous rows of roses, now just blooming, that she had managed to grow by burying soil boxes in the sand. He could see, beyond her house, that the Coast Guard chopper was still thrumming wildly up and down the surf line.

Knowing that it was no use, he banged on the screen door. Finally he opened it and walked in. Her kitchen was immaculate as always. Just being there made him hungry, and he thought he could actually smell the brownie-scent from her oven.

"Minnie!" he called, without much hope.

No answer.

He stepped into the living room, crammed with seashells and pressed flowers. She was sitting at her window, back ramrod-straight, enjoying the aerial activity she had brought to her isolation. Her tawny Siamese stared at him contemptuously, slithered from her lap, and stalked into her bedroom. She still did not know he was there.

"Minnie!" he shouted.

She turned from the window, put her glasses on, twirled her hearing aid, and regarded him wryly.

She looked at her cuckoo clock, ticking in the corner between a lithograph of the *Titanic* and a framed letter from Postmaster General Farley thanking her for twenty years of faithful service. It was dated 1942.

"Good thing somebody wasn't drowning, maybe they were. Or suppose I was being raped?"

"Minnie," said Brody, "are you trying to tell me you'd call us for a rapist?"

"Only if he tried to get away," she said primly. "Now, before you start trying to be a TV policeman, you go out there and look in the upper-left-hand corner of the cupboard, you know, the cookie corner, and—"

"I can't, Minnie. There's just too damn much going on."

"In Amity? That's a lot of BM."

" 'BS'," Marty said patiently. " 'BS' is better, Minnie."

"Whatever." She settled herself. "Now, what do you want to know? Or do we just shoot the wind?"

"Breeze." He took out his report book. "Len logged your call at 10:35. Was that when you heard the explosion?"

It was. And it checked out with the Sunday watchman at the Casino building site, who had seen nothing, but heard a boom at about that time, while brewing coffee in his shack. He'd thought it was a navy jet from Quonset, and had not even bothered to climb a dune to look out at the water.

Jamie Culver, the *Times* delivery boy, remembered a ski-boat earlier, towing a skier. Daisy Wicker had seen it, too, with no skier. Minnie had heard the howl of its engine when she went out on the porch to read her *Times*. She had seen it, too, before she put on her glasses, but it was too far off to tell if it had been towing a skier.

Anyway, once she had sat down in her rocker,

turned off her hearing aid, and put on her reading glasses, boat and everything else disappeared from her universe.

The explosion must have been tremendous, to break through to her private world.

Brody shut his book, accepted a cookie, took a second one for the road, and finally a bagful for Ellen and the boys.

He climbed into the dune buggy, jammed it into 4-wheel drive, and skirted her house. He found a clear shot at the beach, and rocketed to the hard sand below.

It seemed to him that the tide had a westward drift, so he turned west on the beach and began to drive at walking-pace, searching for debris.

He dreaded finding anything. He had always hated looking for floaters, even before The Trouble.

The Trouble was over, though.

Nothing he would find today would be as bad as *that*.

The fat man had not been able to get back to sleep. He lay tensely in the canyon he made in the flabby mattress, listening to the rumble of his wife's snoring.

Next year, *next year*, he promised himself, there would be no Amity. He even hated the name of the town, what did it mean, anyway? Something like the pardon Carter had given the goddamn long-hairs?

So here he was, spending his hard-earned vacation again in a town named after it, or something like it.

Amity . . .

He'd rather be down at the Precinct locker-room, telling lies.

Roughly, he shook his wife. "Look, goddamn it, you going to sleep all day? I'm frigging near starved."

The big cow eyes opened reproachfully. "Huh?"

"Huh, hell. It's damn near noon, and the seals been stirring up the dog and the kid, and you just sleep—"

"Seals?" she repeated.

"Seals! Next year, so help me, I go deer-hunting with the commissioner! You and the kid can spend your summer at Coney Island!"

The big brown eyes filled with tears, giving her that certain passive appeal that only inflamed him. Well, he knew how to close them.

But before he could even get started, the dog began to yelp on the beach. The bedroom door creaked and he went for the .38 on the bedside table.

His little boy was tiptoeing in. He rolled over, slapped the kid across the face, and sent him spinning to the floor. "*Knock*, you knucklehead!"

The child looked up: "You said *quiet*! There's another seal!"

He hit the deck and stumbled to the closet. "Where's my gun?"

He thrashed through the mess inside, threw five rounds of Hi-Speed into the Savage, hiked up his pajamas, grabbed the boy by the wrist, and dragged him out the door.

His wife was howling behind them. She probably thought he was going to murder the kid.

He didn't stop to explain.

Maybe the scare would jazz her up.

Brody stopped the dune buggy and squinted into the dazzle of the surf. Whatever it was that was tumbling in the foam was yellow and looked like part of a fiberglass boat.

He pulled the buggy well away from the tide, got out, and took off his shoes and socks. He rolled up his pants, unholstered his gun, and laid it on the passenger seat.

He had been finding bits of debris for the last five minutes: a styrofoam cooler, a cushion, a blackened, twisted piece of wooden rail.

He walked to the edge of the water. He heard a mighty thumping approaching. The coast guard chopper, hardly higher than his head, reared to a stop over the surf, whipping up a minor typhoon and soaking his pants with salt water. It hovered for a moment. Then the pilot swept his hand around the area, shrugged regretfully, touched his finger to his helmet in farewell, and soared, sandblasting Brody as he spiraled away over the beach.

He'd had enough time in the infantry to expect the contempt of the eagle for the rodent, but he'd never got used to it. He swore until he felt better, and plodded into the surf.

The water was freezing. He had no idea why anyone would come to Amity to dive in it, swim in it, or even ski over the top of it. They were all out of their minds.

He plucked from the wavelets a shard of fiberglass. Its shininess was already scoured from the bottom sand.

He trudged back to dry land. A passing gull jeered at him. He stood for a moment, intending to let his feet dry before he put on his socks.

Pang . . . Pang-pang . . .

Three shots, very loud and close, sounded from behind the western dunes.

Still barefoot, he dove behind the wheel, jerked ahead, spinning his tires, and sped toward the sound. He soared over the nearest dune, jammed on the brake and skidded sidewise, almost landing on a fat man and a boy and showering them with sand.

The fat man was kneeling on a knoll, ready to fire again. The boy stood behind him, fingers to his ears. A huge shabby dog cringed behind them. On the beach near the water, a little pile of beige fur barked plaintively.

The man half turned, swinging the rifle. His eyes were red. Drunk? Brody found himself standing in the jeep, forefinger leveled, gun forgotten on the seat beside him. "Drop it!" he ordered.

The man did not drop the rifle, but he cradled it under his arm. "Hi," he said. He extended his hand. "Charlie Jepps. Sergeant. Fourth Precinct, Flushing."

Brody reached down, yanked the rifle away and tossed it into the rear. He jerked his thumb toward the seat beside him, remembered his revolver was still there, and fumbled for it.

The man seemed amused. "You County, or Amity P.D.?"

"Sit there!" ordered Brody. "You're under arrest."

"Whadda ya mean, 'under arrest'?"

"Township ordinance, for openers." He jumped from the buggy, raced for the water, holstering his gun. A baby harbor seal, high and dry in the sand, stared up at him in wonder. Blood oozed from a wound at the base of its tail. It coughed again, politely, great liquid pupils glazed with pain.

All eyes and agony and a long way from momma . . .

He scooped it into his arms. It was heavier than he'd thought, and smelled strongly of fish, and bled on his khaki pants. He staggered back to the buggy, laid it on the debris in the rear seat.

The man had still not climbed in. Brody drew his gun. "In," he yelled. "Get in the buggy!"

"You don't figure," the fat man suggested, "you better call your chief?"

Brody, for the first time in his life, pointed a loaded weapon at another human being. Nothing happened.

He cocked it.

The boy wailed, the dog barked, and from the porch of the gray house on the bluff a blowsy woman began to bellow.

The fat man got in. He smelled of whisky and beer.

It was all, as Brody admitted afterward, a very unpolicelike operation, but at least he had caught the sonofabitch red-handed.

7

Brody's head felt as if he had just tried to tackle Sean's hero, the Juice. He tried to sort out the chaos that had fallen on his office while the fat man, seated in his pajamas in front of Brody's desk, glared at him. The sergeant—if he *was* a sergeant—seemed to grow redder by the moment.

Maybe he'd have a coronary and save everybody's Sunday. *You'll cool off*, Brody promised him silently. They had turned the township jail cell, over the years, into a storage room for school board records, and Henry Kimble was clearing it out now. *You'll cool off tonight, you bastard . . .*

Brody moved to the dispatch desk, where Hendricks was leafing through a tattered copy of "*Federal Wild Life Statutes.*"

Hendricks pointed out a paragraph. "Once he's booked, I don't think Norton *can* set bail. Not without a federal attorney being here."

"Good." Willy Norton was justice of the peace, when they could find him. Brody turned to Dick Angelo. "Snap it up, Dick? OK?"

Dick Angelo had found the fingerprint cards where Polly kept them. Now he settled himself under the picture of Mayor Larry Vaughan to study the directions. Jesus, did he have to learn it here, in front of the suspect? How come he didn't *know* how to fingerprint, he was supposed to be a cop!

"Christ, Dick, *I'll* print him. Or go see if Polly's home. And tell Henry to get a necktie. I want him to be bailiff if we have a hearing. Where *is* Norton?" he called to Hendricks.

"He was painting his kid's tree-house. He's washing up." The phone on the dispatch desk rang, and Hendricks picked it up. "Amity Police."

"*Police*?" snorted the fat man. "Look, Brody—"

" 'Chief'," grated Brody. He sat down and drew an arrest form from his desk. He inserted the form in his typewriter.

"The animal was attacking my dog," said the fat man.

"What's your permanent address, 'Sergeant'?"

The fat man spit out an address in Flushing. He continued in a monotone: "I was trying to scare it off. I'm an expert rifleman, check with the Flushing P.D. If I'd *wanted* to kill it, I coulda blown its head off!"

"Too bad you couldn't *miss* it. Local address? Never mind, the Smith place."

"You can't hold me on a misdemeanor! You never *seen* me shoot it!" He added that when the State Police Commission heard about this, which would be like tomorrow at nine, Brody would be lucky to get a job *feeding* seals at the Bronx Zoo. "You got false-arrest insurance?"

Brody smiled at him. "I won't need it. It's a *federal* charge, friend. Under the Marine Mammal Protection Act of 1972. A year and 20 grand. That little guy's a harbor seal, not a tin can. A *federal* rap!"

He shook the fat man not at all. The cold monotone never changed: his kid used that beach, *babies* played on that beach, you going to toss a law enforcement officer in your half-assed slammer for trying to protect the public? Seals had teeth, didn't they?

"Not very long teeth, not this one," said Brody. "The vet says he's about three weeks old." He felt his temper rising. His right temple was killing him, and his back was clamping into spasm. He forced himself to relax.

Hendricks was trying to get his attention from the dispatch desk. "Chief?" he mouthed. "Miranda? *Miranda!*"

Oh, Jesus, he had forgotten to read him his rights! Quickly he did so, from a card in his wallet. Then he had Hendricks type them out, hunt and peck, since they couldn't find Polly's forms. He hoped he never had to book another suspect on a Sunday, she was worth more than the rest of his whole force put together.

Hendricks laid the result on Brody's desk. "Doc Lean called. Seal's OK, but he's driving the dogs up the wall. He says we got to go get it." He raised a finger for silence.

Amity Animal Clinic, a block away, was sounding like the hound-chorus from *Uncle Tom's Cabin*, played full-up in stereo. The seal was legal evidence, had to be looked after, but obviously they couldn't leave it there. He called Ellen and told her to pick it up and put it in the garage, with plenty of water.

"OK, you *hear* that, down the street," observed the fat man reasonably. "Now, how you going to sleep? What am I supposed to do, shoot my dog instead? Third seal this morning?"

"*Third* seal?"

"Third today. Two yesterday."

Lying bastard. Amity Beach never had seals. They stayed offshore, barking and laughing at the summer people. This one was a lost pup, obviously, confused without its mother, maybe caught by a wave . . .

Or shot offshore and swept in by the surf?

He chilled, struck by an unspeakable suspicion.

He turned back to the arrest report in his typewriter. His hands were shaking. It might all fall into place . . .

"You shoot at the others?" he asked, pretending faint interest. "Yesterday?"

"No."

"How'd you get rid of them?"

"Showed 'em my badge," the cop smiled thinly.

"Funny you didn't shoot yesterday. Guy likes to shoot seals, seems he'd do it any chance he got. Shoot 'em in the water, even. Why let them *get* ashore, to terrorize the population, chew up the kids?"

The little green eyes flashed hate, but the fat man did not answer.

Brody was so shaky he misspelled his own name at the bottom of the form, and had to erase. He swung away from the machine.

"A little target practice, yesterday, from the porch?" His voice rose. "You're an expert, you told me that, and experts *hit*, man. They don't miss what they aim at. How's your eyesight?"

No answer. Brody's pulse was pounding.

He went on: "Good enough to tell a seal from a diver in a hood? Good enough for that, fat-boy?"

The green eyes widened. "You got me shooting divers?"

"I don't know." He arose, shaking. "If they're there, we'll find them. We'll find them, you bastard, with your Savage and your Hi-Speed ammunition, shooting up our beach. And if we do, we'll send you up for so long you'll *never* come down!"

He sat down. He was sick to his stomach, his

head ached, he wondered if it was Sean's fish, delayed.

The sergeant pointed at the phone: "I get to make a call."

Brody shrugged: "Go ahead."

The sergeant phoned his wife: "Get the commissioner. Tell him to find me the best lawyer in New York State." He paused, smiled coldly, and shook his head. "Don't *worry* who pays for it. There's a jerk right here's going to pay for it." His little eyes met Brody's. "He just don't seem to know it yet."

The sergeant hung up. Hendricks was gaping across the room. He looked scared. Henry Kimble shambled in, wearing his uniform tie for the first time in his career. He'd cleared the cell of school board records, and Judge Norton was in chambers.

Brody nodded toward the fat man. "Book him," he said, "and we'll see what we can do."

He wished he had time for a drink.

The seal weighed almost 200 pounds. She craned her neck from the water, searching the beach. She had been there for almost an hour, though some visceral instinct impelled her to be somewhere, anywhere, else.

She watched the shaggy dog, sniffing near the edge of the water. Her whiskers quivered, but she was safe, here behind the surf line. Safe from anything *ashore* . . .

Every now and then a tiny moan would escape her. She barked once, inquiringly. She sensed somehow that it had not been from seaward that her pup had been snatched. He must have caught her fear and floundered up on the sand, while she, thinking him near her, afraid for his safety even more among the shore creatures than the monster they felt offshore, had paralleled the surf, making for the breakwater where he would be secure from both The Terror and the dogs.

Finally, skimming the cloudy bottom sand, she had known that somewhere in the murk she had lost him. She did not turn immediately. Her fear of what was to seaward was too great for that. She had slithered up on the breakwater, yelping for him, and rested there for a moment.

She was a harbor seal. Unlike the fur seal, she had never known a rookery. Last year she had mated at sea. Three weeks ago, she had borne her pup away from land. She had nursed it far from her fellows, and from shore, romped with it alone and taught it to dive and pluck crabs and lobsters from the bottom, and swallow the little rocks which would help him digest them. She had cradled him in her flippers when he tired, though her own feeding suffered, for she could submerge for 45 minutes and he only 15.

A female seal of another family, like the fur seal or the sea lion, or the elephant seal, might have abandoned him now, knowing the risk and sensing, too, that perhaps in a few weeks she could find an orphan to mother, northward in the summer rookery. But this one had never seen a rookery. To her he was the only pup in the ocean, and for weeks she had known no other being but him. When he had not come to the breakwater, she slid back into the water, although she knew it was far too soon for her own safety.

The signs, to seaward, of a fast white death were still very close. She had ignored them and swum back along the beach, stroking strongly with her flippers and steering with her tail.

When she had come at last to this place she knew it was the spot he had landed.

The dog was still scrabbling in the sand. She backed her flippers and shot ten feet offshore.

She could not see the beach well, in the dazzle of the setting sun, or smell her pup. She listened for his cry, but heard nothing.

She had the sense again of doom from seaward. She floated 15 feet closer to the sand. The dog saw her and began to bark.

She waited, craning, for the sun to sink.

The preliminary hearing, held in the mayor's office because Amity had no courtroom, was over. Willy Norton, justice of the peace, put his feet on Mayor Vaughan's desk and sat back in the mayor's executive chair—$130 from Sears, before The Trouble, and it better damn well last.

"OK, Brody," he said, fixing him with troubled brown eyes. "He'll probably be out tomorrow, but you *did* it."

There was a metallic clang from across the hall. Henry Kimble had slammed the cell door. Brody should have welcomed the sound, but his stomach was jumping and he had a feeling of disbelief. Suppose he'd acted too quickly? A seal was a seal, why lose your cool? And as for the skindivers, suppose he was wrong there? Anything could have happened to them, stoned at the bottom of the sea . . .

"*We* did it," Brody reminded him.

"I don't think you can sue a JP," mumbled Norton. He drove the school bus, led the cub pack, was on the chamber of commerce, headed the PTA: he was a young service-station operator on his way up. Brody hoped he hadn't shot him down. "*Can* you, Brody? Sue a justice of the peace?"

"Nobody's suing anybody," said Brody, rising. "Damn it, he broke the Township firearms ordinance and a federal statute! How the hell can he sue?"

He wished that he felt as sure as he sounded.

He checked to see that his force had properly

worked out a jailer-schedule for the night. If their first prisoner in three years didn't get sprung by tomorrow, Brody would face budget trouble for overtime with the selectmen. And they had to buy the prisoner's dinner, he'd forgotten that, and Polly had the key to the small-change drawer. He gave Angelo three dollars and told him to feed him from the new Colonel Sanders on Water and Nantucket. "I hope he chokes."

He locked up the rifle for evidence, strolled to the cell door for a last silent look at the prisoner, who was sitting on the bunk cursing him steadily. As Willy Norton said, he would probably be out tomorrow, when he got a lawyer. There must be something more they could do to wreck his weekend.

Suddenly he remembered that he had forgotten to inform the Amity *Leader* of the arrest. He glanced at his watch. Harry Meadows, whose gluttony for food was only exceeded by his appetite for work, would be there now, laying out tomorrow's issue. He dialed the paper. Speaking loudly, so that Jepps could worry about the wire services picking up the feature, he briefed Harry on the first police story of the summer.

"That's all he hit, a seal?" Meadows sounded disappointed.

"A *baby* seal," urged Brody. "Look, Harry, you sobbed for half a page Monday about people taking baby *clams*!"

"Nothing else *happened* Monday. Now, we got two divers drowned and a ski-boat blown up, plus three columns on how we got to let the brownies race in the regatta next week, or your wife says she'll never speak to me again—"

"Suppose," Brody suggested, "the divers and the ski-boat got blasted by the same crazy bastard?"

That got his interest. There was a long silence. "Have you *got* something?" Meadows finally asked.

He heard Jepps rise and move to the cell door.

"Well," said Brody, "a pretty good suspicion."

"Can I quote you?"

Brody drummed his fingers. He wished he knew more about libel law, and slander. "Say it's under investigation."

"Good enough," said Meadows, and hung up.

Brody smiled sweetly at Jepps, who was simply staring at him, zapping him with animal hatred. Christ, he thought, if I ever drive through Flushing, they'll shoot me on sight.

He drove home.

The seal was in the garage. Its name was Sammy. Its bandage had slid off. Sean was already its mother, father, playmate, and mentor. He had a bowl of canned sardines and a plate of hamburger and a pot of milk spread out before his charge. He was cradling the seal, who must have weighed 40 pounds, on his lap.

"Daddy, he's *crying* all the time. Look at his eyes!"

Sean's eyes were moist themselves.

Sean was right. The big brown eyes were wet with tears. "I'll check it out with Doc Lean," Brody promised. "Or somebody."

"And he won't eat!"

"He's had a rough day."

"He won't leave the bandage on."

"Nature knows best." Brody's nose twitched. "What the heck?"

Sean rose, red-faced: "It wasn't his fault! He just hasn't learned yet!"

"You are covered, my friend," murmured Brody, "with seal turd." He found a clean place at the tip of his son's nose, bent, and kissed him on it. "Dump your clothes at the kitchen door, streak past your mother, and take a bath. I won't breathe a word."

Sean scurried off.

Brody filled a bucket and began to wash down the garage. Sammy floundered across to him, drank him in with the moist brown eyes, and shook himself like a dog, spraying him with excrement.

Brody hoped the fat sergeant drew life.

8

Nate Starbuck sat on a stool in the darkroom at the rear of his pharmacy, rocking his film tank. He hated the job. He would have preferred, even, to be upstairs in the flat with Lena watching Lawrence Welk. His skinny rump hurt from the stool, his back ached from a day behind the pharmacy counter, and the smell of developer and hypo had sickened him since youth.

But there was an extra dollar per roll in souping it here instead of sending it to Manhattan Processing, and his father had done it before him, and for all he knew his grandfather too, if they'd had film in the nineties. Tourists would pay double for "rush," not realizing that rush was regular. Every cent counted, when half your net went for bank interest, and you'd come so close to going down the drain . . .

He daydreamed. If the gambling law passed, if Amity became another Atlantic City and the Casino another Regency, if downtown property really came back like Vaughan and the other bigshot experts promised, this time he *would* sell and go to Miami. Damned if he wouldn't, and the hell with Minnie's Geritol and Ellen Brody's thyroid and the *parafon forte*, 3 grains, 3 daily, for Willy Norton's back. And the next tourist who came in with a roll of Ektachrome, he'd just tell him to save it and take it home when he left.

He should have sold before The Trouble, when he had the chance . . .

Ellen Brody opened the door between the kitchen and the little utility room that Brody had built two years ago on the back porch. The clothes drier was still groaning away, patiently tumbling Sean's clothes, and Brody's. She thought she could still catch the musty, fishy scent of Sammy's excrement, but she was not sure.

She stopped the machine and took out Sean's torn and faded blue jeans. She sniffed. She heard her husband at the door.

"All gone?" he asked.

She shrugged. "It's relative. They never did smell like *English Leather.*"

"Sean's sorry," he proposed hopefully.

"Wasn't his fault."

"So's Sammy."

"Wasn't his either."

"*I'm* sorry," said Brody.

"Are you?"

"Look, Ellen, the seal's evidence."

"Then the Township ought to keep him."

"Where?"

"In the high school gym, in the municipal pool, in Harry Vaughan's bathtub," she flared. "I don't care. They can't turn my house into a zoo!"

She was being awful, just awful. She liked the seal, really did, he was beautiful and heart-breaking with his big brown eyes, and she was pleased, way down deep, that Sean had taken to him so quickly, and that the seal seemed to regard Brody as its mother. Maybe that was what was wrong. The seal, like Mike and Sean and everything else Brody touched, fell in love with Brody, and she was left out in the cold.

"I'll ask Doc Lean about moving him," promised Brody.

"Oh, never mind. Sean's *involved*, now." Now *she* was sorry. She looked into his face, for forgiveness. He was smiling, gently. Why did he have to be so damn *Christian* about everything? "It's just that you didn't have to rinse them and wash them, and then do it all again to kill the smell.

"I will next time."

No, he wouldn't. Some Town problem would come up, or one of the boys would want him for something else more important, like painting a boat or buying a wetsuit or getting her to take over a cub scout den.

"OK, Brody," she said gently. "Hey, maybe I *need* that thyroid, I seem to be all up tight."

He helped her unload the dryer. His uniform pants were fine, but there were spots on the shirt and they decided he'd have to use it to garden in, or something. They left the clothes on the ironing board and started upstairs hand in hand. She knew what awaited her and felt a warm and pleasurable rush deep down.

At least that, which had once gone bad, was OK now.

Slipping off his shirt, he snapped his fingers. "Oh, hey, Sean told me to ask you—"

Warning flags. "What?"

"About the brownie thing . . ."

"Stay out of it," she warned. "The brownies *are* getting a canoe for the regatta. And that's *it*!"

"Look, *I* gave in on the Moscotti kid . . ." He looked embarrassed.

"With reason." Johnny Moscotti was the lonely little son of a Queens mobster who summered at Amity. Brody, visiting the sins of the father on the son, had wondered if it was wise to let him into Sean's cub pack. He had tried to argue that the

Moscottis were summer visitors and the pack was for permanent kids. She still got angry when she thought of it. "You talk about *unconstitutional*!"

"The brownie thing is different. Sean thinks—"

"The brownies are going to race," she repeated. "In a cub-scout canoe!"

"Sean thinks—"

"He's a conniving, political, male chauvinist piglet." The injustice of it brought her voice up an octave. "The cubs get everything from the Giant's games to open house at Quonset Point, and the brownies sit home and make cookies. *I* was a brownie, and I'm sick of it, and if the cubs race, the brownies race too!"

"And if they don't," finished Brody grimly, "neither does Den Three?"

"You got it, Brody," she said.

Silently, he stripped and got into bed.

She turned her back and pretended to go to sleep.

There would be none of that tonight.

Nathanial Starbuck's wife knocked at the darkroom door. It had taken 30 years, he reflected, but at least she'd learned that. "OK, OK, light's on," he called. She entered.

"Nate? Cod cakes are ready."

Cod cakes! Damn! He wished he'd left his pole alone last night. He'd be eating cod cakes the rest of his life. "OK," he murmured. "Film's ready to hang."

He removed the roll from the wash, squeezed it, and hung it on a film clip. "Is that Brody's?" asked Lena. "What is it?"

He glanced at the envelope he'd taken it out of. It was Brody's—rush—and he hadn't even noticed.

He seldom bothered to look at a roll, unless he knew it was from one of the swinging summer couples that might shoot pictures of *anything*, but the film swaying on the clip, if Brody was right, was the last picture some dead diver had ever taken. Curious, he grabbed the bottom of the strip, pulled it over so that the light would shine through it, and shook his head. "Nothing. Never shot anything."

"Wait! By your fingers!"

He looked down. She was right. The first two frames were exposed. He reversed the film, holding it by the leader so that he would not smudge it. He inspected the transparencies. Suddenly he adjusted his glasses.

The first shot was of a scuba diver, underwater, posing by the stern of the *Orca* wreck. He squinted at the other.

He could hear the water dripping from his washbath. From upstairs he heard the jounce of Lawrence Welk. His stomach growled.

"Lena," he said hoarsely, "magnifying glass? Over the print tray?"

She handed it to him. He inspected the picture again, but he already knew, he had seen it, he just wanted to be sure, it was incredible, but he had to be sure.

"Nate," his wife cried. "What is it?"

The picture was poorly composed and canted crazily. It was underexposed, not too sharp, as if the camera had been moved. The letters on the *Orca*'s stern were red where they should have been yellow and the monster's teeth were grey where they should have been white.

"Nate?"

He sat heavily on the stool.

The thing was still off Amity.

They had not killed it, Brody had lied.

The Trouble was back, had never left.

He thought he was going to be sick.

He came from a seafaring, whaling family. A tiny

Pacific atoll bore his great-grandfather's name. His forebears had known, first hand, the largest creatures in the seas. The lore of oceans ran in his veins.

If Brody had suspected what was on the film, he would probably have tossed it back into the sea.

For Brody might have lied when he said they'd killed it, but not about its size.

It was the biggest, fattest goddamn White any man had ever seen.

He lifted the film strip to let her see. She peered at it for a long moment. She swung her eyes to him. They were wild with fear.

"Oh, God," she moaned. "What'll we do?"

He managed a smile. "Sell," he shrugged. "Shut up and sell. What else?"

PART TWO

1

The White had cruised last night from Amity to Fire Island light. She had traveled steadily at ten knots. She had taken a young bull seal off Sagaponack and hit a school of sea bass off Great South Beach. At Fire Island she had doubled northeast again. In turning, she had surprised a giant squid which, sensing her passing, sank to the bottom to hide in a 15-fathom reef, then resumed his course too soon and died in a blinding flash of white-hot power.

She flushed a sandbar shark off Southampton, lost it because her girth had cut her speed. During the night she had consumed 300 pounds of living protein, but by dawn, back off Amity, she was ravenous again.

She had driven a school of cod into Amity Harbor two days before, and now she found another and herded it into Amity Sound. She was homing in on its greatest mass when a rhythmic *chung . . . chung . . . chung . . .* from the 11:30 Amity Neck ferry confused her sensors and dispersed the school. She was so hungry by then that she very nearly went for the strange, angular shadow passing above her, but she sheered off at the last moment.

She was seen by no one aboard, although the captain's dog, Williwaw, perched on the main deck ahead of the load of six cars, began to bark excitedly.

She skimmed the bottom, her *ampullae* scanning the mud for buried sting-rays. She scooped up a rubber fisherman's boot and shook it. One of the teeth in her upper last row was slightly dislodged, triggering an automatic, convulsive need to swallow. Though her computor-mind recognized the boot as non-protein and she dropped it, synapses triggered by the tooth impelled her to wheel and find it again. She scooped it up and consumed it in a cloud of silt.

In her right uterus the smallest of her brood turned on the largest of his squirming sisters and fought her off.

Brody parked the dune buggy above the high-water mark, near where he'd found Sammy the seal. On the porch of the Smith House the policeman's fat wife glared at him for a moment, then disappeared inside, dragging the little boy. Brody helped Tom Andrews into his diving gear.

The bearded giant had finally agreed to accept pay for looking for the demolished ski-boat. He pulled on his flippers. Then he strode to the water, using enormous, exaggerated steps to keep the flippers from tripping him in the sand. He looked like the Jolly Green Giant in black. When he reached the water he turned and began to walk backward into the surf. He whirled and slid into an onrushing breaker, leaving hardly a ripple. The whole operation looked like the launching of a nuclear submarine at Groton, across the Sound.

Brody picked up his microphone. "Car 3. I'm on Smith's beach, Polly."

"Roger, Martin," said Polly. "Ellen called. She said bring home evaporated milk for Sammy."

"Ten-4." He wrote it down on his ticket book. Sammy had thrown up Sean's morning offering, adding the finishing touches to his previous night's work on the garage. What the poor damn thing needed was a mother's care, and mother was out there somewhere, probably, waiting to provide it. He decided to photograph the wound, for evidence, so that they could turn Sammy loose when he was well enough to swim. It would break Sean's heart.

Phil Hoople's taxi jounced along the Beach Road and stopped at the house. It was Jepps returning to his rented home. A rumpled law clerk from Flushing had arrived this morning, all yellowing smiles and sympathy for Jepps and hostility for Brody. He had left the Township of Amity $500 bail and business cards galore.

Now Jepps, leaving the cab, saw him in the dune buggy, stiffened, and moved thoughtfully into the house.

For a half hour Brody waited for Andrews. Once he stood on the seat of the dune buggy, to see if he could spot the bubbles, but the churning of the surf near the beach was too active. He was glancing more and more at his watch, overcome by a feeling of apprehension, when the shaggy dog burst over the eastern dunes and charged halfway down, barking at him. Jepps followed, his gut overhanging a wisp of a swimming suit so small that for a wild moment Brody thought he had him for nude bathing. He approached the dune buggy. Brody pretended to be tuning his radio.

"Brody?"

"Yeah?"

The fat cop was smiling at him, though his eyes were as cold as ever. "Look, Brody," he began, "I'm up here for a vacation. I come every year. This town needs all the summer trade it can get—"

"Not to shoot up our beach."

"I was *wrong*, Brody! I'm trying to tell you."

Brody pointed out that he didn't *have* to tell him that, he had a guy on the bottom right now trying to find out just how wrong he was. They looked to sea. Andrews was growing from the surf, like some prehistoric monster. The dog yapped louder. The policeman shook his head. "You're still looking for them divers?"

"We'd like to find out," said Brody, "if they got holes in their heads."

In his hand Andrews carried what looked like the remains of a shattered gas tank. It was red. He clomped ashore, pulling off his fins, and put the tank on the hood of the dune buggy. "No divers. I found the engine but I couldn't budge it. And I found this."

Brody studied the gas tank. He was no explosives expert, had never studied ballistics, but the red gas tank was a very odd relic indeed. One side was blown completely out; the other had in it a gaping hole, as if struck by a projectile. He glanced at Jepps.

The fat man was staring at the tank. His eyes bulged. A tiny muscle in his jaw began to work. He swung his little eyes toward Brody.

"Ok, 'chief.' I don't know how you run your police force. I don't know how you run your crummy town. But I know when there's somebody trying to set me up." He tapped the tank on the hood. "Go ahead with *this* and we'll have your *ass*!"

He wheeled and walked away.

"What the hell," rumbled Andrews, "was *that*?"

Brody picked up the can. It reeked faintly of gasoline. He poked a finger through the hole.

"He must have got drunk for the weekend," he mused. "He used our beach for a shooting gallery. He got more ducks than he planned." Angrily, he tossed the can into the rear of the buggy. His voice was shaking. "And I think he knows it, too."

He started the buggy and they rolled along the beach back to town. The headache was starting up again.

What was he supposed to do now?

Nate Starbuck sneaked a glance out the prescription window. His wife Lena was still dusting the cosmetics counter. She had been at it for 15 minutes, with a vacuous, stupid look on her face. She was wasting time, there were other things to do, and her thoughtfulness made him uncomfortable.

He turned back to his inventory. He was counting pill bottles. He had lost track, damn it, with her mooning around, and now he would have to start over. Suddenly he abandoned the task. They had better straighten it out right now.

"Lena!"

She jumped as if he had goosed her. He used to, all the time, a million years ago, just for laughs, and she would start and giggle and pretend to slap him. Jesus, they had been idiots, in those days. She still was, if he let her be.

"Yes?"

"Come here!" He led her back to the darkroom, flicking the red "keep out" light so that Jackie wouldn't wander in and disturb them. He wished he could get *Jackie* in here but she'd probably tell daddy and he'd have the whole Amity police force on his neck.

"Lena, what's biting you? Forget you ever saw it!"

"I *did* see it. And so did you." She looked him full in the face for the first time in years. "Somebody *else* could get killed!"

"I hope it's Brody."

"Nate!"

"Except," he continued viciously, "he don't go near the water, does he? He or his kids."

"*He* never did. Even before!"

He ignored her. "He got *his* money out. *He* got to be a hero. And he sold *his* goddamn land!"

He began to stride back and forth, hands clenching. He had already told her all that last night, she just couldn't seem to get it through her stupid head.

It was a plot, by the ins, against him and the rest of the outs. Mayor Larry Vaughan must have known, all this time, and Willy Norton, the great justice of the peace, and the selectmen. Knowing the shark still lived, they had hidden the fact and taken Peterson and his syndicate for plenty, on the Casino deal. Well, that was his own ace in the hole. He'd sell too, before it was too late.

"I don't *want* to sell!" Lena murmured. "This is our home!"

"Well, we're *going* to. For as much as we can, as quick as we can, and move as far as we can from Amity. I hope the shark eats the whole goddamn place!"

"We never found a buyer, during The Trouble."

"*During* The Trouble? The Trouble never left! And The Trouble never will!"

There was no use trying to explain it to her. She knew nothing about sharks or the sea. His great-grandfather, who had lived to 89, had hobbled with him along Water Street one day, when he was a kid. He sat on a piling on Town Dock—the old wharf, not this one—filled his pipe, and started in again on his tales of the whaling days, and Nate listened, not with his ears—for he'd heard the stories from infancy—but with the pores of his skin.

A Great White off Sydney, Australia, had hit one of the old bastard's whaleboats in 1897 and very nearly capsized it. The same shark attacked a flensed carcass in 1899, a half-mile away. For the White *lived* there.

A White off Tonga had turned the water red with the blood of a sperm they'd taken in '96 and the same shark—still carrying the stub of the old man's flensing knife—had hit another in '98. Same place.

Sharks were jealous of their waters. And they didn't leave.

When the Good Lord made the Great White shark, he was tired. He forgot to give him fear. If he found a feeding ground to his taste, why would he ever depart?

"Suppose we can't sell?" she whispered. "Suppose nobody wants it?"

"I think," Nate Starbuck smiled thinly, "somebody'll want it."

When he had her calmed down, he patted her rump—it felt like the bumper on his old Dodge van—and opened a brand new roll of film. He felt funny exposing it, under the bright light, after all the years of handling it in darkness, and it seemed a wasteful thing to do.

But he overcame his reluctance—it was only $1.30 dealer-price. With the whole drugstore at stake, what difference did $1.30 make?

He developed it blank and hung it up to dry.

Brody found a break in the sand cresting South Amity Beach, downshifted the dune buggy, and went into four-wheel drive. Andrews held on to his air-tank as they ground to the top of the knoll, heading for the Beach Road. Brody felt Andrews' hand on his arm.

"Wait . . ."

Brody stopped and followed his gaze. Far down the beach a group of lanky teen-agers had spread towels on the deserted sand. Most of them were in wet-suits, probably kids from Andrews' Scuba class.

Andrews watched them. "Just wanted to make sure nobody got hold of a tank somewhere, to beat the gun. OK, let's go."

"Wait . . ." said Brody.

His eyes were on the closest boy. He reached for the binoculars in the rack under the dash. He focused.

It was Mike. He was wearing his suit. Further down the beach Larry Vaughan, the mayor's son, sprang from a towel, raced into the water, and flung himself into an oncoming wave. The roller continued in, its crown a sliver arrow speeding under the noonday sun.

Mike watched it come, squatted, and let shallow waters rise to his hips. Larry beckoned him from beyond the surf line. He waved back, took a few steps out, yawned self-consciously. Suddenly he grabbed the back of his leg and hobbled from the water.

The big man regarded Brody uneasily. "He . . . subject to cramps?"

"He'll be OK," said Brody tightly.

He was not going to apologize for Mike to anyone, for anything.

Or tell him, since Mike obviously hadn't, of what, once, the poor damn kid had seen.

Brody faced the druggist across the counter. "What do you mean, you screwed up?"

Nate regarded him with pale blue eyes. "Well, it wasn't me, exactly." He nodded toward his wife, who had a clipboard in her hand and was counting lipsticks in a rack behind the counter. "She opened the darkroom door."

"*Nothing* left on the film?" Brody couldn't believe it.

Starbuck opened a drawer, took a roll of film from a yellow envelope marked: "RUSH: AMITY P.D." He held it up. It was clear from one end to the other.

"Damn," breathed Brody.

"Probably nothing on it *before*. Hear they were drunk."

"And now we'll never know, will we, Nate?"

Starbuck shook his head. Brody felt his blood rising. He had met the dead lawyer's widow this morning. She was a stricken woman with great black eyes. He had promised to send the film when her brother arrived to move the boat.

"Damn it, Nate, it's the last picture the guy ever took! What do I tell his wife?"

Starbuck shrugged. He seemed to be undergoing a mental struggle. His brow furrowed and his fingers tapped. Suddenly, as if he had resolved a painful dilemma, he reached into the film rack and tossed a yellow box on the counter.

"Tell her we're giving her a fresh roll of film."

Brody looked into the blue Yankee eyes, vacant as the sea.

"I'll *tell* her you said you were sorry, Nate. You can shove the film!"

Outside, he discovered he'd forgotten Ellen's thyroid pills again. He was damned if he'd go back.

2

By noon the seal was skirting the Amity beachline, swimming toward the breakwater and the confines of Amity Sound. She had spent most of the night off the spot at which she had lost her pup. Finally she had actually trundled ashore on the beach, despite the dog-smell. There she sensed that she was very close to where her pup had been. She nosed the dry sand. The scent of his blood excited her greatly.

But he was there no longer, and finally at dawn she had reentered the water. She floated offshore for an hour indecisively. She saw the strange two-tailed man-creature enter and dive, heard his raucous foreign gasping for half an hour as he skimmed the bottom like a sandshark searching out rays.

She had no fear of the diver, experience having taught her that he would leave her alone.

When he left, she paralleled the beach until she reached Amity breakwater. She heaved herself up on the rocks, safe from the terror which she still sensed to seaward. She lay under the whitewashed tower of Amity light. A male harbor seal was already sunning himself there, but she paid no attention to him, nor he to her.

She was basking under the noonday sun, still overcome by a tight feeling of loneliness, when some force seemed to impel her back into the water. She swam across the harbor entrance, round the point, and turned up into Amity Sound itself.

This was confining and unfamiliar territory. She preferred, ordinarily, the open ocean. But she had the feeling that her pup was somewhere near, so she stopped a hundred yards from a white clapboard house, floating and craning and letting the feeling of his closeness comfort her.

She did not see, smell, or hear him, but she sensed somehow that he was not too far away.

And so she stayed.

Brody sipped his luncheon beer, watching his sons finish their sandwiches. Sean was scowling at the Amity *Leader*, spread before him. Suddenly he thrust it at his father.

"Read it to me, dad," he demanded. "It's about Sammy."

Brody shook his head. "*You* read it to *me*." Sean hated to read. Strange, when half his own life was books, and Ellen's too.

Sean frowned, but began, in schoolroom monotone:

> *"Amity: A vacationing police officer was arrested yesterday for allegedly shooting and wounding a baby seal on Amity Beach. He was reportedly charged with . . . vilation?"*
>
> "*Violation*," Mike interrupted. He craned to see, grabbed the paper, smoothed it out and commenced, staccato: *"He was reportedly charged with violation of the Marine Mammals Protection Act and a municipal ordinance against discharging firearms in the town limits."*
>
> He cleared his throat importantly. *"The suspect was identified as Sergeant Charles Jepps, 54, of the Flushing Police Department. He is a summer visitor temporarily renting Smith's Sandcastle, 118 W. Beach Road. Chief Martin Brody said the suspect was bound over for*

County Court after a preliminary hearing before Justice of the Peace William Norton.

"According to Brody, the victim was a 3-week-old harbor seal. Brody says he is conducting a further investigation to determine whether shootings by the accused are connected with two missing divers and a boat explosion off Amity Beach (see Page One)."

"Boy," groaned Ellen, "you don't mind sticking your neck out, do you?"

She was right. Though Harry Meadows seemed to have protected the *Leader* with the usual "*allegedly*," "*reportedly*," and "*according to Brody*," his own tail sounded like it was out a mile.

He finished his beer. "Well, I was P.O.ed. But no sweat," he said, trying to project confidence. "He *did* shoot the seal."

"And you put him in jail, right?" Sean prompted, "Right, dad?"

"He wants to get it straight," Mike sighed. "He's bringing Sammy up to date."

Brody nodded: "I put him in jail, Sean. But he's out now. On bail."

Sean's eyes widened. "That isn't fair! Just one night?"

"Tell Sammy I'll do my best to put him back."

Sean shot off to the garage. Brody studied his older son. Mike was toying with his food. He had stayed irritable, jumpy, with the same haunted eyes he had shown for days. Brody decided to take him aside, for he had a good idea why.

Two years before, when The Trouble had hit, Mike and Sean had been as amphibious as frogs. The shark attacks on the first few victims had not had the slightest effect on either: it had been all he could do to keep them out of the ocean off Amity Beach. He had ordained that they swim only off the muddy shore that bordered their back yard on Amity Sound.

At the height of a false panic—and for weeks they had had them almost daily off the beach—while Mike swam in a tidal pond and Sean played in the sand nearby, the White had slithered under the railroad bridge and struck a man basking on a rubber raft not 50 feet from Mike.

The attack had been hideous enough for Brody, as all of them had: there was all *that* mess to contend with. And the effect on Mike had been catastrophic. His older son had been carried from the water in shock, without a scratch on his body, but with a deep and jagged wound on his soul.

They had never spoken afterward of the attack.

After lunch, Brody drew Mike to the solarium and they sat on the back steps, gazing across the water at the minute daytime flicker of Cape North light, far across Amity Sound. Mike's Laser sat stranded and forlorn on its rack above highwater.

"You going to win Sunday?" asked Brody.

Mike shrugged. "If I race."

"What's that mean?"

"If Jackie gets off."

"Hey, what about Sean?"

"Well, he painted the tiller. I got to take him, I guess. *If* I go . . ."

"You can't just *dump* it! You promised him!"

"OK, I'll go, I'll go! No big deal."

Brody faced him. "You got a problem, Mike?" he asked carefully.

"Problem?" parried Mike. He would not meet his eyes. He craned to look at the watch on Brody's wrist. "What time is it? Jackie—"

"Forget Jackie. I think we ought to talk about your swimming off the Beach."

Mike stirred uncomfortably: "Hey! I thought it was settled!"

"Well, it is, kind of." If Brody told him he had seen him this morning, backing out of the water with the "cramps," palpably fake, it would mortify him, and he'd really clam up. "Have you been doing it?"

Mike shrugged: "Tried out my suit, this morning."

"Keep you warm?"

Mike's eyes shifted: "Fantastic."

"Nice to get back in the ocean?" Brady's voice trailed off. These were grounds full of land mines, and he really did not know what to say.

"Oh, wow! Yeah!"

Brody prodded: "No . . . *feelings*?" *Not too much, at one time* . . . "No . . . *worries*?"

It was like trying to entice Minnie's Siamese off a rooftop without scaring it into a 40-foot dive.

"No!" Mike faced him, fiercely. "Look, you *hate* the water! But you went out with Quint, anyway. I *like* the water! You think I'd worry? Now that it's killed?"

From the garage came a piercing bark, followed by a high-pitched yell from Sean. They moved swiftly across the back lawn.

The garage still smelled horribly of seal and sardines. Sean was locked in struggle with Sammy, who was escaping out the door, Sean looked like a defensive linebacker trying to prevent a touchdown with ten seconds to play. Boy and seal were yelling hysterically.

Brody squatted in front of the seal, who shook his head and tried to nudge him out of the way. The three of them managed to ease him back into the garage.

The bandage had slipped from his wound again. If he wasn't ready to swim soon, they had better see if Woods Hole Institute would take him, or the Bronx Zoo.

"He was OK all morning," Sam explained. The

seal was barking plaintively, his eyes still wet with tears. It would be impossible to keep him here much longer. It would be equally impossible, when he left, to console Sean. "We were just playing, and he tried to split."

Brody led Sean out and closed the door. "Give him a rest." Regretfully, he looked at his watch. In the winter his sons were in school, and in the summer there was never enough time for them. He had an appointment at the Suffolk County Crime Lab in Bay Shore in half an hour. He turned to Mike. "So what'll you do this afternoon?"

Mike shrugged: "Fool around with Jackie; it's her day off. Maybe take her for a swim."

His son looked suddenly taller, lankier, and wiser. And Jackie was certainly ripe. And beautiful, behind her braces.

He had a feeling that the ocean would see less of Mike than the little cradled valleys behind the dunes.

"Try to keep your wet suit on," he said, mussing his hair. "OK?"

Mike blushed: "Come on, Dad!"

Brody climbed into Car #1 and headed for Bay Shore.

He found himself hoping that Jackie would keep Mike out of the water altogether.

But that was stupid. The Trouble was over.

Between the shark and his own dad, the kid had achieved a phobia. He had never really had a chance.

Damn, damn, damn . . .

Larry Vaughan, mayor of Amity and the president of Vaughan and Penrose Realty, liked no one to discuss real estate in his Town Hall office. Clients were to be referred to his clapboard realty shack on Scotch Road. He was afraid that if he used his official quarters for personal gain, the selectmen would simply refuse to fund the office supplies and to pay Daisy Wicker, his secretary, whom he claimed he needed in his mayoral capacity.

But Starbuck had somehow bulled past Daisy and was staring at him across the mayor's desk. Vaughan regarded him distrustfully. Though the pharmacist was opening up a prospect of profit, he was always trouble, always a pain in the tail.

"Sell the drugstore?" Vaughan repeated incredulously. He searched for the druggist's true reason, not being disposed to take another's stated reason—especially in business—as true.

"Yup," said Starbuck. "That's what I aim to do."

"Well, Nathanial," Vaughan said slowly, "I'm shocked, of course, but of course I'll handle it. Your price seems high, but maybe in a month or so, if gambling passes—"

"I'm not talkin' about a month or so. I want to sell now."

An alarm bell jingled in Vaughan's head. Though things were coming up rosy; though reasonably Vaughan knew that Vaughan & Penrose and Amity Township itself faced a vista of unprecedented growth and prosperity—he had said that himself at Rotary—The Trouble had sensitized his antennae.

Tourism was fragile. Confidence in downtown Amity was essential if property values were going to increase. At least, until gambling passed and land skyrocketed all by itself, it was disconcerting to know that a downtown merchant who had ridden out The Trouble wanted to bail out now. Perhaps receipts were down.

Vaughan tapped a pencil on the desk. "Nathanial, let's not discuss price right now. What shocks me, there's been a Starbuck peddling pills—" Not exactly the right phrase, the old bastard had his pride—"What I mean to say, handling the town's pharmaceutical needs for, what is it, three generations? So you can see what a blow—"

"Health," said Starbuck.

"Health?"

"Lena." His eyes did not flicker. "Cancer."

Vaughan chilled. Almost 40 years ago, Lena, then a thin teenager with buck teeth, had been recruited as his daytime babysitter when his parents had spent the summer working for a realtor in East Hampton. She had been warm and friendly and had taught him double solitaire.

"Oh, no!" he exclaimed, "not Lena!"

"She'll have to go to New York Memorial. Sixty, a hundred a day, for God knows how long, and Medicare don't near cover it."

Vaughan drummed his fingers. Starbuck's property was the choicest downtown lot on Main. When the Casino was finished and the law passed, anything south of Scotch Road would be worth a bloody fortune. Starbuck had tried to sell it during The Trouble, and of course there had been no takers, and now it was mortgaged heavily. Vaughan himself had assessed it for the bank. It was possible that Starbuck had no idea of its future value. He wanted $50,000: Vaughan was sure that he could sell it for 75. Or keep it himself and wait . . .

"Tell her I'm sorry, Nathanial. I'll list the pharmacy, at 50. I'll call some prospects in New York. And we'll see what we can do."

Starbuck grinned: "Do that, Larry."

Something in the rare, thin smile puzzled Vaughan.

"I'm sure we can sell it," he said weakly.

"I'm sure you *better*," said Starbuck. He arose, placed his hat squarely on his head and left.

Now what the hell had he meant by that?

Maybe the shock of Lena had got to him. Strange man.

Vaughan decided to let him dangle for a week, offer 35 for Lena's sake, and buy the place himself.

The phone on his desk began to flash. It was Albany, from Clyde Bronson, the state legislator of Amity's district. He had just had a visit from the state police commissioner, who had had a visit from an attorney representing a Flushing police sergeant named Jepps, currently charged with a misdemeanor firearms offense and a federal wildlife violation by the Amity Police.

The state police commission, explained Clyde, were anti-gambling anyway and had files on half the legislators in Albany including, probably, himself. If Vaughan thought that pissing *them* off was going to help the gambling statute pass, Vaughan just thought wrong. "*Do you get my message, Larry?*"

He could hear the legislator breathing strenuously. Vaughan told him that yes, he'd got the message.

He replaced the phone and sat back. He had caught the heavy breathing himself as if it were contagious. He lumbered across the hall to the Amity P.D. Brody's desk was empty. Polly was reading *Fear of Flying.* He glared at her, tight-lipped.

"Where is he?" he demanded.

"Suffolk County Crime Lab. Larry, you're all sweaty. Is something wrong?"

"Nothing firing your boss won't cure."

"You can't," she said primly. "We're civil service."

"The *minute* he comes back!" he barked.

He left Town Hall and headed for a drink at the Randy Bear.

3

Brody parked Car #1 beside a Suffolk County paramedic van in the police zone and took out the Savage rifle, the paper bag with the ammunition he had found in its magazine, and the ski-boat's shattered gas tank. He approached the huge gray building, where last year he had attended a police science seminar.

He felt silly, carrying the weapon and the other evidence, as if he were playing Sherlock Holmes in a PTA benefit at Amity High. As he entered the glass doors, the young desk sergeant looked up and threw his arms in the air.

"Don't shoot, Brody, you can have the whole place."

The sergeant made him sign the visitors book, turned the desk over to another officer, and took him upstairs in the elevator.

Brody dipped in his memory for the young man's name, remembering him as the lecturer on County Police Administrative Procedures. That was it: Sgt. Pappas.

They walked down corridors buzzing with activity. Uniformed, plainclothes and civilian personnel moved purposefully through the hallways. Radios crackled in rooms they passed. Telephones jangled in the bunco division office.

"Rat race," muttered the sergeant. "You need another man out there?"

"They'd make you chief," said Brody, "and you'd starve on my salary."

"Try me," murmured the sergeant. He led Brody through a double door into the crime lab.

Brody remembered it from a tour of the facilities three years before. The sergeant signed in the gun and ammunition and gas tank, watched them as a property clerk tagged them, and then moved across a cluttered laboratory, past the polygraph room, to a door marked "Ballistics Lab."

Across an entire wall hung a collection of weapons, from dainty handbag automatics to a machine gun Brody recognized from GI days as a 50-caliber Browning. Above the collection was printed: "COMPARATIVE BALLISTICS TEST SECTION."

On the adjoining wall was mounted another collection of Saturday Night Specials, tire irons, spiked clubs, brass knuckles, sawed-off shotguns, and a submachine gun. On the stock of the last were engraved a crucifix, a peace symbol, and a swastika. Above the second collection, in gold Gothic script, was painted: "The right of the people to bear arms shall not be infringed."

A pretty young black woman, with a triumphant burst of woolen hair, was peering at a pair of bullets through a binocular-microscope. She swung on her stool when she heard them approaching.

"Brody," said the young sergeant, "this is the pride of Suffolk County. Lt. Swede Johansson. Lieutenant, this is Chief Brody of Amity P.D."

She grouped for something in her memory. "Amity . . . Amity. . ."

"The next Las Vegas East," Brody suggested.

She shook her head. "No. That's not it . . ."

"Late hometown of the Great White Shark," Brody confessed. He hated this, and ran into it all the time. The pall of The Trouble, pervasive as smog, seemed to persist forever in the mind of New Yorkers, like some tribal memory.

The lieutenant snapped her fingers. "Ri . . i . . ght," she drawled. She looked at him curiously. "And *you* were the sharkbait?"

"I was there," admitted Brody.

The young woman had small white teeth, bright brown eyes, and a cute upturned nose. She shivered: "You must have been out of your mind!"

"Out of my element, anyway," said Brody, handing her the rifle. "Like now."

"That's refreshing," she said, glancing at the rifle. "You're the first cop who's walked in here in a year didn't claim to know more ballistics than me."

"He wants to know," the sergeant said, putting the shattered gas tank, the bullets and the rifle on her table, "did this cannon and these rounds make *this* hole, or didn't it? Full impact test and report, OK? And an estimate of your time and charges to find out."

Brody felt uncomfortable. Amity, theoretically, had to pay for Suffolk County police services when they were required, which was something like once every ten years. But there was no budget he could tap. He would have to blast the appropriation through the selectmen, who would not understand why he couldn't perform a ballistics test himself.

He licked his lips: "I thought maybe you could just, well, as a matter of professional courtesy . . ."

The lieutenant smiled. She had a great smile. "OK. Lunch sometime," she proposed. "Department cafeteria? $1.35 blueplate, and apple pie á la mode?"

"You're on."

The young sergeant didn't like it, but made no comment.

Brody explained the gas tank, the rifle, the wounded seal and his suspicions. The sergeant raised a finger. "Hey, I read about that today. That guy's a Flushing *cop!*"

"So he can shoot seals? And people?" Swede demanded. She put her finger through the hole in the tank. "Awful big entry," she said dubiously. "More like a magnum. Or a .45. You check him out for a handgun?"

Brody shook his head. Jepps had been in pajamas, firing the rifle, and he'd never thought of getting a warrant to search the house. It was certainly too late now. Embarrassed, he told her he'd assumed that a ski-boat or divers would have been out of pistol range.

"You're probably right." She studied the Savage ammunition. "A spinner, maybe, or a ricochet." She shrugged, and took from under her microscope one of two bullets she had been studying when they entered. It was intact, but it had been made into a dumdum by someone who had filed a cross into its nose. She nodded at its twisted mate, on the microscope slide. "*That* one made a hole as big as your fist. In the trunk of a Patchoque squad car."

"Are people around here trying to kill cops?" Brody asked.

"Not kill, *atomize*," growled the sergeant.

Brody felt sick. The Manhattan disease had jumped to Long Island. He wondered if the cancer would spread to Amity. Another 40 miles to go . . .

"Why?" he wondered. "Why would they do that?"

"Well," the sergeant said acidly, "they did. Makes you wonder why we got to try to stick it to a brother officer, doesn't it?"

"Makes *you* wonder, maybe," said Swede. "He's just another suspect to me." She turned to the microscope. "I'll have a prelim by Wednesday, Brody. Give me a call."

"Thanks, lieutenant," said Brody.

"There are *seven* lieutenants," she said. "Ask for Swede. I'm probably the only black Swede in the building."

He could feel her eyes upon him as he stumbled after the trim young sergeant.

He almost walked into the last lab table, he was so busy holding in his gut.

At 1600 hours, the U.S. destroyer *Leon M. Cooper*, DD 634, was rattling southwest of Block Island. She steadied on course 225° true. The JG on the starboard wing of her bridge passed the watch to his relief, the gunnery officer. As the JG turned over the duty, he saluted. The gun boss, a full lieutenant, did not salute back.

Sloppy, thought the JG. The gun boss was a reservist, drafted for Viet Nam, and staying in for 20. They were all the same. He handed his coffee cup to the quartermaster. "If the Old Man wants me, I'll be in CIC."

The quartermaster, another veteran of Nam, nodded briefly. The JG reddened. "Aye aye sir," would have been appropriate. Even "yes sir" would have been nice. The JG was Annapolis '73. He was irritated that things on this ship seldom went as he had been taught to expect.

But if he reamed out the quartermaster, the gun boss would probably support the enlisted man. They all smoked pot together ashore, he was certain, and shot up God knew what kind of dope while they bragged about their war.

The JG was combat information center officer, and at least he had his own shop squared away. He decided to visit it now, to see if they had studied tonight's exercise, which was to find, if they could, the U.S. submarine *Grouper*, sneaking about in all the vast water to seaward.

Before he stepped into the darkened, fluorescent coolness of the Center, he glanced to starboard. It was hazy now, and would be foggy later. He could dimly discern Montauk off the starboard bow. For a moment he let his mind drift into a familiar dream. A carrier would loom out of the shore mist, dead on a collision course with the *Cooper*. Everyone else would miss it: the officer of the deck, because he was smoking a cigaret on the port wing of the bridge, his own people in CIC because they were brewing coffee, the quartermaster because he was taking a bearing.

The JG would race to the bridge, grab the wheel from the helmsman, slam it over, and save the ship by inches as the skipper tumbled from his cabin wet-eyed with gratitude.

Or perhaps he would spot a Russian torpedo snaking from the deep . . .

He'd simply been born too late, even for Nam.

For a while he observed a helicopter, the other partner in their hunter-killer team, dipping its ball a hundred yards off their port quarter. Well, it was too early to hear the *Grouper*: perhaps he was only testing his sonar gear. A good idea, too.

He stepped inside. He let his eyes adjust to the darkness, stood behind the radarman for a moment to see that he was logging contacts. He could see Montauk on the screen, and he pointed it out and asked the radarman what it was.

"Block Island, sir," mumbled the technician.

He got that squared away, but quickly, and it woke up everyone else. The sonarman turned on his sonar, though it was an hour before he could expect the sub. The airplot man began to pencil bogies out of NAS Quonset on the age-old plastic grid. The radioman began to warm up the TBS.

"Sir?" called the sonarman.

"Yes, Sonar?" the JG said, moving behind him.

"Submarine contact, two-two-zero. Range 6 miles. Closing."

His heart leapt. He glanced at the clock on the bulkhead. Still too early for the *Grouper*, by three hours. And he knew of no other sub in the zone. No other *U.S.* sub . . .

He took the sonarman's earphones. He could follow the beat of the chopper off their quarter, an underseas pounding so loud that it was sometimes supposed to attract sharks. In counterpoint to it he could hear the familiar *ping* of their own transducer. *Ping* . . . and then the fainter echo, *ping*. *Ping* . . . ping. *Ping* . . . ping. He turned the transducer five degrees, centered it on the loudest echo. "*Ping*—ping, *ping*—ping . . ."

Closing indeed. And fast. Too fast for a school of fish. Too fast for anything but, perhaps, a *Keshnov* class sub, sent to spy. To spy, or worse.

"Bass, sir?" asked the sonarman.

"Too big for a school of bass," he said. He took off the headset and reached for the bridge-phone. "Bridge from CIC?"

Nobody answered. That figured, on this turkey.

The sonarman had put on the headset again. "It's too early for *Grouper*. Cod run, I think."

"Too fast. Bridge from CIC!"

"To big for *anything*," the sonarman puzzled. Suddenly he snapped his fingers. "Whale! Finback whale! Heard the same echo in sonar school. It's duller than a ship. Or a sub."

"Whale?" Indecisively, the JG stood, bridge phone in hand.

"Whale," repeated the sonarman, with conviction. "He's sheering off."

"CIC from bridge," the loudspeaker said finally. "You call?"

The JG hesitated. He took back the headset and listened for a moment. The contact was moving toward the beach. It had to be a whale.

He was covered, anyway, by his sonarman's evaluation. He was an officer, and gentleman, not a sonar expert.

"Never mind," he told the bridge. "Belay it."

When he left CIC to wash up for dinner, he saw the chopper chomping off toward shore.

Hunger had again driven her, during the morning, into Amity Sound. She had done her best to clean it of everything that moved. She had consumed perhaps a hundred pounds of mackerel, off Amity Neck. She skirted the breakwater and headed for open ocean.

She sensed, smelled, found nothing, until, as the sun slanted to westward and the light at five fathoms began to dim, she felt the slow pounding, far away, of a low flying helicopter. *Thump . . . thump . . . thump . . .*, and behind it, much less exciting, a feeble, rhythmic *ping* . . .

Blindly she headed for the thumping. The sound, as with any rhythmic vibration in the water, triggered her digestive juices. She became more ravenous with every sweep of her tail. Her need for food became more pressing with every yard she traveled.

Now she sensed another, grinding vibration, the thrashing of propellors. She heard this every day in coastal shipping waters. She followed the thumping instead.

The pinging faded. She had no interest in that. The grinding of screws continued south. She had no interest in that either. She followed the pounding of the helicopter toward the beach.

Larry Vaughan, Jr., the mayor's son, had stopped his mo-ped motorized bicycle on Beach Road when they spotted the bikes chained to a fencepost. Andy Nicholas, Amity's fat boy, climbed off the postillion seat. He rubbed his tail. His swimming suit had climbed up his crotch. Road dust, he feared, was bringing on his asthma too.

"Man, let me drive home, *you* sit back there."

Larry turned off the ignition. "You'd bust the fork, chubby-cheeks." He considered the bikes. "That's his, all right. But who's the girl's?"

Andy shrugged, still rubbing his rear. "You gave me hemorrhoids!"

Larry ignored him. He was looking for a name under the bar of the girl's bicycle. "Mary Detner? Sue Jacobs? That summer fox, whosis, at the Inn?"

"Smell the saddle," suggested Andy.

"Screw you," said Larry mildly. He studied the bike. "Hey! Jackie Angelo? I bet it's the silver-toothed devil herself."

"You think?" asked Andy, with some interest.

"Old *Angelo* will have a fit," promised Larry, "he ever finds out. He'll shoot him up good with that cannon he carries."

"And dump him at sea from his old man's police boat," agreed Andy. His eyes grew sad. "Naw, she'd never let him touch her."

Larry tapped Mike's bike with his toe. "What're they doing here, then?"

"They're swimming, is all," said Andy. "He's trying to show off in his wetsuit."

Larry shook his head. "Not Spitzer. That's the ocean out there, not the Town Pool."

He climbed the wooden fence, scrambled up the sandy bank, and began to reconnoiter the beach from the hummocks along the crest. Andy Nicholas followed, making too much noise. Larry turned on him, motioning him down. The fat boy dropped to his hands and knees, although he was afraid the ground dust would complete the job on his asthma. He joined his companion on the sand bank.

Cautiously, the two scanned the ocean and the dunes below.

Banks of summer fog were gathering on the southeastern horizon. Andy felt Larry poke him. His freckled brow was furrowed and his head cocked. When Andy listened, he could hear a low murmur from the hollow behind the nearest dunes. He could make out Mike's voice, and a throaty chuckle he recognized as Jackie's.

His blood began to warm, but he felt a shiver go up his back. Mike was 30 pounds lighter than he, but sinewy, fast, and strong. "Let's split," he whispered.

Larry glanced at him incredulously. "You crazy, man?"

Larry began to slither down the slope, pulling his body forward on his elbows like a TV commando. Andy hesitated. Then, drawn by some irrepressible force, he began to snake down the hillock himself, the coarse sand working into his swimming suit and the dust threatening his chest.

He was breathing heavily. At the bottom of the slope he paused. Above him, Larry was climbing to the top of the dune hiding the couple. Sand slid into Andy's eyes. But nothing on earth could have stopped his progress now.

Mike Brody shifted his weight on Jackie's beach towel. He stared into the angel face only six inches from his own. The glorious eyes fluttered open. Two heavenly dimples appeared at the corners of the most desirable mouth in the world. Tentatively, he reached out a finger and brushed a strand of shimmering hair from a perfect ear.

He began to tickle the lobe. Did that arouse

women? He searched his memory for chapter and verse of Rubin, and couldn't remember. She was nice. He just wanted to be here with her, drinking in her beauty forever.

She shivered, moaned, and, finally, smiled fully. He even loved the silver braces.

"Mike?"

"Um?"

"Mike, that . . . kind of tickles." She put out her own hand and began to play with the lobe of his ear.

It tickled, all right, or something, Jesus, it did more than that, tickled wasn't the word, it sent arrows of pleasure and longing through him. He couldn't stand it if she kept it up, but he didn't want her to stop, he couldn't bear it if she stopped, and now she was tracking the curve of his neck and shoulders, he wished he'd stuck with the push-ups he'd started last winter. He hadn't, but he had pretty good shoulders anyway, thank God, her hand was slipping under the strap of his wetsuit, and she was massaging the muscles of his back.

"Good?" she murmured.

"I love you," he blurted.

She removed her hand and sat up.

Now why in the name of Christ had he said *that*? He'd blown it for sure.

But he *did* love her, more than his mother, even, or his dad, and a hell of a lot more than Sean.

She was gazing out over the ocean. "Foggy, pretty soon," she said softly. "We could get lost going home."

"Jackie," he muttered bleakly, "you don't want to go *home*?"

She smiled down at him. She was three months and four days younger than he, but today she looked five years older. She reached down and touched his chest, then slid her hand between his wetsuit and his skin. "I don't *ever* want to go home," she whispered.

He took her in his arms.

Chief Martin Brody wiped his forehead. It was hot in the Vaughan & Penrose Realty office, though they had left the door to the street open. A truck rumbled by, bound for the construction at the bank.

Brody took off his glasses, began to polish them, and peered numbly across the desk at Vaughan. "*Drop* the case?" he repeated incredulously. "What do you mean, '*drop*' it?"

Vaughan arose, red-faced, and moved to the county map dominating his tiny shack. On it were shaded commercial areas, residential districts, and state beach preserves. He studied it for a moment, to gain strength. He tapped the Casino site and turned back to Brody.

"Drop it, or we'll lose the Casino. It's that simple."

"What's Jepps got to do with the *Casino*?"

"He's got to do with a state police commissioner—"

"He *says*," Brody interjected.

"He does, all right. The commissioner's got to Clyde Bronson, and Bronson's got to me, and I'm getting to you."

Bronson was not only representative in the State House for Amity and for twenty other little beach towns along the shore, he was also the co-sponsor of the gambling law.

"Damn," muttered Brody. "Damn, damn, damn . . ."

"Politics," shrugged Vaughan.

"This guy's a suspect for *manslaughter*!"

"He's *your* suspect," Vaughan said coldly, "not mine. Be sure you remember that."

"He *ought* to be yours, and everybody else's," Brody growled. "Two divers drown! A ski-boat blows up! There's a hole in its gas tank! Within 500 yards of a guy shooting live ammunition? And reasonable men don't get suspicious? Bull!"

"It wasn't going to stick without a body," Vaughan pointed out.

"We'll find a body," promised Brody, "if we have to drain the Atlantic Ocean!"

"Drop it," sighed Vaughan. "Just drop it, is all."

Brody felt his temper rising. His temple began to throb again. Deliberately, he sat back, tried to ease his legs, his buttocks, his abdomen, his shoulders, his neck—he had read the technique in *Psychology Today*, and had been trying it out when he remembered. It didn't work now. Bitterly, he murmured: "This remind you of something, Larry?"

"What?" The mayor looked uncomfortable.

"The start of The Trouble? When the girl got hit? And I tried to close the beaches? And nobody in the goddamn town would talk to me, or Ellen, or Mike, or even Sean? And the Kintner kid got killed, and it turned out I was right?"

Vaughan returned to his desk, sat down heavily, and leveled a finger at Brody: "There's a difference."

"Yeah?"

"The shark didn't have a single friend in Albany. I'm telling you, Brody! *Drop* it!"

Brody met the mayor's eyes. They were red-rimmed from lack of sleep or from booze. But they did not shift or look away. The pain in his temple flared. He slammed his hand on the mayor's desk.

"Not this time, Larry. Not in a million years!"

He left the shack and walked into the sunlight. Fog would be drifting in soon, he could feel it. So could the horn on the end of the Amity breakwater, which let out a sudden blast.

It had always seemed to him a defiant bellow of protest at the ocean, which for 200 years, in hurricane and winter gale, had tried to drown the town.

He loved Amity. If he had to leave here, he'd have no place to go.

But he was damned if he'd fold again.

4

Andy Nicholas lay in agony next to Larry Vaughan, Jr., behind a bush at the crest of the dune. Dust from the bush was searing his chest and closing his throat. He could hardly breathe. He knew that he had better escape before he began to wheeze, but he could not tear himself away.

Now she had Mike's wetsuit rolled down to his belly, and Andy could practically *feel* her soft, warm body and the touch of her fingers on his skin, as if it were *he* scoring below.

"Jesus," he heard Larry whisper, "*do* it, Spitzer!"

"Shut up," mouthed Andy. If Mike heard them, it was he who would suffer, not Larry, who could do the 100 in ten flat. Larry would escape and Andy would end up in the sand. He squirmed backward a little from the edge, dislodging a rivulet of sand on the couple below. He tensed, but they did not notice.

Andy summoned his courage and ventured another look.

His breath began to come in familiar, strangled gasps. He would have to slither back down the dune and split, now or never. He risked one last glance.

He felt Larry clutch his elbow. "Shut up," Larry whispered in horror. "Shut the hell up!"

Andy shook his head helplessly. Now the wheezing was spasmodic, he could not breathe, a red, familiar tide was engulfing him, worse than he had had it for years, he sounded like a leaky radiator pipe, like a frigging steamboat, a winded horse . . .

The tableau below him froze. Jackie looked up. Mike leaped to his feet. For an instant it was stop-motion, like the replay of a close call on TV.

Then it all exploded into action. Mike was scrambling up the side of the hollow, Larry was on his feet, and Jackie was screaming angrily. Andy rolled in the dust, trying to get to his feet.

Mike reached the summit, somehow got a hand on Larry, slung him seaward down the hill toward Jackie, and drew back his bare foot.

Andy took it full in the pit of his stomach. Between the asthma and the foot in the gut, he thought for a moment that he would die. His vision darkened.

When he could see again, he found Jackie on her knees beside him, patting his cheeks, but none too gently.

"You OK, Andy?"

He managed to nod.

She got to her feet and looked down on him fiercely. "You crummy little *creeps*," she said, she gazed out to sea. He struggled up and followed her glance. At the edge of a fog bank a navy helicopter was dangling something into the water. He let his eyes fall closer to the shoreline.

If Spitzer was scared of the ocean, as Larry Vaughan always claimed, he had got over it in a hell of a hurry.

Larry was splashing to sea, fifty yards past the surf line, swimming fast and thrashing up spray. But 30 yards astern was Vengeance, gaining fast.

"He'll kill him," Jackie said desolately, "and they'll send him to Juvie Hall. He'll *drown* the crummy creep!"

She was probably right. Andy guessed he ought

to be out there, trying to save him. But Mike, once he took care of Larry, might drown him too.

He decided to walk home instead.

He wished that he were dead.

The Great White circled aimlessly. The rhythmic thumping of helicopter vanes which was exciting her had also jammed her computer. She could ordinarily home quite precisely on a vibrating body, zero in on a thrashing fish or a struggling seal. In the deepest reaches of the ocean in the dark of the night, she could find another wounded shark.

The beat she followed now seemed to be everywhere and nowhere. The hunt for its source was fruitless, but she was unable to break from its fascination. Once she swerved to scoop up a giant squid, also confused by the sound of the whirling blades, but mostly she wound in a pointless figure 8, five fathoms deep.

Always, she stayed as close to the source as she could, though it moved toward the shore and the shallows, and hunger impelled her to make a sweep further out.

The navy chopper pilot glanced seaward at the fog banks, and then shoreward at the indistinguishable cottages along the dunes. His orders were to plug the space between water too shoal for the *Grouper*, and the zone that the *Leon M. Cooper* was patrolling to seaward.

He looked at the clock on his instrument panel. 1700 hours, and the fog rolling in. The *Grouper* was presumably well out of New London by now, submerged, and heading into the exercise zone. If she didn't hurry, he'd have to abort his mission and haul-ass back to Quonset before the fog caught him.

It didn't seem a bad idea even now. There was

still time to clean up and make Happy Hour at the club.

He looked, almost furtively, at his young sonarman. "Foggy," he proposed.

"Doesn't look so bad to me, sir," the sonarman said.

The pilot sat back. The kid had seemed so eager and interested in the patrol that he had let him dip his ball early to test the gear. God knew it was hard enough to motivate men nowadays, without discouraging the eager beavers. But now the pilot was getting bored with the whole operation. The young man was an impediment.

"How you doing?" he asked the boy.

"Mackerel, croakers, the usual, I can hear pistol shrimp," said the sonarman. "Everything but the *Grouper*. Let's drag it a little further inshore."

The pilot nodded, eased the stick forward, and imperceptibly twisted the pitch. He felt the sonarman's hand on his arm. "Sir? Hold it!"

He hovered where he was.

"I heard a yell," said the kid, adjusting his headset. "A couple of guys yelling, somebody in the water yelling."

They scanned the ocean ahead. Suddenly the pilot spotted heads in the water. It was almost impossible to fly the chopper hands-off, so he gave his binoculars to his companion, pointing out the swimmers.

"You see two guys? Kids, off the surf line?"

"Yes sir. Hey, one's drowning, or they're fighting, or something!"

"Up ball," ordered the pilot. He heard the winch whine for a moment, checked for a green light on the panel, and swooped ahead toward the pair.

If they really *were* drowning, he'd drop a life vest and call Shinnecock coast guard, but there was no use putting out a false alarm.

* * *

She had been swimming northeastward at 5 fathoms, passing through murky water infested with plankton. She was still hypnotized by the sourceless thrumming from above, and utterly famished. She would have struck at a boat, a bottle, or a lobster buoy if she had sensed one nearby.

There was nothing around, so she glided haphazardly.

Suddenly, beyond the thumping, she heard a surface splashing that galvanized her senses, and a high-pitched yelling that meant nothing. It was as if two large fish were fighting, or two seals mating at the surface.

A chord was struck. She wheeled, tossing her gravid belly upward, and doubled back. The mysterious thumping was far outweighed by this new and more exciting signal.

Her enormous tail began to beat more swiftly. When her momentum was up, she was making a good twenty knots.

Mike Brody, enraged, allowed Larry Vaughan, Jr. to surface, but kept his hold.

"Mike!" screamed Larry. "You turd, you're outta your mind!"

Mike, treading water, stared into the tear-streaked, freckled face. A string of mucous hung from Larry's nose and his eyes were glazed. Mike discerned real fear and a pleading, too, that he could not ignore. His anger fled. He must have damn near drowned him. It was time to quit.

Mike was dead tired, could hardly swim another stroke. But, by Christ, he had shown them that when chased by Mike Brody, the ocean was no sanctuary.

He shoved Larry roughly away, turned on his back, and floated. "Pervert," he spat. "Crummy, creepy, pervert!"

The two lay panting, drifting apart in the ground swell. Mike let his eyes stray to a navy chopper speeding toward them from the offshore cloudbank. The chopper reared, quivered, finally lowered a black sphere into the water. Listening for subs from New London, he knew.

A great elation surged through him. He could be that chopper pilot if he wanted, or one of the men on the sub he was looking for, or a U.S. marine.

He knew no fear of the ocean or anything else.

Jackie knew it, and he could have her any time at all.

The pilot yawned. The sonarman had put down the glasses and said: "They're OK, sir. Just a couple of kids horsing around."

And the pilot had waved at them and eased back on the stick, stopping the chopper in midair. "What say we secure for the day?" he suggested to the young man.

"Whatever you say, sir," his companion said, but he looked disappointed and, what the hell, the kid had probably never had a sub contact in his life and the *Grouper* ought to be due any minute.

"OK, son," he capitulated. "Dangle your ball a while more."

The sonarman grinned, dropped the sphere again, and adjusted his headset.

The pilot yawned. Give the kid a couple of dozen more hours on patrol, and he'd scream to go home at 5 like the rest of them.

He sat back and listened to the whine of the descending sonar ball.

She was not far behind the thumping but she was paying no attention to that, anyway; it was the surface targets that occupied her now. The closer of the two was causing little vibration. It was the further, healthier beating that she instinctively followed, homing in with primitive ears, *ampullae*, *lateralis*-system, and all of the other sensors feeding her brain.

Her smallest male squirmed in her right uterus. Deprivation of food for a few more hours would turn his stronger sisters upon him, and he somehow knew it and eased his body around in the packed organ to a better fighting position.

As if she knew his danger, the mother increased her speed. Now she could hear the splashing very clearly. She began to rise from six fathoms in a gentle ascent toward the target on the surface.

Ahead of her, under the all-pervasive thumping, she heard a sudden *plop*. In the dim light she glimpsed a black shape like an oversized football, descending dead ahead. She rolled, snapped open her mouth, and snatched it between row upon row of serrated teeth. There was a moment of wild resistance from above, as if it were dangled from giant hands. Then she had it free, crushed it, ground it between her jaws, and spit it out in a cloud of teeth, wires, and mangled metal.

She coasted for a moment.

She heard no more thrashing from the surface, and even the thumping was receding.

She cruised the surf line for a while.

Then she turned and headed to sea to hunt.

The sonarman was still quaking and the pilot himself found that he was shaky on the controls. He took it out on the sonarman.

"How deep did you *have* the goddamn thing?"

The boy shook his head helplessly. "Ten, 12 feet, sir! Your altimeter read 50, and the winch gauge read 60 . . . Ten-feet deep at the most, sir."

The pilot climbed. He had only one desire, to get high enough to auto-rotate in case the incredible strains on the chopper proved fatal. At 60 feet, they were dead ducks if the structure collapsed or a vane began to flutter. He had never sustained, in 25 years and 8000 hours, a jerk on a cable as violent as the one they had just survived.

As he ascended, he listened for the telltale blade-dissonance that would spell fuselage or engine failure. The craft had taken a hell of a yank. They would find out how badly it was damaged later at Quonset, or maybe he should land directly on the beach, that would be the safe way to do it; no, everything seemed all right, he'd head back for Quonset . . .

Happy Hour would look good to him now. He wished he'd brought a hip flask in the chopper.

"You dragged the bottom," he insisted.

"No sir!" the sonarman protested. "That ball never got within 25 feet of the bottom!"

"So what *was* it? The *Grouper* grabbed you by the ball?"

The young man looked puzzled. "No," he said uncertainly. "Not the *Grouper*. And not the bottom. You can hear it when it's dragging the bottom. This was something else. I heard a kind of swishing, like, I don't know. You think we fouled a bat-ray or a giant squid or something?"

"No," scoffed the pilot. "You hung it too frigging low. We snagged a reef or a wreck or a goddamn rock!"

He continued to climb, not leveling off until he was at 2000 feet, flirting with the incoming scud. He checked his oil pressure, his tachometer, and his cylinder-head temperature. All seemed OK, but he was still not happy, deep down.

"Damn it, son, you know what those balls cost?"

"Twelve thousand dollars," said the kid. He looked as if he were about to cry.

"Not counting whatever we did to the aircraft,"

muttered the pilot. He heard a high-pitched, rhythmic squeaking from the rotor blade assembly. He didn't like it at all. He searched the fog-shrouded water for the *Leon M. Cooper*. It would be nice to have it around, if worse came to worse. But he could see nothing to seaward but fogbanks. He came gently left, toward Quonset. He pressed the throat-mike button to call the *Cooper*, describe his problem, and punch out from his patrol. Before he could call, the stick began to vibrate in his hand. The collective-stick was shaking so badly it made his palm itch. He should have ditched the chopper the instant he felt the tug.

"Pan! This is a pan call." Pan was a step below mayday. "*Leon M. Cooper* from navy chopper one-four-seven-eight, aborting. Returning to—" He suddenly felt it coming . . .

As a young man in Korea he had snatched wounded marines from the peaks above Pyongyang. Ten years ago he had been plucking navy pilots from Tonkin Gulf. He knew suddenly that after all the danger, it might end here, off a stupid little beach town whose name he could never remember.

He pressed the button again. "Mayday! Mayday, mayday, Navy one-four-seven-eight, calling mayday!" He eased back the throttle. The vibration only increased. Now the sonarman had sensed it too, and was turning to him, tense with terror.

"Mayday, mayday," chanted the pilot. He was pleased to find his voice calm and level. "I'm 5 miles south of . . ." It came to him, suddenly—the shark place—"Amity. Amity, Long Island. I'm going to lose a blade. Commencing descent. Commencing autorotation . . ."

The vane left with a twang like a broken guitar string. He caught a glimpse of it in metallic sunlight, spinning a lazy arc down to the silver sea. The chopper canted crazily, flipped, and his world turned upside down. He saw the fogbanks through the bubble canopy, between his feet. He heard the sonarman scream.

He had a vivid flash of a Saigon girl in a tall-necked dress and a skirt slit to her hip.

Himself, he had seen it all, and done it all, too. The kid had lived hardly at all.

"Near that town called Amity," he managed again, and then he could only hang on.

5

Brody sat in a rickety aluminum chair on his front porch and watched his son cycling up Bayberry Lane. He was peddling very, very slowly, as if exhausted.

When he got closer, parked the bike, and moved up the pathway, it was like seeing a new boy. Despite his apparent weariness, his shoulders were back, his eyes were steady, and a hint of a secret smile played on his lips.

"Good day today?" Brody asked.

"Went swimming with Jackie," he grinned.

Brody looked into his boy's eyes. "*Swimming?*"

Mike colored. "Look, dad, she's a nice girl."

"I know that. I've known her all her life. What are you so uptight about?"

"*You're* uptight, not me. It's like, you know, just because I take a girl for a swim? Do we have to be making it somewhere?"

"Didn't make out," Brody decided.

"I didn't *try*. Just swam, is all."

But something had happened. A weight had been lifted from Mike's soul.

For a moment the two were locked in total eye contact, man-to-man rapport. The moment passed. The Amity foghorn blasted. Behind it Brody heard a cacophony of lesser horns. Mike looked puzzled.

"Sounds like the fleet's in, dad."

Mike obviously hadn't heard. His father told him:

"A chopper went down in the fog. Dick Angelo's out there now. And half of Quonset Point."

Mike looked stricken. "A *navy* chopper?"

Brody nodded. He glanced at his watch. He hoped they'd find something, and quickly, for it would be dark in half an hour. He hated to think of Dick ghosting along between warships on a foggy night.

Mike was listening to the foghorns, thoughtfully. "I wonder . . ."

"What?"

He shook his head. "There was a chopper, when Larry and I were swimming, we were kind of wrestling around outside the surf line . . ."

Brody was glad to hear it. If Mike had breasted the surf, the phobia was dead. Now, if only he didn't get carried away and try to swim to Nova Scotia . . .

"The pilot kind of made a run on us," Mike said. His voice trembled oddly: "I could see him, right through his windshield . . ."

"There are choppers out there all the time," Brody remarked. "Different one, probably."

Mike ignored him. "Maybe he thought we were in trouble, you know, drowning or something, and he came over to see?"

Brody shrugged. "Maybe."

"And then he waved. He waved, dad. Dad, you suppose he got *killed*?"

Brody was sure of it, from what they had told him of the man's last transmission, but there was no use stirring up the kid. He pulled him close and squeezed his shoulders. He reminded him that the odds were it wasn't even the same man, and that they had rafts and wore vests. "They'll probably find him."

Mike was hardly listening: "He waved, and dropped that ball they drag around, you know, to listen for subs . . ." He grimaced, thinking. "And we swam in, and when I turned around to look, from the beach, he was going up again. Funny . . ."

"What?"

"That ball they listen with. Do they leave it in the water when they go?"

Brody shook his head. "I don't think so."

"This guy did. I could see the line he was hanging it from. Just swinging, you know, nothing on it?"

That seemed odd, but maybe they *did* leave the balls, and come back later. Or maybe it had just broken off and sunk. Or maybe Mike was mistaken. Anyway, he'd call Quonset Point and ask.

They went in to dinner. Sean started a drive to make Sammy the cub scout mascot, and finally stormed from the table in frustration when Brody refused to promise to keep him. Brody caught hell from Ellen for letting him go without finishing.

By the time he had calmed everything down, his headache was back and he had forgotten all about the missing ball on Mike's helicopter.

Ellen Brody was, as usual, the only den mother who had come to the pack meeting. She squirmed in her seat in Miss Fairleigh's sixth-grade classroom. The desks were too small for adults. Willy Norton, justice of the peace, president of the PTA and Rotarian, presiding as cub master, had the only decent seat—behind Miss Fairleigh's desk. The whole place smelled of pencil sharpenings, chalk dust, and sweaty cub scouts.

The ambiance made her feel tiny, bringing her back to the Ellen Shepherd of Oak Tree Private School in Pelham. She found herself waving her hand for attention, like an 8-year-old. "Mr. Norton? Willy? The regatta?"

The chair recognized her reluctantly, as if Norton had been down this road before and had no desire to travel it again. Behind her she heard Sean's warning stage-whisper: "Moth . . . er!" She ignored it.

"Yes, Ellen?" Norton said wearily.

"It has to do with Martha Linden's brownies," she began quickly, hoping to get it all in. Behind her erupted a Greek chorus of sighs, wails and boos.

Willy Norton held up his hand. "OK, gang. Pipe down! Ellen, we took a vote last week."

"The vote," Ellen said savagely, "was unconstitutional. There were no brownies here. Did you ever hear of the 18th Amendment?"

"Only three canoes," Willy Norton said with exaggerated patience. "And three dens, right? And I think we decided to lend the brownies the canoes to race *before* the den race, *or* after, or whatever. Equal rights, OK?"

Fatuous bastard. There was a blackboard eraser within her reach, and she briefly considered heaving it at the bland face behind the desk. That would get their attention, even if it triggered a riot behind her, which it would. But she restrained herself.

"They want to *compete* with the boys! For the cup!"

"Then they ought to get their own canoe," piped someone.

"That's right," Sean seconded, stabbing her neatly in the back. "They ought to get their own."

She swung around and glared at him, subduing him temporarily. The time had come to yank off the velvet glove of reason. She turned back to Norton. "There's only one problem, Willy. I'm treasurer of the United Fund. It makes its contribution for the boy scouts, the sea scouts, the girl scouts, the cub scouts, and the brownies. Dig?"

"I guess so."

"As the responsible administrator, if the brownies are restricted from the canoe race, I can't ethically release the regatta hot-dog money. No hamburgers, no cokes. No Hostess Ding-Dongs," she added brutally, for Sean.

That held the little bastards, she thought, in the shocked silence.

Willy Norton was only a service station operator, a glorified mechanic. But he was a politician, too. He had his eye, Ellen knew, on Larry Vaughan's job as mayor.

As a politician, he knew when he was licked, and how to divert the attention of the mob. "OK, gang," he said, glancing at the clock above the blackboard, "a half hour on the basketball court, Pack One against Two, and the winner plays Three. The two best get canoes Sunday. The other den gets to cheer. OK?"

There was a howling rush to the door and the two were alone. The clock on the wall jerked noisily, evoking her childhood again. Norton began squaring up the records on his desk.

"Sorry, Willy," she said. "I know I'm stupid to make an issue of it—"

"No," he shrugged, "and you win." He seemed preoccupied. "Now, your *hubsand's* issue, that's another matter."

She asked him what he meant.

"Jepps." He sat back, studying her. "That Jepps thing is getting out of hand."

"Out of hand?" she flared. "Look, the *least* that idiot did was shoot a helpless baby seal. And he just might have killed those divers and blown up a boat—"

" 'Might have' isn't enough."

"*You* held Jepps over. You're justice of the peace, not Brody. You put him in jail!"

"I wish to hell I'd checked."

"Checked?"

"With Albany."

"What's Albany got to do with shooting up Amity Beach?"

"Ask Brody," Willy Norton sighed. "It seems like every time this town starts moving, it stumbles on the chief of police."

"What do you mean?" she demanded hotly. "A shark starts chewing up swimmers and he closes the beach until he can kill it. A maniac starts shooting up the beach and he puts him in jail! *That's* making the town *stumble*?"

She stared at him, but he didn't look away. His eyes were sad.

She swallowed, close to tears. "You just better hope he's around to stumble on for a long, long time."

"That's what scares me." Willy Norton was shaking his head. "He was right to try to close the beach. Everybody knows that. He's right wanting to prosecute Jepps, probably. But if he does, there'll be no gambling, and they'll have our butts. Brody's butt, and probably mine."

"*Who* will?"

He smiled sadly. "The Casino."

"Peterson's Brody's friend."

"Peterson's *front*."

"No!" She stared at him numbly. "He owns it all."

Norton wanted to tell her something, but seemed strangely afraid to speak. Finally he said: "You'll find out from Brody. So I'll tell you." He lowered his voice. "Behind Peterson," he murmured, "stand some of the best families in New York."

"Well, good," she said, relieved.

"Tuciano," he said sickly. "Di Leone, and our little friend's daddy, Moscotti—"

"Moscotti!" she muttered. By local legend, Shuffles Moscotti was the most vicious don on Long Island, though she liked his little boy. "Who told you that?"

"Peterson."

She was still staring at him when the troops returned. When badges and the pledge were over, she led Den Three to the station wagon.

Behind the wheel, fumbling in the dark to insert the ignition key, she had a sudden vision of the car, Ellen Brody, and Den Three blowing skyward in a tower of orange flame.

She almost wished the Moscotti child was in *her* den, for her own protection.

She gritted her teeth and turned the key. No sound but the engine's. She delivered her squirming charges to hearth and home.

Brody arose, picked up Pete Peterson's empty glass, and took it with his own to the kitchen where he poured them both another scotch. Ellen and Sean should be home any moment. Mike was wiping the last of the dinner dishes, obviously out on his feet from pure exhaustion. Whatever had transpired in the water with his buddies, or out of it with Jackie, had shot him down like a wounded duck. Brody told him to forget the dishes and go to bed.

Then he took the drinks back into the living room. Peterson was sitting on the couch.

"Pete," he said carefully, "I'm sorry, I like you. I like what the Casino's doing for the town. But tearing up a parking ticket outside Starbuck's is one thing. Withdrawing charges against *this* sonofabitch is another."

Peterson shifted his trim little body minutely. He was wearing a denim casual suit and a wide-collared shirt. Brody did indeed like him, though he was always a little too perfectly conditioned, too graceful, and too much on stage. He was more open than any wealthy man had a right to be.

Peterson sipped his drink: "Johnny Walker Black?"

Brody was pleased. It was a $9 bottle, saved for such occasions. "Well, *Red,*" he admitted, "but you've got a good palate."

"Black, red, I never could tell the difference." Peterson swished the ice in the glass and leaned forward. His face was tense and his gray eyes steady.

"Brody, I'm underfinanced."

"Aren't we all?"

"*You* can get a loan."

"That's a matter of conjecture," Brody murmured. He got the drift, suddenly. "You mean *you* can't?"

"Not from the bank." Peterson shook his head. "No more collateral. I've put up the land I bought from you and everybody else, and the existing structure, and a pot full of AT&T, and that's it."

Brody was shocked. His visions of the rebirth of Amity, like a phoenix from the ashes of The Trouble, faded. "You're going to quit construction?"

No, he'd made certain arrangements. But if the gambling law hit a snag, the arrangements would fail. "And apparently, if you don't drop charges, it'll snag."

Brody studied his face. The man had come in from New Jersey, quiet, diffident, with a record as clean as the Pope's. Brody knew, because he had checked it out with Trenton and the state police records and identifications sections, at the Amity board of selectmen's request. It had taken him three days, and he'd felt like Dick Tracy all the time.

Larry Vaughan claimed to have checked him out with the SEC and the State Realty Commission.

If gambling passed, Amity would have only one casino license, and no one professed to want it in the hands of a crook or a half-assed promoter.

Only after all this had the Town Council granted

a building permit. "Well, I can't drop charges, Pete. I just can't."

"Willy Norton's willing to reverse," said Peterson.

"Willy just took the evidence and did his job," Brody pointed out. "Amity's still the plaintiff, and in this case I'm Amity."

Peterson looked embarrassed. He obviously did not like his role. "You're a good man, Brody."

Brody flushed. "Well, I buckled once, on closing the beach. It cost a little boy's life."

"I heard," Peterson said softly. "That's why I'm going to give you some facts."

He moved to the solarium window. Brody followed him.

They looked out across Amity Sound. The fog was thicker and the navy foghorns still audible. Brody felt sorry for the chopper crew, even if they had survived the crash. He heard a familiar blast from across the water. It was the Amity Neck ferry, groping home at the end of her last run of the day. People said that Captain Lowell, who had run it for thirty years, could find his slip when he couldn't see his own bow light, from booze or fog or both.

"I've taken in some partners," Peterson said softly.

Brody stiffened. "What partners?"

Peterson seemed to be having trouble getting it out. "I *said* I had no more collateral. What partners do you think?"

Brody's heart was pounding. "Sharks?"

Peterson nodded.

"Where from?"

"Newark, New York, Queens. I needed three quarters of a million!"

"Who?"

"Balls Tuciano, Tony di Leone." Brody had never

heard of them. "And Shuffles Moscotti," added Peterson quickly.

"*Moscotti?*" groaned Brody. "Oh, Jesus!"

Shuffles was the only don Brody had ever seen in the flesh, an immense, quiet *capo* with a broad smile, bat-wing ears, and a flashing gold tooth. He'd had a summer home on Vista Knoll for years, an immense, storm-beaten mansion that had once belonged to the old town physician. When Clyde Bronson had proposed the gambling law in committee, in Albany, Moscotti had almost bought the Amity Inn through Vaughan. Brody had yelled until Vaughan had thrown in the sponge and stopped the deal. Outside of that, and letting his little boy join the cub scout pack, Moscotti had so far stayed as far from Amity's real pulse as any other summer visitor. That was how it must remain.

Not since The Trouble had Brody felt the town so threatened. Would Larry Vaughan be surprised? Or did he know already? *Was it a set-up, all along?*

"Why are you telling me now?"

Peterson looked into his eyes. "Because I like you. I like Ellen. And Willy Norton's my friend. He has kids too. The only real collateral Moscotti's got—and the rest of them—is in Albany. If gambling doesn't pass—. Damn it, Brody, *drop* Jepps! Forget it!"

"Meaning what?" Brody's fists clenched. "Meaning if I don't, we might get hurt?"

Peterson had guts. He did not flinch, he stood his ground. "I don't know."

Brody wondered, with his superior size and weight, if he could pitch him through the solarium door.

He heard Ellen park the station wagon by the garage, heard Sammy yelp happily, heard Sean bounce into the garage to hose him down. Upstairs he could hear Mike's transistor throbbing with acid rock.

"Get out," he murmured to Peterson. "Get out of my house!"

Brody opened the solarium door, grabbed his arm, hard as a rock, and shoved. Outside, Peterson turned, his face shadowed.

"Please, Brody. Drop it?"

"Move!"

He returned to the living room to find Ellen standing tensely at the kitchen door. "Where'd he go?"

She'd seen Peterson's car in front. "Out. The back way. Ellen, there's something to tell you."

"The Mafia? Norton already did. Oh, Brody, what's going to happen to us?"

"The town? I don't know."

"The hell with the town! *We!* Us. You're chief of police!" She was really scared. "You'll have to resign. Tomorrow!"

She sat down on the couch and covered her face. He sat beside her. Clumsily, he put his hand around her shoulder. He tried to kiss her. His glasses fell off.

"Ellen, don't cry."

"You won't be able to handle this! You don't have the training, or the men, or the . . ."

"Guts?" he asked softly.

"You've got guts! You don't have the instinct for the jugular."

"Guts," he said simply.

"That isn't what I meant."

He felt sick. She was right. "Well, I'm not Serpico, but . . ."

"I don't want Serpico! I want you, in one piece!"

"Look, Moscotti's lived here for years. You got his kid into the cubs. I write him three speeding tickets every season, nothing ever happens. Nothing happened when I blew his deal with the Inn—"

"Nothing *had* to happen! He knew he'd slide in, somehow. Now you're *really* in the way!" She wiped her eyes. "Over a goddamn seal!"

"And a trigger-happy bull who might have killed anybody and probably did kill two divers and a couple of nice young people who wanted to spend another summer in Amity. And he gets home free? No *way*!"

" '*Might* have killed,' " she repeated. "You're right, Brody. '*Might* have.' "

"Well, we ought to know Thursday."

She stood up, went to the kitchen. He heard her pour herself a drink. She drank it quickly, regarded him from the doorway. She shook her head. "You may not be Serpico, but you're one stubborn son of a bitch! Aren't you?"

"*Nowadays* I am. If I think I'm right."

"*I* hope to hell you're wrong." She fled upstairs.

He went out and got the whole bottle. It was a long time before he followed her.

6

She had found the searching warships as evening fell and the depths turned inky.

Devoid of fear, without even the mechanism for it, she was impelled to remain in the area purely by the instinct to stay close to the scene of surface activity. In mammalian terms, she might have been thought of as curious, but she was not: the eons had simply taught her that where there was action there was food.

At 5 fathoms, under the criss-crossing screws of searching destroyers and the higher whine of patrolling launches, she made her giant figure 8s. Every few moments the blast of a vessel's foghorn would penetrate to her depths. She ignored such distractions, as she ignored the churning propellors above, but the horns added to the general din and furor which glued her to the locale.

Her slim, elongated brain was hardly more than an extension of her central nervous system. Lacking any real memory, or the capacity for forethought or timidity, it was straightline efficient, functional, lethal.

As always, when she hungered, she monitored all of the incoming signals—vibratory, audible, electrical, for one that meant protein.

Her flat ebony eyes were highly sensitive in dim light, but it was pitch-black now, and her ocular inputs had been cut off by nightfall. However, they were the least of her sensory aids: she depended only sporadically, at medium range, on vision in daytime when approaching prey.

Her other sensors, as useful in the darkness as at high noon, were tuned by her hunger to their most excitable pitch. Her *ampullae of Lorenzini*, tiny vials of a clear liquid, spaced around her head, could receive electromagnetic energy emitted by her smallest quarry. Sensitized now by need for food, as a radar might be turned up to the highest gain, the *ampullae* were processing every frequency through which she passed, from the changing polarity of salt-water currents to the radiation patterns of the steel hulls passing above.

Her hearing was exquisite, and now pitched by hunger. Though her ears were only tiny ducts, they were, after milleniums of development, perhaps the most efficient hearing organs on earth.

Each ear consisted of three chambers, and in each chamber was a calcified stone connected to hair-thin sensory nerves. In the low-frequency range, her hearing was better than the sonar operating on the great ships thrashing above.

For detection of sounds so feeble and so low in frequency that a man or a porpoise could not have heard them, she had a lateral line of fine canals, filled with a watery solution, from her head along her flanks to the base of her tail. These wire-thin channels, feeling instantly the slightest difference of pressure along her sides, could discern a slowly moving object a thousand feet away.

But all of her receptors together could not equal her sense of smell. Seventy per cent of her computer-brain was devoted to olfactory functions. It was a highly selective system. It ignored the scent of human urine, but zeroed in on minute traces of fish oil. It disregarded human excrement but could smell a cut finger 500 yards away.

Through neuromasts, which were small pits in her skin serving as external organs and monitors of water movement, she sensed the direction of current.

When she caught a whiff of blood, her brain instantly analyzed the speed and direction of the flow that was carrying it to her, and she homed without thought at its source.

She had been holding at 5 fathoms and a steady 3 knots for the last half hour. Suddenly a shiver passed down her length. She peeled off, commenced a gentle climb, and accelerated the beat of her ponderous tail.

Above, behind, below, her world was filled with the startling blast of a foghorn, very close. She did not deviate one degree, and she left the blast astern.

The young aviation sonarman was fading fast. When he had heard the first faint sounds of search he had wasted his voice uselessly, so that now, even if he had had the strength to shout, nothing would have passed his lips.

He had no memory of the actual crash, just a kaleidoscopic recollection of spinning cloud banks, a whirling ocean, and the sound of his own screams above the wail of a runaway engine. He had no idea of what had happened to the gray-haired pilot. He faintly recalled losing the dangling ball, and the climb, and a glimpse of a vane gyrating off toward the sea.

He had found himself clear of the fuselage, hidden in fog. His right arm was lacerated. Automatically he had inflated his life vest. And then had come hope, with the foghorns blasting everywhere, and despair as they moved away.

He had turned on his life-jacket light at dusk, and he still had the whistle attached to his vest, and his arm, though torn and bleeding, had gone numb and that was a relief.

He had heard a helicopter beating somewhere above the fog. He had peered into the black velvet sky, but could not see the chopper lights, only hear the beat.

It did not cheer him. He remembered reading in a navy training manual on survival that the low-frequency sound of a chopper attracted sharks. So you kept helicopters away from the scene of a maritime disaster, if there were swimmers in the water.

He remembered rumors of a shark off Long Island, when he had first been in boot camp. Anywhere near here?

He shivered. He felt vulnerable from below. And when finally the sound of the vanes retreated, he felt more relieved than abandoned.

Now, suddenly, he heard a foghorn much closer than the rest. He fumbled for the whistle and began to shrill with all his might.

The JG stood on the starboard wing of the *Leon M. Cooper*, staring into misty blackness. He hoped that the skipper had seen him there, for it was not his watch, and he was the only junior officer on the ship who had felt obliged to leave the wardroom bridge game to come topside during the search.

He had begun to regret it almost immediately, when the chill penetrated his flimsy summer khakis. But he wanted to be sure he was noticed, so he stayed.

The foghorn 20 feet from his head cut loose with a gut-jarring blast. He thought of the risk of collision with the *Pritchett*, the *Kane*, or the *Karl O. Bergheer*, or any of the other destroyers searching to port or to starboard. He shivered. A horrible thought struck him. If there *were* trouble, if the *Pritchett*, for instance, loomed out of the fog and struck them, could he be held responsible even though off watch?

It was something to consider, and he searched the memory of his Academy lectures for a similar situation. Finding no analogous case, he was about to desert the bridge when he heard the faint sound of a police whistle.

He burst into the pilot house, almost knocking the officer-of-the-deck from his post at the radar hood. The skipper, coffee in hand and pipe in mouth, was sitting on his throne in the red glow of the binnacle light, peering out at the fog.

The JG reported the shrilling, and the captain ordered all engines stopped. They returned together to listen from the wing of the bridge. This time they both heard it, faintly, far off the starboard bow.

"Searchlight!" shouted the skipper at the signal bridge. "Searchlight starboard, sweep it around."

The light went on with a whine, but only showed them a wall of blinding fog.

"Searchlight off," the captain yelled.

They had wrecked their night vision, so they could only stand and listen. They heard nothing more.

The young sonarman in the water had heard the engines stop, far away. He sensed from a rushing bow-wave somewhere beyond the fog that he was very close to rescue. He whistled again, wildly, even managed a shout.

Adrenalin pumped through his veins, cutting his lassitude. He had been lying back in his vest, to save his strength. Now he kicked his feet, straightened up, and craned in the direction of the noise.

He saw a white glow a few hundred yards away through the fog. He raised his hand to wave and felt a piercing pain from his right elbow, where something jagged in the chopper had torn his flesh from bone.

He felt that his wound was bleeding faster, and tried to calm himself. He knew from bootcamp first-aid that shock had slowed his pulse. He lay back, grabbing the upper arm to stem the flow.

Thank *God* they were so close. He would not last long. He envisioned his mother burning a candle for his father years ago.

Thank God she, too, would not have to face that again . . .

A sudden and awful conviction that he was exposed from below, from all sides, struck him. The ocean turned malevolent. He looked around wildly.

Then he lay back. This was not the time to panic. He would be safe on the ship within minutes.

A monstrous force tore him out of the water, tossed him high, arms and legs flailing.

He had a vision of himself, as if from above, enveloped by a dark shadow from the sea. No thought of a shark entered his consciousness: he'd offended somewhere, this was the hand of God.

Mangled and torn, he knew nothing else.

The JG pulled aside the wardroom's dark green curtains and stepped into the lounge. The bridge game had dissolved when the launches and the captain's gig were dropped to search for the source of the whistling. They were still out, inching through the fog.

The cards had been left on the wardroom table. This offended his sense of order, and he collected them and put them away in the wardroom cabinet.

He'd done his part when he heard the whistle: he'd risk no mistakes by staying topside.

He went to his stateroom, undressed, and crawled into the upper bunk.

The stupid chopper pilot had screwed up the whole exercise by crashing, so he might as well get his sleep.

7

Mayor Larry Vaughan got up quickly from behind his desk, crossed the room, and closed the door to his outer office, where his secretary Daisy Wicker was knotting macrame on a wooden frame. He fixed Brody with a bulbous, red-streaked eye. "Jesus, Brody, you don't care what you say, or who hears you, do you?"

Brody shook his head. "I figured everybody knew anyway."

"What do you mean by that?" Vaughan's face was brick-red.

Brody shrugged: "I always assume I'm the last person in town to hear about anything crooked."

"It's not crooked to borrow money. Anyway, *I* didn't know, Brody. I resent the—"

"Cut the crap, Larry. If I hadn't screamed so loud, you'd have sold the Inn to Moscotti two years ago."

"Well, I didn't know about *this*."

Bull, thought Brody. He wondered how many of the board of selectmen had known it all the time. Tony Catsoulis, probably, maybe Albert Morris. Ned Thatcher? Rafe Lopez? Maybe. There was no way to tell. Anyway, Vaughan had known, for sure.

To test the theory, Brody said: "I want you to suspend Peterson's building permit."

Vaughan snorted. "You're off your rocker! I got a wife and kid."

"That's just the point. If these guys get in here, they'll be selling heroin to the church choir at high noon!"

Vaughan looked at him curiously: "And what will the chief of police be doing while all this is going on?"

Probably, thought Brody, teaching high school English or working at the bank.

"Cancel his permit," Brody repeated, "or I'll go to the selectmen."

"The selectmen of this town," said Vaughan slowly, "are not going to flush it down the drain because a minor public servant doesn't think he can handle a small-town hood!"

"Well," Brody said edgily, "I can't."

"Maybe they'll want to find somebody who can."

Brody had a sudden inclination to rip off his badge, unholster his gun and slap them on the mayor's desk. It would make Ellen very happy, until the town started laughing . . .

"Sure," he said. "Maybe you can hire Jepps . . . when I let him off the hook."

"Which, from what you've told me, better be pretty soon."

He asked Vaughan what he meant.

"You're in the way. Moscotti might try to get *you* out of the way. The *hard* way."

Another threat. He'd probably get used to them. "He might, at that, Larry. So let's get the Casino out of town, OK?"

"And put the town back on its ass?"

Len Hendricks knocked and entered. He saluted Brody like a Fort Benning recruit. A navy helicopter had landed a block away, in Town Square. Wasn't that illegal, or something? Or were government planes exempt?

Brody left to check it out.

At least for now he hadn't given up his badge.

Brody pushed through the crowd surrounding an ungainly blue-gray chopper squatting on the grass. He confronted a curly-haired navy pilot. On the collar of his khaki shirt were a pair of gold oak leaves.

The last helicopter Brody had been anywhere close to had blown sand in his face on the beach last Sunday, and this one had destroyed half of a row of azaleas that Minnie Eldridge had planted in the spring of 1956. Brody shook his head.

"Look, major, or whatever—"

The pilot stretched out a hand. He had guileless brown eyes and a cheerful grin. "Lt. Comdr. Chip Chaffey, helicopter safety officer, Quonset Point."

Brody ignored the hand, nodded coolly, and asked him why he thought he could land in the middle of the Town Square.

"It's official business with your department and—"

"Would you land in Central Park if you wanted to see the NYPD?"

"No sir."

A certain pecking order having been established in front of the peasants, Brody decided not to arrest him.

The commander requested a police beach patrol to look for the bodies of the two chopper crewmen lost yesterday.

Brody pointed out that the officer was looking at 50 percent of the Amity Police Department, right now, in the persons of himself and Officer Hendricks, and anyway, wouldn't it have been just as easy to place a telephone call as to blow down half the shrubbery in the only Town Square they had?

"Sorry, sir," said the pilot, disarming him further. The last person wearing gold leaves who had addressed him had called him, not "sir," but a stupid idiot for having dropped an M1 rifle on an army parade ground.

The pilot continued: "I wanted to try to find somebody who might have seen the chopper from the beach, before the accident."

"My son," volunteered Brody.

He sent the commander home with Len Hendricks and left in the dune buggy to sweep the beach for chopper victims, diving victims, explosion victims, or whatever.

It might turn out to be a bloodier summer than the year with The Trouble.

Ellen Brody, serving coffee in the living room to Len Hendricks and the helicopter pilot, caught her older son's eye. He looked away.

Strange, very very strange. She had sensitive antennae to both boys, but Mike more than Sean, because she had known him longer. And she was certain that Mike was hiding something from the jovial man with the golden wings.

"No, Mike," the pilot said. "I doubt if just horsing around with your buddy would have brought him closer. Unless he figured one of you was drowning or something . . ."

"That will be the day," Ellen scoffed. "They're born with gills and they swim before they walk."

The pilot glanced at her. He was on the make, she had sensed it from the moment he and Len Hendricks had arrived at the door. She was used to that, but it was always nice to know that there was someone out there looking.

When she was young, the naval officers had swarmed to her Pelham home from as far as Brooklyn Navy Yard, and the pilots had been the wolfiest of the lot. This one had a warm and tender smile for her.

And of course, he had not the slightest hint that Mike was, for some reason, dissembling. She wondered why he was.

"So just you and this Larry dude," said the commander, "you're the only guys who saw him?"

Mike colored. "Well, Andy Nicholas . . ."

The commander wrote down the name.

"And Jackie," Ellen urged him. "What's wrong with Jackie? She's got eyes, right?"

"Jackie, I forgot."

Forgot, heck . . .

"Jackie?" inquired the commander.

"Jackie Angelo," muttered Mike. "Her dad's a cop."

"Police officer," Ellen said automatically. She glanced at Mike curiously. Was he afraid of Dick Angelo? Wasn't Jackie *supposed* to go swimming? Or what had they been doing out there, anyway? The gulf between 33 and 15 had never yawned more widely.

But the commander seemed satisfied. "OK. We won't bother them." He closed his notebook. "Mike, you know where the wreck of the *Orca* lies?"

"Does he ever!" breathed Ellen.

"My dad was aboard," Mike said, rather proudly, "when she sank."

The commander had a theory. The pilot had been his shipmate in Nam. He was a good pilot. The sonarman was inexperienced. If the crewman had goofed, and dragged his ball too low, it could have snagged in the superstructure of the *Orca*, which was the only wreck around he could find on a nautical chart.

To find the ball and try to decide what had snagged it on the bottom might someday save another pilot's life.

Mike's face lit up. He told the pilot of their diving class. Maybe Andrews, the instructor, might let them search the wreck.

Ellen's heart tumbled. It was one thing to envision Mike, supervised by a capable instructor, skimming harmlessly along a sandy bottom, and another to think of him poking around in the hulk that had very nearly drowned his dad.

The pilot shook his head. Balanced on the verge of laughter, he said no, they'd use a UDT team, whatever that was, from Quonset.

Ellen saw him to the door. When she asked if he thought the crew had survived, he said flatly: "No. Not any more. Too long in the water, even if we find them."

And so the friendly wave from the pilot to Mike had been his final communication with the living world. Even Ellen felt strangely about it, and Mike must feel even funnier. Perhaps that was what was bugging him.

As Len drove the commander off, Mike appeared on the front porch, munching an apple. "What's a UDT team?" she asked him.

"Underwater demolition," he explained, condescendingly.

She asked him if he felt oddly about the helicopter. "It wasn't your fault, you know."

He chewed thoughtfully: "Well, if the guy came over to see if we needed help, and dragged that thing into the *Orca*, it's kind of like it *was* my fault, isn't it?"

Early Catholic training. Search for guilt, and confess. "That's silly. And you know it."

"Except, see, it must have looked like . . . Well,

we weren't just horsing around . . ." He stared down Bayberry Lane. "Wow!"

She followed his gaze. A low yellow sportscar, mirror-sleek and lethal-looking, was slipping under the trees along the street. It drew to a stop at their curb.

"Ferrari 246," pronounced Mike. "That's 20,000 bucks worth of wheels!"

Protruding from the car's passenger window, and jutting back further than the rear wheels, was a familiar fishing pole. Her younger son popped into view, pulling the pole free. As she stared, the driver's door opened and a broad-shouldered, massively paunched figure slid from behind the wheel. At first she did not recognize him, though Brody had once pointed him out in the dining room of the Abelard Arms.

Now, because he was in Bermuda shorts and wearing a sports shirt instead of a suit, it was a moment before she realized who was shuffling up her front walk, with the strange, punchy gait that gave him his name.

Sean ignored her, dropping the pole on the scrubby lawn and heading straight for Sammy in the garage. Mike deserted her, for a closer look at the car. The man kept coming.

"Mrs. Brody? Ellen?"

She stiffened. "Yes?" Her voice was quivering. The enormity of what was happening was just beginning to grip her.

The man smiled, baring yellow teeth, punctuated by one golden canine, set in a wide, full mouth. His head was too big for his body and his ears were too big for his head and his gray hair was leonine.

It was Moscotti. He held out a hand. Automatically, she took it. His grip was soft and wet but absolutely, she sensed, unbreakable. She wanted to jerk her hand away and found herself staring into the man's flat black eyes, like a rabbit confronting a serpent.

"The chief in?" he asked.

"No. Yes. He's coming back any minute."

"Yeah. I guess so. Me and Sean, we had a nice ride. Talked about cub scouts, the regatta, you know, town things." He grinned. She managed to draw her hand away. It felt dirty. He chuckled, watching her. "OK, Mrs. Brody. Don't sweat it. Just wanted to tell your husband something, give him some advice."

She stood mute. She was afraid that if she spoke again she would squeak like a frightened sparrow.

"When I stopped, Sean, he climbed right in. Don't let your kids take rides."

Sean knew that, he *knew* it. He would never have let it happen if he hadn't been dazzled by the car, and by God, when she finished with him it would never happen again.

"They don't," she managed. "They aren't allowed to."

"That's nice," he smiled. "Makes me feel I ain't such a stranger in town." He turned, joined Mike at the car, playfully punched his arm and slid into the seat. He closed the door, stuck his massive face through the window and said, more loudly: "You never know *who* might pick them up."

He pulled the car from the curb. The engine had a deep and throaty growl, like a far-off avalanche she had heard with her father, skiing in the Austrian Alps. The car accelerated, taking the corner at a good 40 miles an hour as smoothly as a model racer on a model track.

It all came out. "Sean!" she shrieked.

He appeared at the garage door, bucket in hand, looking scared. He knew. His face went white when he saw hers. He let out a questioning little bleat.

"Come here!" she cried. "*Now!*"

He sidled across the lawn, terrified. "I . . ."

She met him at the side of the porch. "Don't you ever, ever, *ever*—"

"I *forgot*," he whined. "And *you* let Johnny Moscotti in the cubs—"

She slapped him, hard, like a housewife in a Naples slum. He had never been slapped in his life, and he stared at her in silent shock.

"I'll tell daddy!" he yelled suddenly. Then he whirled and went pounding to the rear of the house, heading for the mudflats bordering Amity Sound.

"Sean!" she called after him weakly. "Honey, come back!"

He was gone. Sammy coughed in the garage. The chunk-chunk of the Amity Neck ferry sounded very near. Mike was approaching the porch from the sidewalk, cautiously, as if she had gone mad.

She ran inside and up to the bathroom.

She could hardly recognize her face in the mirror.

She began to wash Moscotti's touch from her hand.

Yak-Yak Hyman checked the live bait in his shop and decided to replenish it, in case the cod ran again. He walked toward the bait cages sloshing at the foot of the pilings on Town Dock. Abreast of the police launch, he glanced down at Dick Angelo, who had the head off his engine and was working in greasy delight in the cockpit. Angelo looked up. "Hi, Yak-Yak. I about got it, I think."

Yak-Yak considered a nod. He decided against it. It could lead to Angelo's coming by the bait shop to pass the time of day when he finished with the engine, which could lead to his asking for a beer, or even one of the crabs that he already suspected Yak-Yak took in illegal pots off the end of the pier.

Screw Angelo. Screw cops. Screw Rockland, Maine, where years ago he had been picked by the union to deliver a welcoming speech to Muskie, had fumbled it, forgotten it all, drawn a blank, and had to leave the platform. Screw the lobstermen of Penobscot Bay, who had laughed him out of town.

Mostly, screw Amity, with its yammering New York accent, which he could hardly stand, and its inability, after all these years, to decipher plain Down East speech.

He stared down at his live bait cages. They flashed with silvered energy as the mullet, for mullet reasons, wriggled in hysteria. Probably a bonitō or a big-mouth bass, shaking up the harbor.

Laboriously, he climbed over the rail and started down the rough wooden rungs he had nailed to the pilings when first he came to Amity. Halfway down he paused, staring.

The neatly severed head and gills of a sleek fat cod was floating in on the flood, swirling in the oil-mirrored lee of a piling, finally bobbing to his bait cage. He leaned far out and snagged it with his bait-scoop.

It was fresh, too fresh, really, for what he had in mind. He climbed back up the pilings, walked to the end of the dock, and glanced surreptitiously around. He found the yellow polypropolene line he had cleverly wedged in a crack in a piling. He pulled from the bottom a crab-trap dripping mud and muck.

It was empty, so far, but the bait was so rotten that he doubted that even an Amity crab would touch it. He regarded the severed corpse in his scoop. Almost fresh enough to eat himself, but it would rot soon enough. He tossed it in the crabnet and lowered it to the bottom.

Some fisherman with a very sharp knife had chopped the body in two, for bait, maybe, or for cooking. And this half had slipped off his fantail.

Somebody's loss was always someone's gain, that was the ocean.

He looked out over the harbor. He suddenly sensed that there was not a living creature in its whole expanse. There would be no fishermen tonight, not even Sean Brody, who had been turning up like clockwork since the great cod run. So there was no use scooping more bait.

Dick Angelo was leaving, tool kit in hand. Yak-Yak watched him climb into the police jeep and rumble away down the rough wooden boards. No danger of conversation there.

The fog was drifting in again, not the brutal, solid banks of Penobscot, but delicate New York fog, probably laden with germs.

He would have closed up shop, but he had nowhere to go but the chattering bar at the Randy Bear.

He stepped inside his shack, opened a drawer full of jumbled fishhooks. He drew out a pint of Jamaica rum.

He found a copy of *Gallery* that somebody had left on the dock.

Leafing through the pages, shaking his head at the blatant photos—the stuff people would buy, you couldn't believe it—he began to suck at the bottle.

Brody parked the dune buggy in front of his house, climbed wearily from behind the wheel, and spotted his young son sitting dejectedly on the front porch. He had found no bodies on the beach, thank God. The chopper pilot and his crewman must have sunk or drifted out to sea.

Sean, who would ordinarily have been piping the news of the day by now, looked up resentfully.

"What's wrong, Spud?" Brody asked him.

Sean jerked his head toward the door. "Ask *her*!

Dad, can she just *belt* a guy?" His voice was choking.

Brody smiled. "I guess she can. What'd you do?"

"I mean, in the *face*?"

Brody stiffened. He had never known Sean to lie before. "Watch it, Buster . . ."

Sean raised his eyes, and they were without hope. Suddenly he jumped to his feet and ran to the garage. Puzzled, Brody entered his home.

The tension inside was electric. Mike was trying to shut it out by jamming his sensory inputs. He was lying in front of the TV, which was on full-bright and full-loud. His transistor radio blared beside him. He was turning through *Skin Diver Magazine*.

"Where's your mother?" Brody demanded, above the din. Mike jerked his thumb upstairs. Brody took the steps two at a time.

She was sitting at the bedroom window, looking out over Amity Sound.

"What the hell?" he asked.

She turned. Her eyes were bleak with pain. "Did he tell you?"

He put an arm around her shoulder. "Oh, come on, Ellen. You've paddled him before."

"Did he say 'paddled'?"

"Slapped, but I didn't believe him."

"He *was* slapped. On the face. Like a damn fish-wife!"

He couldn't believe it. "What did he *do*?"

She told him. Brody felt his legs go weak.

"A threat? You think?" he muttered.

She stared at him. "Last night Peterson warned you. Today the only hood this side of Flushing picked up Sean. Of *course* it's a threat!"

He looked out across Amity Sound. The sun was setting on his favorite view. The Cape Cod cottages, backed to the waters, had been built in days when marine views were unimportant, when you always faced your house to the street. The sand on the flats glowed golden, blackened behind the hillocks with speeding shadows. The golden cross on the spire of St. Xavier's, last point in town to see the sun, was getting its good-night kiss.

Well, the gun on his belt wasn't wooden and the badge on his shirt wasn't tin. No two-bit hood was scaring him, or anyone else in Amity Town.

"I'm *damned*," he grated, "if it's happening here!"

He whirled, left the room, and flew down the steps.

"Brody!" he heard her call. "Brody, come back!"

He was into the car and halfway up Vista Knoll toward Moscotti's sprawling old mansion when he asked himself what he intended to do.

He kept going. That he would decide when he had the sonofabitch alone.

All afternoon, Lena Starbuck had been trying to gather her courage. She had overheard Mike Brody telling Jackie at the cosmetics counter that navy frogmen were going to dive on Quint's old *Orca*.

Her brother had died in the navy in World War II, of pneumonia, in Boston Navy Yard. She invoked his memory and, after two false starts, managed to tell Nathanial of the navy's plans to dive the wreck. He had looked her dead in the eye, shrugged, and muttered, very quietly: "Ain't our problem, is it?"

"But Nate," she whispered hurriedly, "they're diving tomorrow morning, and they don't even know he's there!"

"If they find out the hard way," he'd grinned, "they'll probably have to go out of business. Just like us. Customer, Lena!"

Now, with trade slowing at suppertime, she decided on a last attempt. Only once in her life had she tried to threaten him with anything. Years ago, she had clamped an embargo on sexual services when he had decided to fire her nephew.

And that had only turned him toward a Portuguese prostitute, with hair as tall as the girl was broad, working—as a cover—as a waitress in Cy's Diner. Lena approached her husband again.

"Nathanial, we have to tell *somebody*!"

"Tell who, for Christ's sake?"

"Brody."

"Brody," Starbuck laughed bitterly, "*knows* the shark's still there. Or alive, anyway."

"Larry Vaughan, then."

"He probably knows it too."

"Then Harry Meadows."

"He won't print it."

"He'll have to if you tell him you'll tell the *Long Island Press*, or something. And show him the film."

"It's too late. And anyway, I *burned* the film."

That was a palpable lie. Nathanial never burned anything, never threw anything away. The drugstore cellar was full of things he might someday find use for again. And someday he would use the film, or sell it, or something.

It was in his safe, she was sure, with the morphine, cocaine and seconal, secure against the drug-crazed burglar he expected every night when he bolted the door of the pharmacy.

"You've got to tell Mayor Larry Vaughan," she insisted. "Then, if something happens, it isn't your fault."

"I'll tell Larry," he said grimly, "when he sells our store. Look, you have a customer. Go take his money, *I'll* handle the shark."

She went to the register. When she returned, he was in the back, squatting in the corner.

He was changing the combination on the safe.

There were homes and rentals in the knolls behind Amity Beach that Brody expected to be summoned to three or four times each summer. Some of the weathered beach cottages seemed to attract conflict and tension no matter who rented or owned them. And there were others that he knew only by the names outside, and which he had not had occasion to visit since he took over the force.

Moscotti's home was one of the peaceful ones. Brody last had driven up the winding length of Vista Knoll Drive to attend the dying gasp of its original owner, the town's former doctor, old Roger Ruskin. Maybe Moscotti got enough action in Queens during the winter. The hood's domestic arrangements were as impeccable as those of the Rev. Wickham at Amity Presbyterian.

He parked in front of the sprawling home, in a well-lighted portico. Moscotti's newest acquisition, a Ferrari, lay in his headlights. He could almost sympathize with Sean. He would have loved to have ridden in it himself.

Inside, a dog began to bark. Brody pressed the bell. It chimed musically. The door opened. A boy of about ten, with Moscotti's broad mouth, big ears, but with soft Latin eyes, looked up at him. Brody had never noticed him, but it had to be Johnny, of the Amity Cubs. Brody was surprised. He had expected to be greeted by half the Mafia of Queens, assembled for battle. The boy smiled, and it was not a bad smile at that. "He's watching TV. You want to come in?"

The Moscotti's had left Doc Ruskin's furniture, old leather easy chairs and worn rattan, as they had found it. A dowdy woman in an expensive black slack suit was curled in front of a stereo, selecting records. She got up, awkwardly, and approached Brody.

"Chief Brody! Would you like to sit down?"

Brody shook his head, told her that he was not here socially, and would like to see her husband.

Moscotti, apparently, did not bring his office problems home or she would have known why he was here.

Moscotti opened the door of what had been old Ruskin's medical office. He motioned Brody inside. The gangster had turned the room into a den. Books lined the walls, a big desk glowered massively in a corner, and a TV faced an overstuffed easy chair.

Drawn next to the easy chair was a smaller one, and on it sat a hulking, fresh-faced youth of perhaps 25. He wore a flowing moustache, had pink Italian cheeks. He seemed delighted at Mike Douglas guest-gushing on his show.

Moscotti turned down the TV. The giant seemed not to notice. "Dummy," Moscotti explained. "Nephew from Palermo. Don't speak Italian, don't speak English, don't hear either, nobody told me." He shrugged. "Family. What am I gonna do?"

"Keep your rotten hands off my kid!" blurted Brody.

The gangster's eyes widened. He sat behind his desk, swung in his swivel chair, presenting his back while he took a pipe from a rack on a bookcase behind him. When he turned back he was smiling, gold tooth flashing, but his eyes were rock-hard. "Hell, I thought you come up here to thank me."

"For what? That he got home at all?"

Moscotti studied him. "Poor little guy, carrying that pole."

"He can make it."

"Just thought I'd be neighborly."

"How long you summered here?" lashed Brody.

"Three years," grinned Moscotti. It was no grin at all. "Three fun-filled years in the Amity sun."

"And after three years, the night after you find out your casino might not get to *be* a casino—"

"*My* casino? Hey, I ain't got a casino." He snorted. "You think Albany'd let *me* have a casino?"

"—might not *be* a casino because I'm stirring up heat in the Legislature, *then* you get neighborly? Bull!"

"Funny thing," Moscotti ruminated, studying the smoke drifting from his pipe. "The casino's to bury the shark, save the town. Ain't that right? Everybody told me Amity was *for* a casino."

"Sure. Backed with Chase Manhattan's money. Not *yours*."

"Hey!" Moscotti began to laugh. He slid open his drawer and drew out a stack of $100 bills. They were bound in a paper collar. On the collar was printed: *Chase Manhattan Bank.* "Hey, this *is* Chase Manhattan's. See, maybe you don't understand, Brody. Chase Manhattan wants, like stock certificates, title to your car, mortgage on your house, your arm, your leg, Peterson don't have none of them things left. *I* trust *people*. Outside of that . . ." He shrugged. "Same money."

"It's dirty."

Moscotti let his mouth gape. He picked up the stack and pretended to look at it. "I don't see no dirt." He tossed it across the desk. "You see dirt? Take it home, look at it good."

"You son of a bitch," murmured Brody. "*You* take it home to Queens. *We don't want it here.*"

"Who's this 'we'?"

"Amity."

"Amity? You know what Amity is?" Moscotti stretched and yawned. "A fat-assed mayor that can't make up his mind if he wants to be straight or a two-bit scam artist. A half dozen 'selectmen' you wouldn't hire to run a funeral parlor. Twenty 'merchants' that couldn't sell Kona Gold at a rock festival. A couple hundred more yucks that know if the Casino *don't* come in they'll be digging clams in a month." He moved back to the TV set and turned Mike Douglas up. "And the 'chief of police?' Hell, you couldn't get the beaches closed when the shark was chewing up tourists faster'n the Cannonball Express could bring 'em in." He smiled. "*That's* what Amity is."

"This town," grated Brody, "*beat* the shark. It beat more hurricanes than you got soldiers on the streets, and the blizzards of '88 and '77 and the Crash and gas rationing in '41 and it'll beat *you*, Moscotti, if we got to blow your goddamn casino all the way across Long Island Sound!"

"That's nice," murmured Moscotti, puffing his pipe. "That all you come up here to say?"

"No. Don't let my kids even *see* you again." Brody leaned on the desk. "Do you read that? Loud and clear?"

The black eyes studied him. "Hey, Brody?"

"What?"

"You don't have no other summer kids in the cub scouts. Who let Johnny in?"

"What's the difference—"

"Norton, or your wife? Your wife, right?"

"She couldn't see why a kid should get hurt—"

"And what did *you* have to say?"

"I didn't like it."

"I figured."

"All right. About *that*, I was wrong."

Moscotti smiled: "Ain't fair, take it out on a kid. Very happy you figured that out. You should be happy, too. Very, very happy." He got up, opened the door, and waited. "Don't push your luck."

Brody had a wild impulse to pistol-whip the

broad mouth to a shattered mess of broken teeth. He turned, slammed from the house, and took out his anger in a winding, tire-torturing run down Vista Knoll Drive. He almost drove some poor summer klutz into the culvert at Spoonaker's Creek.

It was surprising that he got home without killing himself or someone else, and then he and Ellen fought for an hour about turning in his badge.

8

Brody sat opposite Harry Meadows in Cy's Diner and watched the fat editor drown his after-breakfast cigar in his half-filled coffee cup.

"They're in, Harry," Brody told him. "The families are in. And you and me have to get them out."

Brody had left home early to catch him here, rather than to brave the smell of the editorial cubicle in the *Amity Leader*. Here in Cy's Diner the air was bad enough, heavy with burned grease and stale coffee, but Harry's office was insufferable. And reminded him, too, of the hours spent there in the time of The Trouble. He needed no more of that.

"I already heard about Moscotti," Harry belched. "So what else is new?" He shifted, making the table between them screech and spilling the customer's coffee in the next booth. "Hey, you tried the bear-claws here?"

"No, and you better not either." Brody regarded the yellowed smear of three fried eggs on Harry's plate, a lonely shoestring potato, a rind of ham, a crumb of toast, a dab of jelly, and some cream cheese from a last-minute bagel. "Harry, you're a slob!"

"I've heard that too, Brody. Now where did I hear *that*?"

"Your wife. Your doctor. All those who love and revere you."

"You're concerned?"

"You're killing yourself."

Meadows speared the potato. "There are worse ways to go. You could strangle in the trunk of your car. You could fall out of an office building. You could blow up with the morning paper."

"Has Moscotti been talking to you?"

"He doesn't have to. And he knows it." Meadows signaled the waitress and ordered a bearclaw.

Brody told Meadows sarcastically that he was aware of the *Leader's* courage and its glorious record in legislative reporting. He admired its concern for the public good, as exemplified during The Trouble by its refusal to print the news of the first shark attack. But if the *Leader* wouldn't help now, and Vaughan wouldn't help, who would?

"Nobody. Hey, Mitz! Make it two!" He smiled at Brody. "You just *got* to try one of these, with butter, lots of butter."

"No thanks. Harry?"

"Um?"

"Print it."

"There's no *story*. Peterson needed money. He had to go to the Families. It isn't *news*!"

Mitz returned, flouncing her foot-high hair and smiling through cheery Portuguese eyes. She was the only practicing prostitute in town, had come all the way from Providence across Long Island Sound, and Amity was a little proud of her. She ran, Brody thought, a clean operation: he had never heard any complaints. She was unobtrusive in her role as a waitress and absolutely impartial in her clientele, which ranged from Mayor Vaughan at the affluent end to Yak-Yak Hyman at the poverty level.

And she was the best waitress in town, besides. She set a warm bearclaw before Brody and another before Meadows.

"Morning, Brody," she said in her flat Rhode Island twang. "Say, if you'll eat with him, how come you won't make it with me?"

"Let me know when it goes on sale."

She grinned and swished off. Meadows looked after her, jowels perpetually moving. "You don't try to run *her* out of town. Why Moscotti?"

"That's a stupid question, Harry."

"It isn't stupid. *You're* stupid. A town this size always has a pro. It *always* has hard porn, like at Starbuck's. It *always* has an after-hours place, like the back room at the Randy Bear. You don't raid *it*."

"No," admitted Brody. "I wish the front room was as quiet."

Meadows ignored him. "And if it's going to have gambling, it's always going to have gambling money, and that's Mafia money, you better believe it. And there isn't a damn thing you or me or anybody else can do about it, and the town should have known that going in."

"*I* didn't."

"Well, *I* did. And Vaughan did, you can bet your ass. And Peterson sure did. Vegas or Atlantic City or Nassau or Amity—gambling equals Mafia. Period."

"Then block the gambling law!"

"It looks like *you* will, if you just keep rousting Jepps. Who's he know up there?"

Brody shrugged. "State police commissioner, or somebody."

"And you're willing to have goats grazing on Water Street and Main, just to put him away?"

"I don't know."

Meadows noticed that Brody was not eating his bearclaw. He slid it onto his own plate. "That story on Jepps—"

"I read it."

"You practically *wrote* it, and don't you forget it. How *is* your homicide 'investigation'? What did you *have*, anyway?"

Brody told him. Every time he spoke of his suspicions, they sounded weaker. Meadows sat, fork suspended, shaking his head. "That's all?"

Brody nodded. "Enough."

"No! To go to county ballistics, maybe. But you didn't have enough to get me to go to *press*! You ever hear of *libel*?"

Brody nodded tiredly. "Since you ask, noble scribe, yes, I have."

"Then hold your fire until you get that ballistics report," Meadows growled. "And pray."

Brody studied him for a moment, then stepped out onto the street.

He left the diner. He had never seen Meadows more serious.

Lt. Comdr. Chip Chaffey, helicopter safety officer at Quonset Point, braced himself on the miniscule bridge of the AVR aviation rescue boat anchored over the *Orca* wreck. He was nauseated from the ground swell. Years of shore duty had lost him his sealegs. He had last been to sea on a carrier in Tonkin Gulf, the same carrier the dead chopper pilot had flown from. And a ship was more like a city block than a vessel anyway; this heaving toy, cluttered with diving gear and swarming with UDT divers, was churning his insides so badly that he was about to disgrace his wings.

He accepted another cup of coffee from the skipper of the divers, a big, broad-chested ensign in a wetsuit, who should have been playing noseguard for the Steelers and looked as if he could stay below for ten minutes without a tank. The ensign had been sulking from the beginning.

"You know, commander, how very futile this is."

Chaffey flinched. *How very futile* . . . A new breed. Harvard, or Yale?

"Where you from, mister?"

"OCS. Then UDT San Diego."

"I mean, before?"

"Georgetown."

What a waste of muscle. Chaffey wasn't sure they had a football team. He put down his cup. "OK. *You* think it's futile. But those guys you got over the side, and your friend the porpoise, you got *them* thinking it's futile?"

"The men, frankly, don't care. It's bottom-time, and they need it. But yes, they think it's futile. They know the ball will roll, and they know the currents, and the tides . . . It's *been* 24 hours."

"And what about the dolphin?"

"Well, he wasn't exactly eager, was he?"

The team had managed to launch the porpoise, pride of their unit, at 10 a.m. His name, imaginatively, was P-19. He was a Pacific bottlenose, trained to locate lost torpedoes, sunken subs, and stray nukes from plane crashes. If anyone aboard knew what secret suicidal missions lay in store for him in actual combat, they were not about to tell a mere helicopter pilot.

P-19, from the moment they anchored, had been an unenthusiastic participant. He had struggled as they eased him from his tank into his sling, chattering peevishly at his keeper. And when finally he had been winched over the rail and into the water, he had refused for five minutes to leave his padded cocoon.

There had been great puzzlement. P-19, his handler explained to Chaffey, was a perfect porpoise, a regular Tom Swift among dolphin, trustworthy, loyal, helpful, obedient. He had once found a practice warhead in forty fathoms off Norfolk, and a ditched fighter off Key West. Last week he had followed the submarine *Growler* all night long at 20 fathoms and 18 knots, surfacing every quarter hour on the minute to beep his location to the pursuing forces.

Chaffey had stared down at the reluctant animal. He was nuzzling the side of the AVR as if it were his mother. "Maybe he wants a better pension plan."

Everyone had smiled, though thinly. It was no joking matter. The pride of the unit was at stake. Whatever had demotivated him, they had better find out, but soon.

His handler, circling in a rubber raft with a big outboard engine, had finally pried him loose with an oar. P-19 had slow-rolled away from the sling, tossed its flukes high, and disappeared.

No one had seen him since, though he was supposed to surface every fifteen minutes. Now the handler was charging desperately back and forth between the AVR and the beach, stopping every few moments to shrill on a whistle. As Chaffey watched, the keeper broke off and zoomed up abeam.

"Sir," he yelled to the ensign. "He's 20 minutes over!"

"He's gone," muttered the ensign. To the handler he said: "Give him another 5 minutes. We'll call in and secure." He tossed a lighted cherry-bomb into the water to recall his divers. "Damn!" he moaned, as the divers began to climb aboard. "You wouldn't believe the paperwork I'll have to do."

"They split very often?" asked Chaffey.

The ensign shrugged. "Sometimes, obviously. Sex, usually. Not this one, though. Neutered."

"He must be very grateful," observed Chaffey.

The ensign was in a real snit. "Well, he was worth a hell of a lot more with no balls at all than the ball full of junk he was looking for!"

Chaffey was tempted to point out that the ball

full of junk might have held the key to the death of a man who had spent more hours under enemy fire than the ensign had in the navy. And the key, as well, to teaching others to avoid whatever mishap had befallen him.

The hell with it, for today. The pilot was gone, for good, and if he had to depend on the UDT they would never know why.

Chaffey tossed the contents of his cup over the side. The ponderous, gentle breathing of the groundswell heightened at the beach to spume-blowing pants of rage. He glared at the surging water, then at Amity Beach.

No, he was damned if he'd give up. He'd somehow get Disbursing to post a reward for finding the ball. That would attract commercial divers, maybe, or at least amateurs. His heart sank at *that* paperwork, but he owed it to his friend.

Bad show, all around.

The porpoise had been ten miles to sea, and now, sensing that he had lost the shark, he was streaking back to land. He scanned, as he went, the world ahead, using his high-pitched clicking voice to envision the shoreline and the wreck of the *Orca.* Half a mile ahead, he sensed that the vessel carrying his keeper, who was also his God, was departing.

He had been born in a tank and all of his friends were men. He loved to swim with them, and to find their toys on the bottom when they lost them, and to shadow the enormous ocean-piercing playthings, too, that they liked him to follow through the deep.

He was a sensitive, impressionable animal, and at present a little confused. He had sensed a shark while he was still on the boat. He had squirmed under the gentle hands of his trainer, picking up vibrations of danger, perhaps through the hull of the vessel, or from the air around.

He had no real fear of sharks. But into him had been trained a desire to warn divers when one was about. This he would have liked to have done on the boat, for he could hear and see from the preparations that it would be playtime shortly, with his friends spilling into the water in their hilarious, clumsy way.

There was no way he could warn them until he was launched, so finally, after protesting every way he knew, he had permitted himself to be slung and hoisted.

As always, the water had been cool on his dry, sun-baked skin. But instantly, while he was still in the sling, he sensed the shark presence again, and knew that this was no sand shark or tiger or mako or white-tip, but a creature so enormous that none of the rules applied. He was suddenly reluctant to leave the boat.

Ordinary sharks avoided him. Instinctively, if he had sensed one near a school of dolphin with young in their midst, he would have attacked with the rest, at lightning speed, snout centered on the one soft shark-target, the ventral zone. With each of the adults battering his 200-pound mass at 25 knots into the area of the shark's liver, they might actually kill a mako or a tiger, or drive it off.

He had of course never cruised with a dolphin school, and his friends had not taught him to attack sharks, only to play at assaulting the gigantic steel toys he shadowed when they failed to beep properly. His brain began to marry the unprogrammed instinct to the learned program.

Suddenly, as he vascillated next to the boat, he caught the shark echo loud and clear. It imprinted on his massive cerebellum so monstrous a picture that for a moment he was immobile with fright.

It was approaching very swiftly. He knew instantly a good deal about the fish. He learned it from vibrations that had nothing to do with sound or sight, sensed it in his genes. He knew her sex, and that her purposeful speed meant that she was feeding and desperate and would attack anything that moved, his own kind or his friends when they plunged in, or perhaps the boat itself. So he had pressed for a moment close to the hull, chattering cries for help. No one had understood. His keeper was prodding him away from the boat, so he knew he must go, but it was not until he heard the *klunge . . . klunge . . . klunge* of his friends as they dropped butt-first into the water, and glimpsed them passing below trailing their bubbles, that he knew he must act.

So he had taken a last look at the keeper poking at him with the stick, gulped a deep breath, rolled clear of the sling, and dived. He had headed to sea.

He computed a course straight for the oncoming White. She sensed him coming, and he sensed that he was locked into her perceptions, and that there was room for nothing more in her brain, and that he had her complete and unwavering attention as he flashed toward her. Her imprint on his cortex, sketched by his hearing on a paralimbic lobe of his brain that even his human playmates lacked, grew clearer with every stroke of their tails.

By the time he visually glimpsed her bulk, a hundred feet away and closing fast, he knew that she was not going to flinch like a normal shark to present a target. She was simply too big to care, or too hungry. He had stopped his echo-locator, using eyes now that he was close enough.

In a flash she was on him, an enormous mouth studded with rows of teeth, a barnacled head and a black staring eye. Unthinkingly, he twisted, spun, and felt the lash of her tail, lacerating his dorsal with its sheen of deadly little skin-teeth. He headed seaward. Now he was crying in alarm, shrieking for other dolphins, men, anything to help him. He had no more thought of attack. He was afraid to slow for air, although he needed it. He was flashing at full speed. He had no idea where she was and was afraid to try to find out. Dead aft, he was almost deaf, and could not echo-locate, but he was afraid to turn to bring his sonar into play, for fear she would gain.

He knew one thing, from senses that had nothing to do with his ears or his clicking sonar, but only some deep network of psychic unity with his pursuer.

She was still locked onto *him*, and nothing else.

He had bored seaward for ten minutes, starved for air but afraid to climb. Finally, 5 miles from the beach, he broached, taking a sonor reading as he did. She was a full minute behind him. He lengthened his lead and began to curve toward shore, half afraid that his friends would leave without him, half afraid to draw the white death into their midst. But by the time he was fully headed in, she was six minutes astern and losing. He began to click his sonar, scanning the shoreline with his ears.

He skimmed past the wrecked fishing boat on the bottom. His own boat was gone. His God had left. Confused, he circled. He had an excellent sense of direction, and no fear that he could not overtake the vessel, but he let his sonar rove for a moment, disappointed that his friends had left without letting him play. With his echo-locator he caught something lying on the bottom, and zeroed in on it.

A hundred yards toward the beach from the wreck lay a battered, round toy caught in a rocky crevice. His great brain switched from the shark to the metal ball. This was what the game was about. He broached, glimpsed the distance, departing boat, breathed and dove for the plaything again.

It was the toy they had come to find. He nuzzled it, but could not move it. Now he was puzzled, with the boat gone, how to announce to his keeper that he had found the ball. He paused for a moment, drifting and entranced.

First he would catch up with the boat . . .

In his last moment he realized he had been caught from astern. He knew an instant very much like regret, as he twisted and tried to surface.

He wished they knew he had come back.

9

The Casino was growing, without any apparent effort, it seemed. A lonely carpenter banged nails into a portico. A half dozen men were gathered at a lunch wagon. No one else seemed in sight.

Brody clambered over a joist laid in the sand, scaled a pile of two-by-fours, and dropped into the hollow in which Tony Catsoulis, Amity selectman and owner of Amity Building Contractors Inc., had placed his construction shack, low and out of the wind from the sea.

Brody found Tony inside, phone jammed to his ear, hard-hat pushed back, and bell-shaped body perched on a chair that looked as if it had been unsuccessfully used in a lion-taming act.

Tony waved at him vaguely, as if offering him some place to sit down and wait. There was none, so he stood.

"Now, Vern," Tony yawned, "I *know* I said Friday, but the check's in your mail today, I mailed it Monday, you look in your mail today? Oh . . . I see." He yawned again. "Well, look tomorrow, ya wanna? You got my absolute word. On my mother's grave!" He hung up. "Greedy bastard. Electrical subcontractor. Someday, I'm going to plug 220 volts into him, see how he's wired. So, what can I do for law and order, chief?"

"Plenty." Brody took a breath. Tony Catsoulis

was his last chance. He had tracked down every selectman on the Town Council. He had dug up old Ned Thatcher at the Aberlard Arms, who could barely hear him, had apparently never heard of the Mafia in general or Moscotti in particular, and couldn't care less, if only business would pick up.

He had found Rafe Lopez, champion of the minescule black population of Amity, and proud token of democracy on the Council. Rafe didn't care whose money got into the Casino, as long as Peterson made good on his promise to hire blacks for waiters and himself as maitre d'.

Albert Morris had winced when Brody mentioned Moscotti, and pointed out what a well-placed firebomb would do to his hardware store, and Fred Potter merely said he didn't want to hear about it.

Brody's vague hope of getting the building permit suspended seemed stupider every hour. Tony was his last prayer.

"You know who's paying you?" Brody asked.

"*Nobody's* paying me," replied Catsoulis. "Peterson don't pay me, and I don't pay my subs—" he waved at the phone—"and everybody ends up paying the damn lawyers. Normal construction job. Next time around, same thing." He sighed. "You don't know how lucky you are, no headaches, city job . . ."

"You want me to keep it?"

That got his attention. He sat straight up. "Who's going to take it?" he growled.

"Ellen wants me to quit." That was certainly true, but he felt guilty to lay it on her. He honestly didn't know whether he was afraid for his family, or scared of Moscotti, period. Both, perhaps.

"You quit," Tony agreed quickly, "we'll put in Hendricks as police chief, and I'll hire you."

"As what? As night watchman?"

"Foreman, administrator, manager, you name it. As partner, when you get your general contractor's ticket."

He looked into Tony's eyes. They seemed perfectly sincere. "Thanks," he said, moved. "But I'm afraid not. No experience."

"You make $7,200 now. I'd start you at $15."

"Fifteen what?"

"Fifteen thousand. Eighteen? I don't give a damn."

Brody stared. His heart began to pump. He saw a Kenmore dishwasher, a TV they didn't have to squint at, and Mike at Yale . . . Well, NYU. He cleared his throat.

"Why?"

Tony shrugged: "You don't steal."

"Is that worth twice what I'm getting?"

"Everybody *knows* you don't. That's what's worth it."

Brody shook his head, to drive the vision of affluence away. Catsoulis seemed serious. But he might be too sanguine about the ability of a small town police chief to learn anything about construction. Or too optimistic about Amity's future . . ."

"Suppose the rug got yanked out from the Casino?" Brody asked. "Would you hire me then?"

"Don't worry about Peterson," Catsoulis snorted. "He 's solvent."

Brody asked if he was sure, wondering if he'd heard about Moscotti yet. Catsoulis moved across the shack like a small bulldozer with feet, to a coffeepot rattling on a stove. He poured two cups and laced them with bourbon against the chill from the sea. He handed one to Brody.

"Brought in the *Families*," Catsoulis beamed. "You hear about that?" He lifted his coffee cup. "To Peterson."

When Brody did not lift his, Tony drank anyway. "Hey, you asked if I knew who was paying me. Why?"

Brody drank his coffee. The whisky tasted stale. His mouth was dry. He had been talking all day, to Meadows, and then to Lopez and Morris and the rest. He was all talked out.

"I don't know, Tony," he said wearily. "Just passing the time of day."

Brody seated Lt. Swede Johansson across the table from him in a quiet little restaurant in Bay Shore. When he had seen the thickness of the file she had prepared on the Savage rifle, the ammunition, and the blasted gas tank, he had refused, blue-plate special or not, to simply take her to the department cafeteria.

The file sat on the table between them now, as they sipped martinis. He wondered what lunch would cost, and if he could get it back from the selectmen.

From the thickness of the file, it would be worth it. He ordered a club sandwich for her and a calorie-watcher hamburger for himself. It had been years since he had taken a woman, outside of Ellen, to a restaurant. "And two more martinis," he added.

She grinned. Her teeth flashed in the dim light. He wished it were brighter, she was so pretty.

"So, what have we got?" He lifted the file.

Her amber eyes twinkled in the darkness. "Drink up while we're still friends."

He chilled. "Is it that bad?"

Playing with her cocktail glass, she nodded at the file: "I did a complete ballistics." She had test fired three rounds from the Savage into the lab water-barrel, and another two into a replica of the gas tank, same gage steel, same manufacturer. He would see the difference, she told him, in entry diameter in the report. "Entry holes on the duplicate tank showed a diameter 30% smaller than the entry on the exhibit."

He rubbed his temple. "Suppose what I brought you is an *exit* hole. Wouldn't that be bigger?"

"It's not an exit, it's an entry," she said simply. "I'm sorry, pal, it just doesn't do it."

"Hollow-point?" he begged, thinking of the slugs she had shown him Monday, from the squad-car shooting, "or dumdums?"

She shook her head. "I tried that, too. I filed the noses on two of his slugs and fired them. No discernable difference. It's no soap."

Brody stabbed viciously at the olive in his new drink. *What had done it then?* "*Something* blew up the tank!"

She shrugged "I tested a .45," she went on. "I tested a 357 magnum. I even tested a g.d. elephant gun we confiscated from some crazy in East Hampton. That's quite a hole in that can, Brody."

"What *did* it?"

She asked him how much he knew about the water skiers.

"The guy was an engineer from Grumman, wife was a secretary there, pretty girl, I'd noticed them around town over the years, just a nice young couple, is all."

She wanted to know their reputation.

He shrugged. "Grumman says he was very competent, a quality-control type. The coast guard tells me he used to check in with Shinnecock Bay every time they'd take the boat out, just to make sure the radio worked."

He paused. A dim memory had been triggered. He tried to chase it down, wishing he had not had the martini. Something about flags . . . He snapped his fingers. "You know, I saw them the day before?

They were buying a ski flag at the water sports center."

"Why?"

"A safety device. You're *supposed* to fly it when you're towing, so nobody cuts too close astern. Nobody flies it much around Amity."

"But this guy did?"

"Apparently."

The waitress brought their lunch. Swede was deep in thought now, her coffee-colored brow furrowed, jabbing her club sandwich with a toothpick that held it together, not eating at all.

"You find any flares?" she asked suddenly.

"*Flares*? No."

"A man that careful, he might have had flares, OK?"

"Well," he said, "we didn't find any."

She sat back. She still had not begun her sandwich. "Brody, the spectograph analysis showed it first. Whatever hit that can was loaded with magnesium. The paint around the entry hole was scorched. Maybe from the explosion, maybe from muzzle blast, but anyway, scorched. And *loaded* with magnesium."

Brody regarded his half-eaten hamburger. He didn't feel like finishing it. "OK! Tracers? Tracers, maybe, from the Savage?"

"I checked the barrel. Every land, every groove, from muzzle to breech. I spectographed the follower. I ran a grease-analysis on the chamber lubricant. I even checked the magazine. There's no trace of magnesium in the *rifle* at all."

"Damn," Brody said dully.

"Brody, it came from a flare pistol." She placed a hand on his. "A standard navy Very pistol, probably surplus, Mark IV, mod 2, 1942."

He studied her face. She was dead certain.

"Why in the name of Christ," he demanded,

"would a man fire a flare into his own gas tank?"

She began to nibble at the sandwich and didn't answer.

"Why," he continued, "would he even have it *loaded*, around gasoline?"

"Well, maybe he wouldn't, ordinarily," she said. "But a flare pistol's a firearm. Firearms and careful people mix just fine. Except when?"

He'd been a cop long enough to know the answer. "Except in an emergency, when you need them. But what kind of an emergency? He didn't call Shinnecock."

She shrugged. "That's not ballistics. That's a field problem. You're the guy in the field."

"Yeah."

"You better start over, my friend."

He paid the bill, returned with her to the ballistics lab and picked up his useless evidence.

They'd forgotten, she reminded him, the pie a la mode.

"Next time," he said softly. "And speaking of forgetting . . ."

"Yes?" she smiled.

"I got another charge on this suspect. It'll stick. And I'll drop my manslaughter, of course. But I'll still look awfully stupid. Do you think you might . . ."

"You have the original," she grinned. "I'll try to lose our copy. We can't be tarnishing the image of the Amity chief of police."

He signed the rifle, ammunition, and gas tank out with the young sergeant at the desk. The sergeant asked him again if there was a vacancy at Amity.

"There just might be, if this hits the fan."

"What did she find out?"

"She tested my manslaughter charge out of existence."

Speeding north on the Southern State Parkway,

he decided finally that the water-skiers must have started a minor fire with a cigaret, panicked, loaded the flare pistol to signal for help, and discharged it into the tank as they were trying to get out of the boat.

And their bodies?

Blown to bits? Burned?

And what had happened to the two skin divers?

It was none of his business. His responsibility stopped at mean high tide on the sands of Amity Beach.

And as for the case against Jepps, thank God he still had the wounded seal.

Lt. Cmdr. Chip Chaffey, helicopter safety officer at NAS Quonset Point, bellied up to the officers' club bar, slung a foot over his favorite barstool, and ordered a Moscow Mule.

In the breast pocket of his worn green aviation uniform, which would probably get him kicked out of the club if the duty officer happened in, rested the report on the chopper crash which the yeoman in his office had just finished.

It was a nothing report. He knew as little about what had caused his old shipmate to die as when he had started. He did not even know whether the whistle that the tin-can sailors had heard off Amity was his friend's, or his friend's crewman.

Academic, now. Whichever of the two it was, he was long dead, swept to sea, and his body, probably, would turn up on some Hampton beach, bloated and scoured by the shifting sands.

He sipped at the vodka and ginger beer. He was a bachelor, divorced. Like his old shipmate, he was one of a vanishing, hard-drinking breed who would never get any further in the navy and had no desire to do so. His future stretched interminably. Countless hours aloft, listening for subs which were hardly ever there, hours here at the O Club bar, equally endless, striking-out with the lonely navy wives who grew younger every year.

Until, perhaps, a random engine failure or a fatigued engine bolt would strike him down. Or whatever had happened to his friend, and it would all end in a crazy, spinning ride to the sea.

The young UDT ensign wandered in, properly wearing civvies, and escorting a long-legged blonde who looked like Vassar or Bennington, and was probably his wife. They sat at a table, shuffling through bingo cards and readying themselves for the forthcoming nightly game.

The ensign's eyes met his and fled. He sure didn't want him at *that* table, whether from pique because he had lost his dolphin, or because he didn't want to share the attentions of the broad.

The hell with them. He scanned the bar. Two lone navy wives, noses already burrowing into their bingo cards, sat together. Their husbands were probably at sea on the *Grouper* or one of the tin-cans.

The hell with them, too. Navy wives seemed to get more faithful every year. His eyes fell again on the ensign. A phony, him and his lacquered blonde. And phonies, too, his UDT team, who had quit too early. Even their crummy dolphin was phony. He hoped it was still AWOL.

He decided tomorrow to buzz over to Amity. The police chief's wife had been cute, and he might see her again. He wondered if Brody ever left town. Anyway, he'd find the chief's kid or his diving instructor, and try to scratch up some enthusiasm for another search for the sonar ball.

He could imagine the ensign's chiseled, Flash Gordon face, if a bunch of kids on their first dive found the ball. You never knew . . .

The drone of bingo numbers began over the club's PA system, and he slugged down his drink.

Next to the useless report in his pocket was a letter from Disbursing. He had asked for a $2,000 reward for anyone finding the ball: they had, predictably, authorized him to promise $1,000. Well, that ought to stir interest in Amity among the younger set.

He left for his sack in the BOQ.

Tomorrow was another day.

10

Brody awoke at 7, to the blast of the Amity Neck ferry leaving her slip on the other side of Amity Sound.

Since it was running so early, he knew instantly that today was Saturday.

Summer and Saturday. For a long moment he lay still, certain that today would not be a good one, not at all.

First, the damn ballistics report. He would simply let the whole thing slide. Manslaughter charges against Jepps were dead, but there was no reason that Jepps or his lawyer had to know that the first homicide investigation in the history of Amity had laid an egg. The problem would simply drift away if no one rocked the boat, and he still had the federal and local charge.

He stirred, unwilling to get up. Today Mike joined the muscular, seal-skinned ranks he saw in the pages of *Skin Diver Magazine*. This afternoon, he would slither further away from childhood into a space that Brody was afraid to enter. He did not like the image, and stirred restlessly in bed.

The last of today's problems would be that of Sammy the seal. The wound was healed. He and Ellen had decided that this was the weekend to pry him loose, send him back to the ocean if he seemed capable, or to the Bronx Zoo or Woods Hole Institute or to the state game commission if he didn't want to swim.

Maybe the anticipation of tomorrow's regatta would soften the blow for Sean.

He glanced at Ellen. She was snuggled into a ball. A bronze strand of hair shivered in the breath from her nose. He brushed it aside, with his finger.

The telephone rang. *Damn!*

He swung his feet over the side of the bed. Today was shaping up as a rerun of last Saturday, in full living color, only worse He stumbled to the desk by the window and picked up the telephone. "Brody! Yeah?"

"Good morning," said Harry Meadows. He sounded edgy, even for a newspaper editor at seven in the morning. "Look, can you come up to my office?"

"Do you know," Brody asked sweetly, "what time this is?"

"7:08," Meadows said. "We're in trouble."

Brody wondered what possible trouble he could share with Meadows or the Amity *Leader*. "Who's 'we'?"

"Mostly, you."

"Me?" Brody demanded. "What's going down?"

"Brody," Meadows said tiredly, "just get down here, OK?"

Press relations were important to a police department, but he didn't have to put up with *that*. He told Harry so.

"You have my apologies," Meadows replied. "On the other hand, you are approaching a crisis in your career. You may need all the help you can get from the Fourth Estate." He suggested that with that in view, and their well-known friendship, could Brody get his ass down there by, say, maybe eight?

"Maybe." He hung up. He regarded Ellen. She was still asleep, and the curve of her hip under the blanket stirred him. He slipped back into bed, slid a hand under the cover, and let his fingers trail along her thigh. Her eyes bounced open. She smiled.

The alarm blasted by his bed. In the next room Mike's transistor awakened, blaring at the new day. Outside the open window he heard Sean, on the flats by Amity Sound, yelling at someone or something. He gave up, touseled Ellen's hair, and arose for good. "I'll get your breakfast," she murmured and plopped back to sleep.

He turned off the alarm and leaned out the window. Sean was hurling rocks at the water. "Hey, Spud, what do you think you're doing?"

Sean spun guiltily, as if he had been caught picking his nose.

"Nothing. Just . . . skipping rocks."

Brody, puzzled, dressed and went down to feed himself.

Brody waited for the coffee to perk and watched his older son prowling around the kitchen. First the boy had dragged cornflakes from the shelf, studied the label, and put it back. He had poured a glass of milk, drunk half of it, and the rest sat now on the kitchen sink. He had finally taken a coffee cup from the shelf and placed it next to Brody's on the counter, although Brody had never known him to drink coffee before.

"Today's the day," Brody remarked. His own hand trembled on the coffee pot, as he poured. "Right?"

"The check-out?" Mike yawned, as if he had forgotten. "Yeah . . . I guess so. Briefing at the Aqua Center, one o'clock, then saddle up and go."

Brody thought of something. "Has Andrews got flare guns for sale down there? For boaters, yachtsmen, you know?"

"He's got them," said Mike. "Hey, what time is it now?

He told him. Mike seemed disappointed that it was so early. He yawned again, impressively, watched his father sugar coffee for both of them, then yawned once more. "Any word on the navy's ball?" he asked suddenly.

"I don't know."

"Dad," Mike confessed, "that pilot came in to see if somebody was drowning. Larry Vaughan. Dad, I nearly *drowned* him!"

"Why?"

"He's a slimy *yuk*!"

"It runs in his family. What did he do?"

Mike clamped his jaws and shook his head. "What difference does it make? But we *were* in trouble, *he* was, anyway. It's like yelling for help, and the lifeguard drowns!"

"You told the commander everything that matters. Forget it."

"OK," murmured Mike. He took his father's wrist and twisted it, to look at the watch. "Have a good day."

The screen door slammed behind him.

It was too late to have a *good* day. Brody hoped he could just get through the one he'd have.

The editorial office of the Amity *Leader* had, years before, ceased rocking to the beat of the presses below. The machines lay idle. The paper was actually printed now in Port Washington, or Great Neck, or some other dismal place that Brody could never remember. But the stench of printer's ink from ancient linotypes still penetrated the upstairs editorial offices, which overlooked the inactivity of Main Street.

Harry Meadows' tiny cubicle had the worst smell of all, for he often had his salami-infested hero sandwiches sent up from Cy's Diner when he was hardpressed on a deadline. Their odor seemed to have penetrated the woodwork and the jumbled piles of telephone books, layouts, and back-issues stacked on desk, floor, and file cabinets. He sat in a smog of cigar smoke.

As Brody entered, he was staring out the window, an elephantine mound of moody flesh. He swiveled his over-sized chair, which shrieked in agony.

"What's the flap?" asked Brody. "I'm supposed to open shop at 9—"

"You may not *have* a shop much longer," Meadows growled, "unless you can think of some way to get me and the *Leader* off the hook."

Brody was tired of people threatening to get him fired, and told him so: "To start with, outside of Hendricks, you'll never find anybody else stupid enough to take this job at $600 a month and smart enough to write a traffic ticket."

"Don't count on *that*," Meadows said. "When gambling comes in here, every vice squad dick in Manhattan will be crying for a job just to get in on the ice."

If Moscotti had truly bought Casino control, he was probably right.

"OK, Harry," he muttered. "What have you got?"

Meadows flicked a sheaf of papers across his desk. Brody recognized it instantly as a Xerox of the ballastics report.

"When'd you get this?" he demanded. "*How'd* you get it? It's confidential! Why'd you *want* it?"

"It's the *last* thing I wanted. Did you ever meet Hollerin' Halloran? Counselor-at-law?"

Brody hadn't.

"You will. Probably today. About two feet high, a voice like the Amity ferry, and a mouth like an asshole with teeth."

Brody winced: "Jepps' lawyer?"

"You better believe it. Well, he brought me this."

Brody picked up the report. "How'd he get it?"

"Suffolk county police sent it to him. Yesterday."

"I don't believe it," murmured Brody, stiffly. He felt as if someone had offered him the best seat in the house and pulled it out from under him. "Let me use your phone."

He called Bay Shore and found that it was Swede Johansson's day off. No, they didn't give out home numbers, how did they know he was *really* a police officer, on the phone? He could leave his number and they'd try to get the message to her, if she hadn't taken off for the weekend.

"Skip it," Brody said bitterly. It didn't matter anyway. He'd been sand-bagged, but good. He hung up the phone. "OK. So they have the report. If he didn't shoot at anybody, he already knew he was clear. What difference does it make?"

"And he *didn't* shoot at anybody; did he?"

"Just the seal."

Meadows sat back. "Thanks . . . You're the stubbornest S.O.B. I—"

"OK. What's the hassle?"

"Libel."

Far away, Brody heard a blast as the Amity Neck ferry left her slip near Town Dock, bound across Amity Sound. Faintly, through the window, he could hear the beat of the nickelodeon in Cy's Diner. A car horn honked.

"Bull."

Meadows sat back. "I don't retain a lawyer. But from my point of view, and the paper's, which as you know is all I got, libel means bankruptcy."

"It's not libel, Harry. And you know it! You were quoting me. All you said was I was investigating it. And I was! Where's the libel?"

Meadows shook his head sadly: "I'm not saying I'd *lose*! I'm saying I can't afford to fight!"

Brody moved to the window, looked out at the street. Albert Morris was sweeping the walk in front of Amity Hardware, not trusting it yet to his son, who worked as his clerk and was almost as old as Brody. Yak-Yak Hyman was leaving the diner, heading for Town Dock. To Brody's surprise, he saw Nate Starbuck, who should have been opening the pharmacy, parking his delivery truck in front of Town Hall. A license fee to complain about? City taxes? No, this was Saturday. Another parking complaint, maybe, this one to be delivered in person.

Brody looked at his watch. It was time to finish here, visit the Aqua Center, and then take his place behind his desk in Town Hall to await the blows of a summer Saturday.

He turned back to Meadows and asked him what he wanted him to do. Meadows rolled a story from his typewriter. He slid it across to Brody. "*POLICE SERGEANT CLEARED: Amity Police Chief Martin Brody revealed today that his investigation into manslaughter charges against Flushing Police Sgt. Charles Jepps, 54, of Smith's Sand Castle, revealed no evidence of a connection between the inadvertant discharge of weapons by Sgt. Jepps on the beach and the disappearance of two scuba divers and a boating couple last weekend.*

"*Ballistics tests on debris recovered from the skiboat proved conclusively that the explosion off Amity Beach last Saturday was the result of a flare gun fired into a gas tank, apparently by one of the occupants.*

"'*Evidence exonerates Sgt. Jepps,' Brody said. 'All charges have been dropped.'*"

"Did I say this?" Brody asked.

"You will, won't you?" Meadows handed him a pencil. "Just initial it, OK?"

Brody tapped the pencil for a moment on the desk. "'Inadvertant' discharge?" he complained. "No!" He crossed out "inadvertant," drew a line through the entire last paragraph, and wrote in:

"Federal wildlife and firearm misdemeanor charges still remain."

He signed his name and tossed the story back to Meadows.

"I was afraid of that," Meadows said miserably. "You don't want to change it back?"

"*You're* off the hook. Why worry?"

Meadows shrugged. "Because I like you. I hate to see you go down the drain for a stupid seal, and I don't understand it all all."

"I got a couple of kids," said Brody, "who wouldn't understand it any other way."

He left and headed for the Aqua Center.

Mayor Larry Vaughan looked up into the gaunt New England face. He groaned inwardly. Starbuck had called three times in the last three days, and the pharmacist knew that he hated to use the town office for private business. It made him nervous. It was unethical. He might get caught. Which was probably why Starbuck had cornered him here.

"Damn it, Nathanial," Vaughan exploded, "I've asked you not to bug me. Not here. Not about real estate. This is a *township* office."

"I pay township taxes," shrugged Starbuck. "Any offers on the pharmacy?"

It was time to explain to Starbuck something of the facts of life, reality-wise and realty-wise. Vaughan began to tick them off on his fingers. First, Vaughan had phoned a Manhattan realty company specializing in resort properties, and another which concentrated on locating pharmaceutical retail stores and chains.

He hadn't, really, but there was no way that the druggist could check.

"They both wanted to know our chamber of commerce figures on last summer's trade. And you know how last summer went."

Starbuck merely stared with the cold blue eyes. He made Vaughan uncomfortable. He toyed with the idea of making his own offer now, just to get the old bastard out of his office. But no, it would be best to let him sweat it a little longer, let Lena's illness back him further into a corner . . .

"I know it's urgent," he finished. "And I have feelers out. How is she, Nate?"

Nate waved his hand. "Worse. Don't worry about that. Just sell it. 'Mayor' . . ."

There were quotes around the title, as he said it, and a threat behind the bland face. It was time to drag out into the open whatever Starbuck thought he had. Vaughan was suddenly sure that he knew. The old bastard must have found out, somehow, about Moscotti. Probably, next to the bank, he'd heard Peterson had been turned down, maybe seen him with Moscotti. Approaching things backward, as always, Starbuck must have perceived the gangster's involvement in the Casino as a threat to business, instead of the opposite.

And he must be thinking of it as a secret, which it was not. And must have understood it as something that would embarrass Vaughan, lose him the next election, perhaps.

It was laughable. Amity would elect him mayor as long as the summer trade held up. With the Casino safely operating, he'd win until hell froze over.

He sat back. "When's Lena going in? *If* she is?" he asked slyly.

"Never mind. Sell it."

"When's she scheduled for Memorial?"

"She ain't. Git rid of the drugstore for me, or you'll wish you had."

So he was right. Starbuck thought he had something on him. Vaughan relaxed, hiding a grin.

"And why's that, Nathanial?" he asked easily.

Starbuck smiled. He moved to the leather couch Vaughan used for afternoon naps and settled himself comfortably. He made a great ceremony of filling his pipe, sucking on it, and immersing the room in a smog of Sir Walter Raleigh. "I *could* be talkin' about listin' with Amity Realty."

"You could," agreed Vaughan. "But if *I* can't sell it, *they* sure can't. You know that, so I guess you're not talking about that, right?"

Starbuck nodded agreeably. "You're maybe right. Maybe I'm talkin' about droppin' the other shoe, as they say."

"What other shoe is that?"

"Maybe there's people in this town don't know everything you and Brody, and maybe some others, know about this 'rebirth' we been waitin' for. Maybe they'd *like* to know. Maybe guys like you and Brody, on the inside, would like me out of town before it hits the fan, like they say. You sell my store, or buy it yourself, and I'll *be* out of town. How's that strike you?"

The notion of Starbuck leaving town was so attractive that, properly organized, a drive to buy him out by popular subscription might be successful. But Vaughan kept his eye on the ball.

A little brainwashing was obviously necessary. At that he considered himself a master.

"Nathanial," he said heavily, "you're right. Unfortunately. About what's likely to happen."

Starbuck raised his eyebrows, puffed noncommittally, and waited.

"I don't know how you found out about Moscotti," Vaughan continued, "but—"

"I didn't say nothing about *Moscotti*," said Starbuck, apparently puzzled. Then his face turned impassive.

Vaughan studied him, a little puzzled himself. Well, you couldn't figure out Starbuck.

"He's got us *all* scared," Vaughan conceded. "He may save the Casino. But," he lied, "it's not going to help legitimate business one damn bit. You're the first to see it. I got to hand it to you, you spotted it before anybody. The trouble is, word's going to get around—"

"About Moscotti," Starbuck interjected thoughtfully. "You mean about Moscotti? Getting into the Casino?"

Vaughan nodded. "When *everybody* knows, there *might* be a selling panic. You're right."

Starbuck made no comment. He seemed almost to have lost interest. A strange man . . .

Vaughan went on: "You know Lena used to take care of me when I was a kid?"

Starbuck shrugged: "I guess."

"She was very kind. Lonely boy, big house, folks away half the summer . . . *You* know."

Starbuck shifted uncomfortably. "What you tryin' to say, Larry?"

"Well, I want to help. Even if Lena's OK, I know you want to sell. I realize the risk. *I'm* willing to bet on Amity. Nobody from the *outside* is likely to make that bet, after the shark thing, and now Moscotti . . ."

"The shark thing," nodded Starbuck. "Right. Let's not forget the shark thing, Larry."

Well, if Starbuck thought the taint of the shark still lingered, fine. Vaughan sat back, contorting his face in thought. He got up and paced for a moment. He sat down again and drummed his pencil. He made notations on a sheet of paper, pretending to add numbers.

Starbuck sighed heavily: "Cut the bull. What's your bid?"

Avaricious old son of a bitch. Vaughan looked up, as if hurt. "Twenty-five," he said. "Thirty . . . I can maybe go 30 . . ."

"The price is 50," said Starbuck tartly. "And I wonder if Moscotti knows *everything*? He still summer here?"

"What do you mean, 'everything'?"

"He still vacation up here?"

"Look, Nate, you aren't going to offer it to *him*?"

"I'm going to sell. If you can't handle it, I'll handle it myself."

"Don't quote me," Vaughan said cautiously, "but having him in the Casino is one thing. Giving him the town *drug* store, for Christ's sake, that's another. I mean, narcotics and all? All he has to do is find a crooked pharmacist . . ."

"Maybe I won't *have* to sell it to him," Starbuck said mysteriously. "Might be I can sell him something else, instead. He's in the Ruskin place?"

Again, there was a threat in his voice. Vaughan said: "Yeah. What are you trying to say?"

Starbuck chuckled dryly, but only shook his head and left. Vaughan watched him go. The hell with him, and his paranoia. When Moscotti threw him out, he would make another offer, lower.

The buzzer on his desk hummed. "Mr. John Halloran, attorney-at-law," Daisy Wicker announced. "Representing Sgt. Jepps."

For a wild instant he thought of escape through his ground-floor window. He groaned and flipped the switch. "Send him in, Daisy. And get Brody."

Trapped in his lair, he awaited the onslaught of the legendary Halloran, prince of judicial darkness.

There had been a time, when Brody tried to close the beaches at the start of The Trouble, when he could have got his chief fired.

He wished he had.

11

Brody parked Car #1 outside the Aqua Center. On the windows had been added, in new gold script: "Your Headquarters for Scuba, Surf, and Sail." No one was visible inside. He hoped that business would pick up as the summer progressed.

He walked in. He heard voices in the rear. They came from an open door marked: *"Air. No Tanks Filled Past Purge-Date."* He went in.

Tom Andrews towered over a 55-gallon topless drum filled with water, set next to a whirring air-compressor. Immersed in the water was a Scuba tank, attached to the compressor by a tube. Ringed around Andrews, already suited in their diving gear, were Mike, Andy Nicholas, Larry Vaughan, and a half dozen other potential mermen. They looked up at Brody in alarm, afraid, no doubt, that he was going to throw another wrench into their dive.

Brody asked Andrews whether he had sold any flare guns since he opened up shop. Yes, he had. To whom? He'd have to check his records. He pulled out a Diner's Club draft. "Last Saturday, to R. L. Heller, 1433 Myrtle, Lynbrook—"

"That's it," said Brody.

Brody told him that the shattered gas tank he'd found in the surf had been torn by a flare, and Andrews winced. "So it wasn't that cop? From Flushing?"

Brody shook his head. "He still shot a seal."

Andrews nodded thoughtfully. "But I hear things, political things . . ."

"What do *you* think I ought to do?" asked Brody, curiously.

Andrews looked at his store. Outside of the kids, there were still no customers. He glanced at the skimpy file of invoices in his hand. "Second week into the summer," he murmured. "I wouldn't mind a few slot machines in here myself."

"Drop it?" murmured Brody. His mouth was dry.

"Some of my best friends are seals," grinned Andrews. "Hang the S.O.B.!"

The door jingled. Ellen and the Quonset Point safety officer walked in. Surprised, Brody introduced them to Andrews.

"He turned up in Hoople's taxi," Ellen volunteered, "so I brought him down."

She said it a little too quickly. Brody felt a fast stab of jealousy. He wondered if she would have been as eager to chauffer the commander if he were ten years older, with a potbelly. He stifled the feeling quickly. During The Trouble, there had been a thing, maybe, with the young shark expert, but Brody had been too distracted by the shark to go into it.

The boys were poking around the tank racks and windowshopping the knives and depth-gauges in the display cases.

"Mr. Andrews," announced Chaffey, "there's a $1,000 reward for finding that navy ball."

"Wow!" yelled Mike. "We'll look. There're 13 of us, and—"

Andrews glared at him. "You look," he promised, "you try *anything* but exactly what I tell you, today, and it's your last dive. I'll tear up that pretty exam you took and you won't get your card and you'll be high and dry. The *navy* can't find it, and you guys want to try?"

Mike blushed. Brody felt the need to protect him. "OK, Tom. He understands. It isn't the money. He was the last guy to see the chopper."

"It's the money, with *me*," Andrews told the commander. "I'll take a look next week."

Chaffey apologized for bringing the matter up in front of the class, and Ellen volunteered to drive him back to his chopper, which this time he had landed well out of town, on the abandoned navy airstrip between Amity and Montauk Point.

"I'll take him," Brody said, too quickly.

Rumbling through the center of Amity with the commander, Brody justified himself. He hadn't been jealous, the only reason he was driving him back was to stay out of his office. He had a gut-feeling that between Jepps, Moscotti, and the g.d. *Leader*, the longer he stayed away the better.

Since striking the porpoise the day before, the White had circled aimlessly in a triangle 20 miles on a side, formed by Block Island, Fisher's Island, and Montauk Point.

She was patrolling the northeastern entrance to Long Island Sound, for she had scoured clean the seas off Amity. She was within a day or two of bearing her young. Her hunger, which would cease instantly when she birthed, to protect her offspring from her appetite, was flaring for one last time. She had consumed, during the previous 24 hours, the dolphin, 20 pounds of snapper, a 100-pound nurse shark, a basking blue, and three diving egrets. She had hit a lure off Quonochontung and yanked it free of its shark-hook so quickly that the fisherman above assumed that he had hit a snag and thought nothing more of the incident. The hook was lodged in her upper jaw, irritating it.

As she glided off Montauk Point for another sweep near Amity, a remora fastened itself by its suction-cup mouth to her lower jaw, hanging like a living whisker and nearly driving her into a frenzy.

Unsuccessfully, she had tried to scrape it off on an underwater rock near the Montauk Point light. She had failed. Now it hung listlessly, still alive and irritating her, but lost in her tunnel-vision need for food.

She rounded Montauk and headed southeast along Napeague Beach, sniffing the offshore currents, reading the flowing water with her lateral lines for vibrations, scanning the electromagnetic spectrum as well.

By the time she was off Amity, she had not eaten for two hours.

In her wombs her young squirmed to be free of each other, and of her.

The remora sucked relentlessly.

Her hunger was white-hot, searing.

She was triggered and ready to explode on anything that moved.

Hollerin' Halloran was, at first, soft-spoken. He seemed simply a gnome with a bald head, thick bifocals, and a crimped, prissy mouth. Brody wondered, for the first three minutes in Mayor Larry Vaughan's office, where Halloran had picked up his nickname.

He did not have to wonder long. "So, chief," Halloran smiled, "have I described the situation? That you didn't *see* the shots fired? You only heard them over the dunes?"

Brody pointed out that he'd arrived on the scene within seconds, had spotted the accused kneeling and ready to fire again, with his little boy holding his ears and his dog cowering behind him.

"It's all in my report," said Brody. He had taken the witness stand in trials perhaps half-a-dozen times in the last ten years: hit-run, wife-beating, marijuana busts, a couple of contested drunken-driving citations. He had an instinctive distrust of lawyers, prosecutors or defense. He cautioned himself to stay cool.

"But there are *two* reports," murmured Halloran, more softly. "One from Suffolk County, a ballistic report. Ordered by you. Now, did you *see* my client fire at a skin diver?"

"Of course not."

A little louder: "A ski-boat?"

"Nope."

"Anybody *else*?" A bark, with overtones of hysteria.

"Look, Mr. Halloran. This isn't a courtroom! When I'm a sworn witness, you can pull this stuff, if the judge lets you. Not now!"

Halloran gave no sign that he even heard him: "If you didn't see him shoot at anybody, if *nobody* saw him shooting at anybody," he yelled, "then why did you call the Amity *Leader* with this?"

From his briefcase he yanked the previous week's *Leader*, smoothed it excitedly, and poked it into Brody's face.

"I told them I was investigating," said Brody, fighting for his cool. "And that's what they printed."

"That's what you *asked* them to print." The little man was bellowing now. Larry Vaughan's face grew red. Brody winced. Everybody in town, and people passing on the street, must be hearing every word through the open windows. "What you actually said —and my client heard you—was 'I got a pretty good suspicion that the divers and the ski-boat got blasted by the same crazy bastard!' Do you deny that?"

Brody was silent. "Good," said Halloran, so softly that they could hardly hear him. He grinned, like a squeezed lemon. "That's slander. When he printed it, it became libel. The question is, why did you volunteer that? There has to be a reason."

"Your client was shooting up our beach. I like to let people know the police department doesn't approve."

"Look, Brody," cautioned Vaughan, "I don't think you ought to get in any deeper—"

"He *is* in deeper," yelled Halloran. "Your whole town's in deeper. My client was falsely arrested, imprisoned; your chief of police tried to set him up with phony ballistic evidence, and the "confidential' report he got back completely exonerates Jepps." The voice swept to full volume, high-pitched, like a giant fingernail scraping a blackboard: "But why did Brody slander him? You know why?"

Vaughan stared at Halloran dumbly, as if hypnotized. He shook his head.

Halloran leveled a skinny forefinger at Brody. His voice fell again, dramatically. "Gambling's coming in. Or was, until your boy here fouled it up. It'll be a gold mine for an ambitious chief of police. Jepps has summered here for years. He retires from the Flushing P. D. next year. You couldn't *find* a better chief. Brody knows it. Your two-bit local boy is afraid for his job. *That's* why!"

Brody found himself gaping at the little lawyer, like a yokel at the county fair shell game. "Say again?" he asked weakly.

Behind the thick glasses Halloran's eyes shone, triumphantly. Despite himself Brody took a step toward him.

"Brody!" warned Vaughan. "Watch it!"

He relaxed. "Don't worry, Larry." He studied Halloran. "Larry, is this guy crazy?"

Vaughan looked uncomfortable. He addressed Halloran. "Listen, Mr. Halloran, if Chief Brody can be persuaded to drop the federal charges—"

"It's too late," said Halloran. "The damage was

done with the newspaper article. My client's a very angry man. I doubt if I could turn him around."

"Let's try," begged Vaughan. "Right, Brody?"

Brody looked into Vaughan's face. For a moment, the mayor's eyes held his own. Then they dropped.

"No," Brody said quietly. He turned on his heel and left.

Andy Nicholas, half in and half out of his wetsuit pants, lurched against a tank rack in the stern of the *Aqua Queen*, raising a welt on his butt.

He looked like a sausage in his wetsuit and knew it. When the class suited up, he was always the last to succeed in cramming his porcine flesh into the tight neoprene pants. The fat on his arms rebelled at the tight grip of the wetsuit upper.

Now he had one leg encased, and the other foot jammed halfway down a vise-tight rubber leg. He looked around helplessly. Larry Vaughan was busy brown-nosing Tom Andrews as the giant lowered the anchor on the forepeak: probably asking to make the first dive in the class, or more likely asking to dive with someone other than him.

That was OK, the crummy bastard. Larry always put you down anyway. He glanced at Mike Brody, who was ready as usual, tank already strapped to his shoulders, sitting quietly on the gunwale, gazing at the deep green waters.

"Hey, Mike?" Mike flopped over to him in his fins. Thank God, he didn't seem to be sore anymore at the stupid, childish spying on the beach. He grabbed Andy's pants cuff, rolled it back, and by sheer sinewy strength pulled the foot through and the pant-leg smooth.

Mike was worth three Larry Vaughans. He had sure scared Larry that day, it was a wonder he hadn't drowned him, and nobody was going to call him 'Spitzer' again, and if he ever got into another fight, Andy would back him to the limit. "You want to pair up today?" Andy begged.

"If you'll keep your eyes open for that thing, OK?" Mike murmured. "The chopper-ball, you know?"

Andy had grave doubts whether he'd be able to keep his eyes on anything but the closest comforting human form. He intended to let Mike do all the thinking, just hoped he could keep up with him.

Andrews returned to the cockpit. "OK, pair up. And one last time: *What do we do going down*?

"Breathe," everyone chorused. *"In and out!"*

"And what do we do coming *up*?"

"Breathe *out, out, out*!"

"Again, louder?"

"Breathe out, out, out!"

"And how fast do we rise?"

"As slow as our slowest bubble!"

Andrews stuck up a thumb, looked around, and, God, thought Andy, he was picking them first, he was going to pick Mike and him first. . . .

"Brody and Nicholas, in the drink!"

They switched on each other's air valves, wheezed into their regulators to test them. At least, reflected Andy, there was no dust down there to start the asthma. They spit into their masks to clear them.

Mike suddenly twisted and dropped into the water. Heart pounding, mouth dry, Andy shut his eyes and followed.

He plunged and sank. God, with his tank, weight-belt, diving knife and fins, he must weigh about two tons. He felt a stroke of panic, almost jettisoned his belt, then bobbed to the surface anyway.

The world before his mask was a smeary jungle of bubbling green. He heard his strangled breath in his regulator. Suppose he had an attack down there? He couldn't see. What was wrong? He remembered suddenly. He let water into his mask, deliberately swirled it around by shaking his head, expelled it through his nose-valve.

Life turned brilliant. Mike Brody, already spiraling into the emerald void, jumped into clear focus in a storm of dancing bubbles. Mike paused, looked up, and beckoned.

Andy followed.

The seal had spent most of the last five days bobbing helplessly in the placid waters of Amity Sound, off the mud flats, for she sensed her pup's presence nearby. When the wind turned southeast, she could actually smell him, along with the man-smell, if she poked her nose high enough and craned her neck.

She had eaten very little. The catch was scarce in the Sound at all times; she knew this and had made a few excursions to sea, but never far, and never successfully. Had the pup been with her, or had she reconciled herself to her loss, she would have been far to the north by now, away from the white death which she sensed always when she broke from the neck of the bay and into open ocean.

Devoted as she was, there came finally a time when her hunger simply impelled her to head to sea and hunt. So, this morning, she had barked farewell and broken away. She skirted the shoreline of Amity Sound, shot for Amity light at the end of the long granite breakwater. She saw no cod, no haddock. This was strange, and could mean that the White was closer than she had felt.

She doubled and headed back to Cape North, where nervousness impelled her to beach herself on the rock-strewn base of Cape North light.

Here she rested for a while. But she still had not eaten, and finally hunger drove her again into the water. This time, she headed arrow-swift for the entrance to Amity Harbor, where she had once feasted with her pup on mackerel.

But today the harbor entrance, busy with the sounds of man, was bare of quarry. She made a quick, harried sweep within, all the way to the pilings of a pier she knew well. Then she left the harbor for another tour outside.

She passed the mournful Amity bellbuoy, clanging bleakly, and turned southeast along the beach. She sped to the place she had first lost her pup, but now she was intent upon only one thing. Food.

She was in the middle of a 15-minute dive along the bottom when she surprised a school of mackerel darting seaward. She sped the short, rowing-stroke of her flippers, soaring into the dark shadow of the school like a hawk attacking a flock of pigeons.

She took the largest fish she could see through the murky water, sensed a lightning communal decision of the school to turn north. She cut across its path, and took two more. Appetite sated, she began to ascend.

All at once she sensed great danger. She had got too far from land. She turned shoreward. Turning, she craned her neck to see if the white death was close.

She saw nothing, but all of her instincts drove her toward shore. She shot for the surface, trailing bubbles, gulped a huge breath of air, arched like a broaching torpedo, and dove again. She was faster underwater than on the surface.

This time, when she craned back, it was there, a dim gray shape homing on her, matching her speed.

Knowing in her core that it was no use, that it was all too late, she tore onward. Somewhere ahead, she began to hear the strange rasping man-sound of divers.

Having no fear of them, she shot toward the sound.

Perhaps she sought mammalian comfort, or to draw her pursuer toward another source of food.

Andy Nicholas was ecstatic. Trailing Mike Brody's left hip, matching him kick for kick as their great flat flippers sped them along the bottom, he knew suddenly that he had found his world.

He was no longer apprehensive. No asthma here, no dust, pure air from the tank on his back. His breath was steady and easy. A fat boy could swim as well as a skinny one, down here, more comfortably, perhaps, warmer under the layers. Tom Andrews was layered, too. His own seemed a different kind of fat, but perhaps when Andy got older it would firm.

He took his eyes off Mike and began to look around. The Long Island Shoals were not the sort of thing you saw in *Skin Diver*. No reefs or fish or waving coral. Mostly mud, flat as a flounder, with only a few dead shells to break the monotony.

A brief flash at the edge of his vision sent a thrill through him. It was a stingray. He moved closer to Mike's speeding form. If Andy grew to Andrews' size, his courage would probably grow proportionately.

But now he was losing ground on Mike. He turned on every bit of speed he had, and found that he was hardly keeping up. Damn it, they were supposed to stay together.

Slow down, slow down, he protested silently. He should never have let him gain in the first place. It was happening again: Tail-End Andy, puffing last always, on scout hikes, in gym classes, on bike rides. *Damn, damn, damn . . .*

Suddenly, off to the left, he spotted an oblong, man-made object on the bottom. He knew immediately that he had found the chopper-ball, though he could not really credit it, not a thousand dollars worth, not found by him when so many others had failed. He had an impulse to yell after Mike, underwater, even managed a squeal into his mouthpiece to try to attract his attention.

But Mike, intent on things ahead, swooped onward. Buddy-system forgotten, Andy swam to the thing. It was the chopper-ball, all right, black, mashed, with wires and a strand of broken cable protruding from it. It could be nothing else.

He simply could not believe it. A thousand dollars, and a hero's place in Amity legend! Brody had missed it, heck, the *navy* hadn't found it.

Now he was faced with problems. How to find it again, once he'd surfaced? He'd have to keep his place over the ball, somehow, get Andrews' attention in the boat. But then, having deserted his partner, he'd probably never get his diving card.

He approached the ball for a better look. He was poking at it cautiously when he sensed a shape approaching. For a moment he thought it was Mike returning. He had a flash of jealousy: the ball was his discovery, and now Mike would get half the credit, and half the reward. He didn't care. They'd end up friends and partners for life. The shape took form. It was not Mike, no diver at all. Astonished, he saw that it was a diving seal, hurtling toward him. He cowered. Did seals attack humans? No, from what he had read in *Skin Diver*, they might try to steal speared fish, but they were harmless to man.

It was almost on him. He waved it ineffectually away. It passed within 5 feet. He glimpsed a soft brown eye flicking toward him, had the strange impression that the seal itself was frightened. Of him, or something else?

He peered into the murk. What he saw sent an electric shock of terror through his nervous system, overwhelming his training, obliterating the hours he had spent wearing a tank, purging him of all but the simple instinct to leave this hostile jungle.

A mammoth shark was tearing toward him out of the murk. He had a flash of an ebony eye, profoundly unthinking, and great tail lashing dimly.

He squeezed his own eyes shut, gulped in a great breath of air, held it, and shot for the dim surface light far above. His weight belt was slowing his flight. He fumbled for the quick-release, found it, sent the belt slithering away off his hips. He yanked the lanyard on his air-vest and felt it fill, tugging him faster to the surface. His lungs grew larger, as if asthma had cut off his larynx, there was *something* he was supposed to be doing . . . Breathe *out*, that was it, but would there be another breath, would he somehow run out of air?

Before he broke the surface he knew certainly that the shark had been after the seal, had not even seen him, and he knew that whatever he had done to his body—embolism, bends, or paralysis—had been done for nothing, nothing at all.

Surfacing, he exhaled. But by that time, it was too late. He tasted blood. The world went dim, and then black.

His inflated life-vest rolled him over, floating him on his back. He must look like a dead baby whale.

His head began to grow and grow and the pain began, and soon he did not care.

Mike Brody turned. He could not believe his eyes. Andy had been within touching distance, practically fastened to his legs, not two minutes before.

Now he had disappeared.

His first thought was that he must find him before he surfaced, or they would both lose their cards. Andrews had told them that two partners must be fastened together by an invisible rubber band. In good visibility, the band could stretch to 10 or 15 feet; in murk the wing-man must not wander more than 5 or so. In really bad conditions, they should be within touching range.

He tried to retrace his path. If Andrews saw them surface separately, they were dead. But he was completely disoriented. He had no wrist compass. There was no way to tell, in the featureless waste, which was north, south, landward, or seaward.

For a while he swam mindlessly below, reluctant to expose their stupidity. It wasn't his fault: Lardbutt, as usual, simply hadn't kept up.

He searched for perhaps three minutes, then, truly concerned, he rose slowly to the surface, no faster than his slowest bubble, breathing out, out, out. The water around him blended from brown to jade to aqua. Golden spears of sunlight lanced down at him, and suddenly he broke into daylight.

He craned around. He spotted the *Aqua Queen* not 50 yards away. He had thought they had swum a mile: maybe they'd circled.

All at once he saw his partner, ten yards off. "Andy, you idiot!" he called, not too loudly. "Where the hell—"

He stared. Andy's nose was streaming blood. His eyes were closed. From his mouth a trickle of saliva was turning red. Mike swam to him and grasped him. Blood from his left ear was oozing around the jawline of his wetsuit hood.

He arched himself from the water like a broaching marlin, shrieking for Andrews. He saw the giant run forward, slash his anchor line, and hurtle aft to start the engine. There was a thunderous roar as it caught.

Within a minute Tom Andrews was reaching down from the diving-step. He plucked Andy from the sea like an air-filled rubber doll, laid him in the cockpit as Mike scrambled aboard. In a moment they were roaring home with Andrews on the radio demanding a coast guard chopper to fly the victim to the decompression chamber at the New London sub base.

Mike crouched in the stern. Whatever had happened, when Andy had needed him, he had not been there.

Andy would probably die.

He wished he had never heard of the diving course. Everything he touched lately seemed to come apart in his hands.

Brody sat frozen with fear at his desk. Shinnecock Bay coast guard did not know the name of the diving victim.

He hung up, rushed from the office, and rocketed down Main to Water, siren yowling. He skidded onto Town Dock, scattering fishermen.

Aqua Queen was tying up. Everyone in wetsuits looked the same. Andrews rose from a knot of divers in the stern, carrying a body.

But . . . a fat body. Brody almost collapsed with relief. A fat, sausage body, not Mike's. Andy Nicholas.

He cleared his throat. "Get him in my car," he told Andrews. "Chopper will land in Town Square."

"Convulsion," grunted Andrews, as they swept down Main, siren wailing. The giant's agonized eyes met Brody's in the rear-view mirror. "Air bubble must have hit his brain. *Move* this thing, Brody."

Brody, making 55 through the Saturday traffic, pushed it up a notch. They reached Town Square. The chopper was spiraling down over the homes on Amity Knoll. As Brody helped Andrews remove the rotund body, Andy's eyes flicked open and met his. Brody reached out and brushed back a strand of hair.

"OK, Andy, OK, son . . ."

The boy seemed to try to talk. His mouth opened, his tongue worked, but he failed. Brody bent close. "Yes, Andy? What happened, Spud?"

Andy's eyes filled with tears. He tried again. Brody heard only a faint sibilence, then an awkward croak, deep in his throat. "S . . . awk . . ."

All at once the body went stiff, writhed, and convulsed. It was all Brody could do to keep hold of the head and shoulders. When the spasm passed, Andy grew limp.

They loaded him into the chopper. Andrews climbed in beside him.

In three minutes the whirring blades had disappeared over the top of the Knolls.

Brody drove back to Town Dock. Mike was handing up tanks to the wharf. When he saw his father, he scrambled ashore.

"What happened, Mike?" asked Brody.

Mike made a move, as if to come into his arms, then remembered the watching kids. "I was with him," he muttered. *"Dad, I was his buddy!"*

"What happened?"

"I *lost* him. How do I know what happened?"

"I have to tell his folks."

"Tell them their son couldn't keep up with the local Spitzer. Way it goes, tell 'em."

"Lay off yourself, Mike, OK?"

"And put the same damn thing in your g.d report!"

"Mike!"

His son, fighting tears, turned away. Then he stooped, heaved a tank to his shoulder, and started down the dock.

12

Nate Starbuck parked his delivery van behind Moscotti's Ferrari on the sweeping drive of the mansion. He still thought of the gray, crumbling place as Doc Ruskin's. Years ago, when the old doctor had had his offices here, Starbuck had delivered here often, up the dirt road.

But now the roads of Amity Knolls were paved, and would soon be paved with gold as well. OK, that was what he was here for, to get some of it. But looking at the immense building, which Doc had probably built for $10,000 and which must be worth 10 times as much now, he felt apprehension.

There were supposed to be hoods and bodyguards and Doberman pinschers all over a mobster's home, from what he had seen on TV. When none of these appeared, his reaction was one of fear. Moscotti must have dozens of what was it—"contracts"?—out on him. The mobster's apparent fearlessness was impressive.

Suppose, instead of paying for Starbuck's information, he simply had him killed? "Bumped off?"

Ridiculous. In Amity?

Starbuck took a deep breath and jabbed the doorbell. In a moment, a little boy opened the door. A tall, broad-shouldered young man with a flaring moustache towered behind him. He had a pleasant smile. He looked nothing like a TV mobster.

"Want to see Moscotti," Starbuck said, "Shuffles

Moscotti." Oh, Christ, why had he added that? Suppose Moscotti didn't like his nickname? "*Mister* Moscotti," he amended.

Apparently, he need not have worried. The young man pointed to his ears, his lips, and shook his head. Starbuck could hear the mumble of voices behind the door to old Doc Ruskin's surgery.

Mrs. Moscotti, whom he recognized from her drugstore visits, appeared from the kitchen. She was wiping a plate.

She smiled but shook her head. "Well, but Moscotti, he is not in."

He *was* in, or someone was.

"I have something to tell him. It can save him a lot of money. It can maybe *make* him a lot of money."

"He will be downtown tomorrow. I can ask him to see you."

For a moment he stood irresolute. The deaf-mute stood smiling. The Moscotti kid went back to shuffling records by a stereo.

"He better come down," Starbuck said, feeling foolish. "I'll be in the store all day. Important."

The door closed gently as he left. He turned and glared at it. No-good foreigners. His grandfather would have run them out of town at the end of a flensing knife.

He opened the door of his panel truck, stood lost in thought for a moment. He had given up on selling the store. He was sure that Vaughan was playing with him, letting him dangle. When the next swimmer got hit, the mayor would try to pick up the pharmacy for a song.

OK. He'd resigned himself to default on the bank loan. But Moscotti would pay his way to Florida, and more besides.

God knew how much Moscotti had in the Casino, and how much it was worth to him to get it out.

If the dago bastards were going to treat him like a delivery boy, they could pay for that, too. He'd been going to ask $10,000 for the picture.

On second thought, he'd ask 15.

Shuffles Moscotti leaned back in the swivel chair behind his desk and studied the thin sour face of Hollerin' Halloran, then glanced at Jepps. The fat bull's florid jowls were working angrily.

Ever since Moscotti had got his foot into the Casino's back door, he had heard of the heat in Albany. He had expected this meeting, down-deep.

He had paid enough ice over the years to cops like Jepps. He expected no pig to miss an opportunity, nor a shyster like Halloran to dissuade a client from a blackmail attempt.

Amused, he lit the jet on his desk lighter, played it over the coarse tobacco in his pipe-bowl. "Let's say," he puffed, "I *did* lend Peterson some money. X dollars, say." He loved the phrase. It made him sound like Chase Manhattan or a government economist. "X dollars," he repeated. "Then I find out I ain't got nothin' for collateral because a tank-town cop stirs up Albany, so there ain't going to be no gambling after all."

"What tank-town cop you talking about?" growled Jepps. "I hope it's Amity."

"Take your choice, sergeant," smiled Moscotti. He watched the smoke rise, happily. He knew precisely what was coming and how he would deal with it.

The door opened and his nephew came in, heading for the TV set as if there were nobody there at all. Moscotti beamed at him. The young man lived in innocence, behind his veil of silence, in a world Moscotti almost envied. He had grown to love him like a son.

He caught his eye, pantomined whisky pouring

from a bottle. Instantly all three were sipping bourbon on the rocks.

The boy settled himself in front of a Saturday-night movie, volume off, enjoying the show as if he had had his hearing.

But the young man's presence bugged Halloran. "He staying?"

"You got something you don't want heard?" asked Moscotti.

"He's a dummy, Halloran," scoffed Jepps. "Can't you see that?"

"No," Moscotti said softly. "'Exceptional'. You understand?"

His eyes met Jepps' little green ones. Christ, the guy *looked* like a pig, behind the folds of fat. The sergeant shrugged, but did not look away. A pig, but no coward . . .

"So get it off your chest," Moscotti yawned, "I want to go to bed."

Halloran explained that his client was facing a possible federal term and a fine. If he had a defense fund, of say, $20,000, he'd be inclined to risk the fine and even federal prison, and not to rock the boat further.

"Bull," grinned Moscotti. "He ain't going to jail. Shooting a seal? And the fine ain't going to be nothing."

Halloran looked away. "You never know."

"Now *your* fee, Halloran, I can see that might worry him a little." The whole charade was suddenly boring. "So you want 20 Gs. And that's the *only* way you can think for me to protect my collateral? My X dollars?"

Halloran's voice rose. "I can state categorically that unless the charges are dropped, which nobody seems to be able to accomplish—"

"That's interesting, that you should bring that up. I was just thinking . . ."

"Thinking what?" Jepps broke in heavily.

"If Brody's the *only* one wants to press charges, there's a cheaper way."

Halloran stood suddenly. "I don't want to hear about it. Neither does my client."

"Don't be too sure," muttered Jepps.

Moscotti sucked on his pipe. "Tell me, Fat-Boy, what'd you like better? Twenty big ones for your 'defense fund,' or Brody goes up in smoke?"

Moscotti caught a quick, speculative gleam in Jepps' eye. "Good question. Your problem, not mine."

Moscotti finished his drink. He put down his pipe, shuffled to the door of the den. "You find your way out, OK? I'll give the 'problem' everything I got."

"When'll we know?" asked Halloran.

"Tomorrow," smiled Moscotti. "Tomorrow, latest."

He watched his wife see them out the front door, stumbled back to his desk. He could have been the best light-heavy to come out of Brooklyn in 20 years, built like his nephew, he'd been . . . Damn legs.

He sketched a rough map of South Amity Beach, placed on it a mark for Smith's Sand Castle, and offshore, inscribed an X. He shot a rubber band at his nephew's hulking back. The boy was at his desk in a flash.

He handed him the map, and the keys to the Ferrari. He swiveled and drew from a file cabinet a 12-gauge shotgun with a foot-long sawed-off barrel and a six-inch sawed-off stock.

He pantomimed a beerbelly, pointed to the door through which Jepps had left. He put a thumbnail to his teeth and shot it toward his departed guests in a violent, vicious motion.

It was the first real task that Moscotti had entrusted to the boy. Tears of gratitude gathered in his nephew's eyes. He took keys, map, and weapon.

Impulsively, he bent and kissed Moscotti's cheek, and then he was gone.

Maybe it wasn't the safest solution, reflected Moscotti. The death of a Flushing police sergeant would cause more heat than the death of the Amity chief of police.

But Brody's wife had let Johnny join the cubs.

Brody drove Car #1 halfway up his driveway, switched off the ignition, and sat for a moment gathering strength in the twilight.

He had broken the news of Andy to Phil and Linda Nicholas, had detailed Angelo to speed them across Long Island Sound to New London in the police launch, saving them hours of driving. Linda had taken the news better than Phil, the town plumber.

Brody was sure that he would find his own house in emotional shambles, with Mike's guilt and Ellen's preparations for tomorrow's regatta. And he faced the impossible task of reconciling Sean to banishing Sammy.

Finally, he slid from behind the wheel and moved reluctantly through the side door, past the overworked washer—smelling of seal, still. He built himself a blast of scotch. He carried it into the living room. Mike sat in front of the TV, staring blankly at the tube, taking in nothing.

"You tell them?" he muttered hopelessly.

Brody nodded. "They were OK," he lied.

"They sore at me?"

Brody shook his head.

Mike asked dully: "Is Tom Andrews?"

"Nobody is. But you."

"I don't want to race tomorrow."

"Sean hopes you will. *I* hope you will. OK?"

Mike finally nodded. "Dad, is he going to die?"

"He'll be fine." He wished he felt as confident as he sounded.

"Dad?"

"Yeah?"

"I think he saw the ball."

"Why?"

Mike shrugged: "He'd have kept up with me, you couldn't have *tore* him loose, if he hadn't seen *something*. He's chicken."

Something . . . Brody tensed. The ball, that would have been fine. But suppose he had seen something else?

He looked into his son's eyes. Did the kid, scarred like himself by The Trouble, think of sharks when he was in the ocean?

To ask him would start the whole lousy scene again: should he swim in the sea, should he dive?

It was better for Mike and for himself to leave it alone. Comparing Andy diving to Mike was like comparing a tomato to a cucumber: the fat kid was an accident waiting to happen. Mike was an athlete; Andy was a buffoon.

Brody, drink in hand, drifted to the solarium where he could hear the chattering of Ellen's sewing machine. She glanced at the glass in his hand. "You couldn't wait for me?" she asked.

"Rough day," he growled.

"Tough," she said callously.

"Next time somebody gets the bends," he flared, "*you* tell the next of kin."

She told him that she'd had a rough day too, not the least of it stemming from a call she'd made to the hospital at New London about Andy. So he wasn't to scream at the phone bill. They had told her that Andy was paralyzed, conscious, but couldn't articulate. There was an air-bubble in his brain.

"That goddamn commander!" blurted Brody.

"What's he got to do with it?"

He told her that Mike thought Andy had seen the navy ball and surfaced carelessly, unthinkingly, to report it. "A kid thinks he sees a thousand dollars lying on the bottom? What do you expect?"

"You can't blame Chip Chaffey," she protested, "for what a 15-year-old does when he's excited."

Chip, yet . . . Wasn't that chummy? He didn't bother to reply.

She stood up, leaving a bright orange pennant in her machine. She began to recite the woes of the day: Mike had told Sean he wasn't going to race tomorrow, Sean had thrown a fit and was talking about scraping paint off the tiller he did, the seal had been crying, and the dumb sewing machine of his mother's that she was trying to sew racing flags with wouldn't take the material. "And I don't know why *I* can't have a drink too! Is the bottle getting low?"

She glared at him and began to stomp upstairs.

"Honey, I'll mix you—"

"Don't bother," she said from the landing. "And, oh yeah, one Swede Johansson, as she calls herself, ballistics lab at Bay Shore, called. Her home number's by the phone."

So that was it. "Thanks."

She whirled and tramped upstairs.

He moved to the phone, studied the slip of paper. He wondered how Halloran had got the report, had got to the girl. Political leverage, perhaps, or an out-and-out bribe.

The heck with it. He wasn't mad enough any more to bitch. He headed for the garage.

Sean was trying to teach Sammy to sit up and beg. But the seal was listless, dispirited, and looked sadder than the day they had found him.

"He's tired, "Sean said. "He's happy here, now, though."

"He's been trying to break loose for a week," Brody reminded him.

"That was before—no, he likes it here now."

Something had been going on, with Sean and Sammy, and it had to do with the tidal-flat waters below, and he hadn't had time to look into it this morning. "Spud, what were you throwing rocks at this morning?"

"The water."

"Why?"

Sean's face went dead. His lower lip came out. "Just . . . throwing."

"Cub's honor?" Might as well give it the acid test, right off. Sean nodded. His eyes skittered away.

"Let's see," urged Brody. He held up his own two fingers in the cub scout sign.

Sean couldn't do it. He seemed on the verge of crying.

"Another seal?" Brody murmured. "His mother?"

"I don't know," squeaked his son. "How do I know? A seal, is all."

"And you threw rocks at it?" Brody murmured. "Hey, Spud . . . That wasn't right!"

His son was suddenly in his arms, crying. He patted his head. "Sean, tomorrow, before the regatta, we have to let him go. OK?"

"Suppose she's gone?"

"She'll find him."

His son pulled away. He looked at Sammy, then his father. "You think?"

Brody nodded. "I promise."

Sean looked suddenly older, like a smaller Mike. "OK."

13

Sergeant Charlie Jepps lay in bed, eyes bleary and open, listening to the hated boom of the surf on the beach. His stomach gurgled.

Tomorrow, thank Christ, they were heading back to Flushing. He hoped he would never see Amity again. If he hadn't paid in advance for the crummy cottage, they would have been gone the moment he met bail.

He belched. He had had bourbon at Moscotti's, and then, after Halloran had dropped him at home, had sat alone for hours at the kitchen table drinking beer.

Every night since Brody had arrested him, it had been harder and harder for him to forget Brody's lean, boy-scout face and to drop off to sleep.

And his wife compounded his insomnia. She snored every few minutes all night long. He tossed sleeplessly when she was at full volume and almost as restlessly when she was not, waiting for her to start.

She began suddenly, like a Diesel truck. He knew that if he rolled her on her side, she would quit, but it was like trying to wrestle with a waterbed to budge her, and he was too tired to try.

From the beach below, the sound of a breaker began, with a distant ripping sound, building, building, then ending in a crash like the incoming shell that had terrified him on an Anzio beachhead almost 40 years ago. He had learned to hate it there, and even more in Amity. It shook Smith's Sand Castle to its beams. The next one would do the same, and the next and the next and the next.

His wife snorted like an anxious mare. The Amity foghorn bellowed. Cape North horn groaned back, far away. The dog began to howl at the flitting moon. *Christ* . . .

He rolled over, tried to sleep, rolled back, and stared into the night. He had a hangover already, before he even got rid of the buzz. Moscotti's crummy bourbon. He ought to stick to beer.

At least, the Moscotti thing looked good. He thought of Brody stuffed into an oil drum, or sprawled in a Suffolk County ditch, and his spirits rose.

He was drifting off to sleep, despite the cacophony of surf, foghorns and wheezing wife, when the dog, chained outside, began to yelp.

Another seal? Or a prowler?

He scooped his .38 from the bedside table, grabbed the flashlight next to it, and padded onto the sagging porch. Still half drunk, he banged his shin on a broken beach chair the kid had left blocking the steps. He dropped the flashlight, cursing, grabbed his leg. He began to feel for the light on the weathered planks.

The porch creaked behind him. All at once he knew that he had blown it. After thirty years, he had let down his guard. Habit took him into a combat crouch, gun instantly cocked. He was too late.

The enormous diameter of the muzzle pressed behind his left ear told him that it was a 12-gauge and that he had walked into the valley of death. A long arm reached around him, almost gently, and removed his revolver. An enormous paw urged him from the steps and the gun-barrel stayed right where it was.

A giant? *The dummy!*

He could see nothing, but it had to be the dummy . . .

No, the real dummy was himself . . .

Prodded from the porch, he stumbled onto the sand. He almost fell. His assailant grabbed him, kept him on his feet. He smelled Aqua Velva and mouthwash.

"Look," he began uselessly. "Look, *paisano* . . ."

He tripped again, on a scrub-crested hummock halfway from the porch to the pounding surf. He fell to his knees. The barrel jabbed him. Somehow he scrambled up.

"Hey," he choked. His tongue was thick. "Come on, lay off," he bleated. "OK?"

The barrel caught him across the back, sending a flash of pain up his neck. He staggered seaward. His mind was clearing.

He remembered a shootout on Northern and Roosevelt, years ago when he had worked Traffic. A young black holdup man, stoned to the eyeballs, had been trapped in a liquor store robbery. The jerk had taken a clerk hostage, a rugged young man as black as himself and bigger.

From behind a squad car, Jepps had watched the hostage march to a subway entrance. Everyone, including the victim, knew what was going to happen. Jepps had even thought of writing off the hostage, trying for a head shot, knowing he could do it, too, but not stupid enough to risk his badge by trying.

He had wondered, since the clerk knew himself doomed, why he didn't try to go out in glory, whirl, take one last crack at life and break for freedom.

Now he knew why.

You never willingly cut one second off your time . . .

They were plodding through hard, wet sand and still the muzzle jabbed him onward. The disembodied figure behind him crunched inexorably toward the water. Jepps' pajamas grew wet at the cuffs with the last retreating wave.

They sloshed further into the water, he uncomplaining and docile, his murderer unheeding. What was he doing? Why couldn't he fight? He was leaving life like a sheeney toward a gas chamber, a lamb toward the altar, a pig trussed for the knife.

His limbs were limp. Everything moved slowly. He felt the rising water. He could hear the giant splashing behind him. Now was the time, *now* . . .

He was belly-deep, fighting for balance in the outrush of water, and still incapable of turning, even to face his murderer.

To seaward a giant comber was gathering in the moonlight. So apparently the dummy understood sound, was waiting for the boom of surf to drown the sound of his weapon, and the wave was growing, combing, reaching . . .

The breaker collapsed with a roar like a 37mm howitzer.

His brain met the sound in a red-orange blast that, for him, would span eternity.

The young giant watched the headless corpse disappear in a froth of rushing water. He hurled the cop's revolver as far as he could to sea, followed it with his own weapon. He turned and struggled ashore.

On the beach, he crossed himself. He had understood the signs, the map, made not a single mistake, done exactly as his uncle had asked.

He dropped for a moment to his knees, thanking God.

Trudging over the dunes on the beach, he watched the house. No lights. The surf had done what he had thought it would do, deafen the world to the sound of the shot.

How this was, he did not know, but it had worked.

He took off his soaking trousers so that they would not wet his uncle's seat, climbed into the Ferrari, and drove carefully home in his shorts.

The Great White cruised north, gliding through ebony waters at the six-fathom mark. Her passion for food ebbed and flowed. Her young squirmed more and more violently to be free. When they were active enough, her appetite left, as it would leave at the instant of birth, to protect them from herself.

And so, as her smallest male, blockaded in the anterior of her right uterus, slashed in self-protection against his sisters, the quick stiff strokes of her tail diminished in speed. She cruised aimlessly, not hungry at all.

When the furor subsided, and the fetuses had adjusted their differences, she was famished again and accelerated.

Off South Amity Beach, where she had earlier in the day taken the big female seal, she scented a trace of human blood.

She banked and turned, slashing forward through the surf for its source.

When she found it, some subtle signal told her that the meat, though fresh, was already dead. By then she had severed a haunch and groin and taken part of the abdomen. She worried the headless torso for an instant, tearing through gristle and fat.

Her hunger left. Tonight, carrion did not interest her. But she continued north, with her trophy, as if undecided.

In 20 minutes she would be starving again.

But her ancestor *Carcharodon megalodon* had been a hundred feet in length, had teeth a half-foot long, a jaw six feet wide, and weighed 50 tons. And his world had been full of fresh food, available when he needed it. Little in her universe had changed from his in 50 million years.

Though she was not as large as he, his nervous system was hers. Her neuronic network was not designed to anticipate hunger, nor make provision for the future.

So after a mile or so, she shook loose the body in a cloud of viscera.

She swam on.

Brody had been trudging the moonlit edge of Amity Sound for half an hour, barefoot. He had done this during The Trouble, for he had found ease from the pressure here, when he was the town villain for closing the beaches.

At the tip of Amity Point he found a boulder he remembered. He sat down. The surf was up. He could hear it pounding at Amity Beach. In three hours or so, with the moon so full, the tide here would be in raging battle with the sea, all the way across the entrance of Amity Sound, to the great tide rip off Cape North. He could see the Cape North light now, five miles away.

But now the tide was slack and tranquil.

The urge to be here seemed somehow tied in with The Trouble. He tried to dredge the problem to the surface of his mind. All afternoon, it had slipped away when he had tried to grapple with it.

Now he saw himself bending over Andy Nicholas, as the vanes on the helicopter beckoned impatiently.

Whatever Andy had tried to say, he was *not* reporting that he had spotted the navy ball.

"S . . . *awk.*"

Sawk? Sock?

Shark?

Ridiculous. The shark was dead. If another had come, they would have known by now.

He started home. When he reached Mike's Laser, he paused below the house. The boat was bone-white on its rack. The moon was flirting with the shadows. Low scud was suddenly racing in from seaward. There would be fog by dawn, and if the sun didn't burn it off, they would have to postpone the regatta. That would charm Ellen no end, after all the trouble with the racing-buoy flags.

He checked the Laser. Nobody had done anything about tuning the rigging, and there was a crack in the deck from Mike's collison during the last Frostbite Race, but it wasn't serious enough to warrant repair, apparently. Mike knew more about it than he.

He looked up at his house. Ellen had gone to bed before he left, still sulking about the phone call from the mysterious Swede. He could have removed the source of conflict by telling her the whole truth: Five minutes in the ballastics lab, a lunch and cocktails because she was supposed to be doing him a favor. But he was damned if he would explain: let Ellen imagine whatever she wanted. It would do her good, the way she was bitching lately.

Mike's light went out as he watched.

S . . . *awk?*

Brody was tired. But he had a feeling that he could not sleep yet. He climbed the bluff, went in through the utility room, washed his feet in the laundry sink so that he wouldn't track sand, and went upstairs.

Ellen, by moonlight, was as beautiful as a princess and as glacial. He moved silently to his desk, turned the light on low, and drew a book from a pile above it.

Then, because he didn't want to awaken her, he took the book below to the dining room table. He popped a beercan and sat down.

It was *The Book of Sharks*, by Ellis. It was beautifully illustrated with the author's paintings. It had cost him a fortune: $17.50, discounted at Amy's Book Nook, during The Trouble. It came out of his own pocket, the Town Council having rejected his plea for reimbursement.

It was so beautiful that he had kept it, though he got rid of everything else that reminded him of those frantic days.

He leafed through it, looking for the Great White, illustrated by a painting he remembered of the author's. When he found it, enormous and chilling in pursuit of a sea-lion in the surf, he tensed.

A few clippings soared from the pages. Most were from the Amity *Leader*, first villifying him for closing the beaches, then extolling him as "Amity Man of the Year" when the shark was destroyed.

Great . . . Just great. And suppose there was another?

There was a clipping somewhere, from the *Sunday Times . . .*

He flipped through the pages, finally found it, a yellowing, brittle feature from deep in the bowels of the paper.

"GREAT WHITE SHARK TERRITORIAL? Wood's Hole, Mass. Aug. 15: Dr. Harold Lamson, marine biologist, chief of the shark statistical section of Wood's Hole Oceanographic Institute, reported today at a symposium on shark behavior that recent findings cast doubt on the migratory habits of Carcharodon carcharias (the Great White Shark).

'Tagging of this species off the Great Barrier Reef of Australia, the North Island of New Zealand, and Catalina Island off Southern California, is making us take a second look,' Dr. Lamson said.

Lamson reported that while certain individuals were observed to stray as much as 1000 miles from areas where they had been tagged, others seemed to remain near reefs and shoals where there was a good food supply. 'They seldom leave it, and even, possibly, protect it from other predators.'"

He put the clipping back into the book.

The shark was dead. He had seen it die.

But if he had *not*, himself, seen it killed, what would he be thinking now? In seven days, two divers had disappeared, a ski-boat skipper had apparently panicked and blown up his craft, something had snagged the dangling ball of a navy helicopter hard enough to structurally damage it, both crewmen, presumably wearing lifejackets, had disappeared, cod had run for the first time in Amity Harbor—for refuge?—seals had begun to crawl onto dry land, despite dogs and man, a faithful porpoise which had known none of its own species had disappeared—chased off or eaten?—Andy Nicholas, stuffed with new-learned lore, had forgotten it all in a mad dash for the surface. Terror or exuberance?

If he had not seen the shark killed, he would have thought it back.

His beer was finished. Savagely he crushed the can. His worries were stupid. There was no shark, or they would have had proof by now.

He turned at a movement behind him. Ellen, sleepy and provocative in a shorty nightgown, stood looking down at him from the steps.

"Brody?"

"Yeah?"

"Come to bed. I'm sorry. I've been bitchy."

He sighed: "I've been kind of a bastard myself."

"What you reading?"

"Just browsing." Thank God, she didn't pursue it."

"Brody," she confessed, "it *was* that girl. She's pretty, isn't she? I could tell by her voice, almost."

"Yes. But just lunch. You know that. She's black," he added, for no apparent reason. "Or tan, anyway."

"Racist," she grinned. "Just don't try to change your luck."

He closed the book carefully, on sharks and other nightmares.

There *were* no sharks. The shark was dead.

"My luck's already changed." He carried her upstairs, laid her gently on the bed, and afterward slept like a child.

PART THREE

1

Brody awakened reluctantly to the sound of Sean's outraged voice drifting up from below. He looked at the clock. 7:15 a.m.

Ellen lay coiled beside him, smiling in her sleep. Sunlight shafted through a rip in the window blind, spotlighting the upturned tip of her nose. He kissed her, got up, looked out the window.

Already the night fog had burned away. It seemed that the regatta would be on. She would be glad to have it over with.

He heard St. Xavier's chimes, insisting that he go to mass. He thought of Andy Nicholas, across Long Island Sound, perhaps paralyzed, perhaps dying. He was almost impelled to drive to church to light a candle.

Silly. Superstition. The hell with it. He went downstairs.

He spotted the shark book on the dining room table. But the dark shark thoughts of the night before were gone.

The shark was dead. They were territorial. When you killed the one you had . . . you were safe.

His sons were in the kitchen. He stuffed the shark book in the downstairs bookcase, under a pile of paperbacks.

Sean wandered from the kitchen and confronted him. "Daddy, he wants to take Jackie!"

"I'm *taking* Jackie," called Mike from the kitchen. "If her old man will let her. If Sean wants to tend the sheets, OK."

Sean's voice trembled: "She weighs about a thousand pounds! We won't win doodly-squat!"

Brody reminded him that the captain's word was law. "And don't forget, today's the day we launch Sammy."

He led the boy to the garage, tried to gather Sammy in his arms, and could hardly budge him. The seal must have gained twenty pounds. His back went out on him with an agonizing flash of pain. He straightened, cursing. "Go get Mike."

Sean shook his head. "Sammy!" he called.

The seal shot Brody a look of scorn and floundered toward the boy. Sean flipped him a mackerel from a bucket filled yesterday at Amity Market. The seal caught it expertly: In Brody's mind, a cash register rang up 80¢ a pound. Sammy gulped, reared his body, and clapped his flippers modestly.

"Cute," said Brody. His throat was tight. "But let's go, chum."

Sean's china-blue eyes pleaded for a moment with his own. Then the boy capitulated.

Taking the bucket of fish, Sean led the way. Sammy wallowed after him. Down the bluff, across the hard sand, and to the water's edge, the two marched.

To Brody's surprise, Sean was right. The seal didn't want to go in.

He heard Ellen calling him from the bedroom.

"Brody! Len Hendricks. Morning emergency!"

Brody hobbled toward the house. "Leave him," he called back to Sean. "He'll go."

His anger rose with every step. Poor Sammy, Sean's agony, their stinking garage, and his aching back, which was going into spasm and shortening one leg, were all Jepps' fault.

He picked up the downstairs phone. "Yeah, Len?"

"Missing person. Wife just called."

Christ, couldn't Len handle *that*? "Who?"

A pause. "Charlie Jepps."

"Oh, God," moaned Brody.

Limping toward Car #1, he wished he'd gone to mass.

Lena Starbuck faced her husband across the walnut dining table—almost her entire inheritance 20 years ago when her mother had died.

Below, she could hear Jackie Angelo opening up the store, dusting the cases and neatening up. The poor girl wanted the day off. Lots of luck . . .

"Nate," she said doggedly, "we *have* to tell now."

He chewed away, mouth opening and closing noisily, at the last of the breakfast codcakes. He claimed to hate them, like everything else she cooked, but he stuffed them in as fast as she could get them off the skillet.

" 'We *have* to tell,' " he mimicked, falsetto. " 'We *have* to tell . . .' That's all you been sayin' the whole week long. We don't *have* to tell nobody nothin'."

"Andy Nicholas," she said definitely, "that *could* have been the shark!"

" 'Could have been.' Could not have been, too. All he did, he blew out his lungs with their stupid tank. Didn't have to be a shark. Kid like that, he's too stupid to learn to do it right, remember when he ate his asthma pills?"

"He was 3 years old!" protested Lena.

"They shouldn't have let him dive anyhow. Ain't his ocean down there. You see sharks walkin' on Main Street?"

She was clearing the dishes now, piling them into the sink to wash tonight, after the store closed.

"We have to tell somebody," she insisted.

"I am, today."

She stiffened.

"Who?"

He began to pick his teeth with a long fingernail, stained with developing fluid. "We'll talk about it later." He glanced at his watch. "Time to open up."

She had promised Jackie to ask, so she tried, hopelessly. "Jackie worked last Sunday. She'd like today off."

"OK."

"*What?*" She could hardly believe Jackie's fortune.

"Let her off. Moscotti's coming in. That ain't so good for my image. Why let her daddy know?"

She gaped at him. "You're telling *Moscotti?*"

He looked at her as if she were an idiot. "You find a diamond in the street, you don't try to sell it to the newsboy." He dug out whatever morsel was stuck in his plate, inspected it, and flicked it away. "You sell it to somebody that wears diamond rings."

She stared at him as if he'd lost his mind. Finally, shaking her head, she went down to release Jackie before he changed his mind.

Brody sat in Smith's Sand Castle on a broken rattan couch and filled out the Missing Person's Report. The enormous woman had quit sniveling and the boy was playing with a jackknife outside, carving grafitti in the Smith's rotted porchrail. The dog had quit howling.

"You checked *all* his clothes?" he asked.

"Yes."

"And you're sure he took his revolver?"

"It's with him, wherever he is. It's *always* with him." She had cow-like brown eyes, not unattractive, but reddened with tears and full of fear.

If Jepps had simply jumped bail, he had prepared the stage well. He must have left barefoot and in his pajamas, without funds. She had found his wallet on the bedside table. Its contents were spilled on the couch beside Brody: $12.37, Flushing P.D. ID card, badge, cards for the VFW, BPOE, Police Pistol Club, business cards from three aldermen, and one from Halloran, two lottery tickets, a tattered picture of the woman in much better days.

No picture of his son, which might explain the kid's happy vandalizing, outside, while everyone else was panicked . . .

"We'll put out an APB," he promised.

She'd been docile, bearing him no further malice, apparently, for her husband's arrest. Now she said: "Will you call in the Flushing P.D.?"

"If he doesn't show in 24 hours, yes."

"Twelve? Twelve hours?"

He nodded. "OK."

Her affection for a slob like Jepps was touching.

"The boy," she said suddenly.

"What about the boy?"

She shook her head. "If something *happened* to Charlie . . . It could happen to the boy."

She suspected what? Some long-forgotten arrest Jepps had made? Or the Mafia? Moscotti? Jepps was bucking gambling in Amity.

Christ, thought Brody suddenly, *so am I* . . . He almost dropped the notebook.

"He knows Shuffles Moscotti?" he asked suddenly.

She looked away and said she didn't know.

He pressed no further. God knows how many blood enemies Jepps had made in 30 years of conflict. Moscotti was too obvious, Moscotti wouldn't dare . . .

Suicide? Eating the gun was a cop's occupational disease.

But no body, and no note.

If he'd gone somewhere to kiss the world goodbye with the muzzle of his gun, he'd have left a note, probably blaming Brody.

No, they knew from the beer cans that he'd been drinking. He'd simply got drunk, taken the gun for protection, wandered down the beach, was sleeping it off behind some dune.

Brody hoped he'd freeze.

He left. Passing the small boy on the porch, he smiled down at him and mussed his hair. The boy grinned radiantly. No problem there. He looked as if he hoped he'd never see his dad again.

Brody climbed into the dune buggy and began to cruise, at walking speed, along the beach, checking every dune and hillock.

Shuffles Moscotti watched as his son and nephew lifted Johnny's Laser off the trailer behind his Farrari. They carried it together down the Amity Boat Club ramp and launched it. He noted a gay little power cruiser tied to the dock, festooned with pennants. On it a banner read: COMMITTEE BOAT. FINISH LINE.

Little girls—the brownies, he assumed, that Johnny had complained of—were paddling a canoe. They had just lost a race to a canoe full of boys—Johnny's cub scout pack.

When the boys saw Johnny, they waved. Moscotti glowed. His boy had no friends in Queens, so far as he knew. Amity was another matter, and he felt a surge of affection for the town. Well, gambling would keep it alive, and he'd done his part last night.

He noticed Ellen Brody at the end of the dock, dressed in a den-mother uniform. *Bellissima!* Great hips. Long legs. He liked the way she moved. His own wife, with only one kid, had a body like a barrel of olive oil.

He moved down the dock to where Ellen stood

talking to another woman in a brownie uniform. She shot him a startled glance. Her eyes grew hard. She turned away.

He should have been angry, but instead found himself amused. He had a crazy inclination to tell her that he had just saved, or at least spared, her husband's life, and murdered Brody's enemy.

He grinned widely, glanced at a row of cheap trophy cups glittering on a weathered bench outside the clubhouse. He took a fifty from his wallet, dropped it into the largest cup. "Bonus. Maybe Johnny'll win it."

"Amateur race," Mrs. Brody said grimly, plucking it out. "Keep it."

"For hot dogs, then, OK?" he flared.

"Come on, Ellen," pleaded the other woman.

Mrs. Brody colored. "OK," she said finally. "Thanks."

He shuffled back up the dock. Amity was good to him, he was good to Amity. He climbed into his car to wait for the start. His nephew slipped into the seat beside him. Affectionately, Moscotti punched him in the arm. He waved his hand at the misty, sunlit scene. It was Palermo, but better. "Bono?" he mouthed.

The kid understood. He nodded enthusiastically. Moscotti leaned back, closing his eyes. Fine boy. Fine son. Fine sunshine. Fine town.

After a while, he dozed.

Tom Andrews had spent the night in the decompression chamber with Andy Nicholas. It had brought to mind another night, years before, when his abalone partner had died screaming in a tank in Port Hueneme, California, driving him east to forget.

Now, bare-chested and still wearing wetsuit pants, Tom stood with the Nicholases in the X-ray lab and watched Andy wheeled from the room. *Number two,* he reflected, *and the last . . .*

The tall, white-haired neurosurgeon was supposed to be the best in Connecticut. Stepping to the viewer, he radiated confidence. He wanted to enter the frontal lobe and relieve the pressure on the left hemisphere, caused by one of the two air bubbles which showed on the film as a dark mass. The trouble was, it was a high-risk procedure.

He went on, paternally, speaking as if to children and only occasionally falling into medical jargon: "So, we see this large defect on the upper left hemisphere, accounting for the paralysis of his right arm and leg. His eyes deviate to the left. There seems considerably more weakness in his right facial muscles. That's why he dribbles—"

"As if he'd had a goddamn stroke," broke in Andy's father. "At 15!"

Andrews felt the bottled rage toward himself, the doctor, the sea, and perhaps the world at large. And he did not blame the man at all.

"I'm afraid so," said the doctor. He glanced at Andrews, who felt the same hostility there.

But the kid had been trained as well as anybody could train him. Whatever had happened, it was not Andrews' fault.

"On the plus side," the doctor continued, "the circulation to the *motor* cortex seems to be improving. Meaning that this *upper* bubble is resorbing. His *paralysis* is leaving. It's the pressure of this *lower* embolie here—" he pointed "—Embarrassing circulation to the Wernicke Area—his *speech*—that concerns me. I think we have to relieve it."

"Will it work?" begged Linda Nicholas. She was holding up well, but her eyes were puffy from sleeplessness.

"It's our best shot," the doctor said simply. "Asphasia is living death."

"We're not wealthy," blurted Andy's father. "You should know that . . ."

"I can help," cut in Andrews. "I'm closing up, but I've got gear in stock and a boat. If I have to I'll dive scallop."

Linda's eyes filled with tears, and before she could thank him, he left the room. He had been a fat little boy himself.

He wanted to say goodbye to Andy, and, if he could, lend him strength.

Ellen Brody joined Willy Norton, race committee chairman, at the end of the boat club dock.

He was studying the haze to seaward. The committee boat was returning from Cape North light, having anchored the racing buoy in the shallows of Amity Sound, a quarter mile off the lighthouse.

Ellen had been up half the night making the orange pennants for the buoys and she squinted into the distance to see whether her flags showed through. It was too far away. Even the Cape North light seemed dwarfed, but maybe younger eyes in the dinghies and Lasers could make out her work better.

"I don't know," Willy said doubtfully. He turned and scanned the spectators on the wharf, shoreline, and perched on the boat club railings. He spotted Yak-Yak Hyman, chewing on a hot dog at the refreshment stand.

"Yak-Yak," he called, "we going to have fog?"

Yak-Yak looked at him in amazement. Obviously, to expect a man of his dignity to reply in public at such distance was almost more than reason could bear. He shrugged, shook his head in disgust, and wandered back to his bait shop on Town Dock.

"Going to get foggy?" Willy asked Harry Meadows. The editor, temporarily sports reporter, smiled kindly. "I don't know. I never read the paper."

"Oh, Willy," exploded Ellen. "For God's sake! You've lived in Amity all your life! Can't *you* decide?"

Willy looked at her reproachfully. He turned and surveyed the dinghies, Lasers, Flying Dutchmen, and classless vessels jostling the pilings below. There were 14—no, 15—entries, Ellen noted, and Larry Vaughan, Jr., was going to win. He sailed alone, and handled his craft like a pro, as Mike could do when he wanted. Larry weaved in and out of the multitude, his eyes on his sail, his feet in hiking-straps, his hands on his tiller, and his body hiked far over the side. He was a nautical fighter-plane gone berserk, and he had scented blood the instant he saw Mike's craft.

Her eyes fell on Mike's poor *Happy Daze*. Burdened with Sean and Jackie, it had only an inch or two of freeboard. "Sean," she called, as quietly as she could over the water, "ask Larry if he'll take you to crew. You guys are going to *sink*!"

"Tell her, not me! I *earned* a spot on this crummy boat."

Jackie grinned up at her in a flash of silver bands. Ellen felt a tug of jealousy. When the bands were off, Jackie would be queen of the town.

Lithely, the girl rose and gasped the mast. Judging the distance to the rungs along the pilings, she seemed ready for sacrifice. "I'll watch, Mrs. Brody. I don't want to—"

Mike reached up and grabbed the seat of her trunks. Ah, thought Ellen. It's not the first time . . .

"You stay," said Mike. "Nerd-head can go if he wants."

Sean, insulted, looked around wildly. Ellen heard him ask Johnny Moscotti if he could sail with him. Johnny nodded, brought his boat alongside, and

Sean leaped in with a wild, froggy movement that almost capsized them both. He flashed his brother a quick finger that Ellen wasn't supposed to see.

Ellen turned away.

"Is it yes or no?" Ellen demanded of Willy.

Reluctantly, he nodded and sent the committee boat to anchor a hundred feet over, for a starting line. Through a bullhorn borrowed from Brody yesterday, he lined up the crazy armada below. Ellen hoped they wouldn't spread all over Amity Sound; no amount of handicapping could even things up.

Mostly, she hoped the fog would stay out. They lived with the sea and the Sound, all of them but Johnny Moscotti, and they would never get lost, but the Amity Neck ferry was another matter. She hoped Captain Lowell was sober enough to keep watch.

The one-minute warning blew, then the 30-second warning, then the flag and the gun, and they were off.

Incredibly, Mike had taken the lead. But Larry Vaughan was in hot pursuit.

"I like that ballast Mike's got, Ellen," Harry Meadows said, squinting after them. "But Larry is going to pass him like he's standing still. She going to cook, or what?"

" 'What,' I think," she said sweetly. "Larry has *his* values, Mike has his."

"What about you, Ellen?" Harry leered. "All these years, we never discussed yours."

She tapped him on the tummy. "Lose some of *that* ballast, Harry. You can never tell."

Incredibly, the old goat's eyes lit. A blow for Harry's potential widow, in favor of the *Last Chance Diet* and low cholesteral.

Maybe she'd saved his life.

2

Andy Nicholas lay in the strange hospital room, drinking in his hero with his eyes as the bearded giant towered over him.

Andy knew that Tom Andrews had sat with him all night, rubbing his agonized joints. He remembered this through the dreamy haze of a strange, foggy coma.

He could not move anything but his left hand. The right side of his face felt droopy. He was very much afraid that the searing pain in his joints would return. He could think quite clearly sometimes, recognize mother, father, and Tom by sight, and had even somehow pegged a tall, white-haired man as a doctor, although he had forgotten everyone's name and even the words for what they were.

And there was a nurse, too, who had, to his dreamy astonishment, bathed him in bed.

He could not talk. This he had realized almost from the first. He could not understand why.

What he heard made sense for an instant and then disappeared forever just as he was beginning to understand, like the time Larry Vaughan had found the pot and they had smoked joints in the alley behind the Randy Bear.

Now, everyone might have been talking French, for all he knew. The words were familiar, but the meanings lost.

With perfect clarity, he could recall his dive. He

had been following Mike through the green murk, and he could see Mike's bubbles now, like the pearl necklace which Jackie Angelo wore behind Starbuck's counter. The bubbles soared away to the surface above, and then he had seen the round, beat-up object on the bottom, crushed like a punctured football, with its rows of scratches—scratches he associated with the horror he had seen later—but which he could not name.

And the terrified thing like a dog with flippers—he could not remember what it was called—and then . . .

Andrews was looking down into his face. He seemed sad. Andy wanted to tell him what he had seen. He tried to remember what the things were called, the ball, the seal, the shark. What were their names?

What was his own? What was the bearded giant's? And the man and woman who had been standing there earlier? They were a *part* of him! He'd begged them to stay, with his eyes. Maybe that was why they had left, he couldn't say it and they thought he didn't care . . .

The bearded man wiped Andy's mouth with a Kleenex. He looked tired and very unhappy. He brushed Andy's forehead with a hairy paw and stood studying him for a moment.

"So long, Andy. Good luck."

Andy peered into his eyes. He knew that he had failed the giant, as he had failed in everything all his life. He wanted to explain that anybody, *anybody* would have panicked . . .

The Thing had been as big as an airplane, and coming just as fast. He tried to say it with his eyes: the gaping mouth, full of gleaming teeth . . .

"Tee . . ." he managed.

Andrews stared, grinned suddenly. Excitedly, he pushed a button hanging from the bed. A nurse came in. In a daze, Andy heard him ask if he could have tea.

No, no, whatever that was, it wasn't what he'd meant . . .

The nurse shook her head. "Pre-op. Nothing." She looked startled. "He *asked* for it?"

"I think so."

"Wonderful!" she cried, and left.

Andy tried again. It wasn't fair. Even Mike, if he'd seen the ball, would have forgotten everything—"

"Baa . . ." he gasped.

Andrews was at his side in a moment. "Baa . . .?"

Andy lifted his left hand, shakily, so that he could see it from the corner of his eye. He tried to form it into a round thing like a . . . called a *what*? Already he had forgotten.

"Ball?" yelled the giant. "*Ball*, Andy?"

Andy felt faint. He could not think, could not remember. For a moment he had no idea what the bearded mouth had said.

The giant stood up. "I'll dive on it. I'll damn well find it for you, Andy."

Andy's mind drifted back, suddenly. Dive? No! Danger there, the thing with teeth . . . *Shark*?

He had the word on the tip of his tongue, fumbled with it, and lost it.

Then he floated into sleep.

Tom Andrews stared down at the chubby, whitened face. He had no idea what the operation would cost, but a thousand bucks should help.

OK. It was the navy commander, with his big mouth and one-track mind, who'd been the agent of Andy's disaster, and his own.

And he'd get his stupid ball back. The least the son-of-a-bitch could do was fly him home to dive for it.

He called Chaffey at NAS Quonset Point, collect. Then he went upstairs to the hospital heli-pad to wait.

For half an hour Ellen Brody had been sitting at the commodore's desk in the boat club shack. She had been adding points: jousting, Hobie-sailing, finally the great canoe race, which had been lost to the cause of women's rights when little Jeanie Enzensperger had dropped her paddle to grab at a falling curler.

She had totaled receipts at the hot dog stand and sent three honest teenagers to the deli with Moscotti's $50 to buy hamburger meat and rolls.

When she finished she looked out the window and chilled. She could still see the sails bobbing toward Cape North light. She could even glimpse the orange flash of her brave little pennants.

But behind the Cape the ocean blended imperceptibly with a gray pall that meant, to her at least, that fog would shortly be oozing into the mouth of Amity Sound.

She took her list of prize-winners and wandered outside to look for Willy Norton. She found him drinking a beer with Larry Vaughan, lounging in the shade of the refreshment stand. She drew their attention to the haze forming to seaward.

Willy walked to the dock railing, studied the seascape, and strolled back. He seemed worried.

But Larry Vaughan said: "Hell, Ellen, nobody gets lost in Amity *Sound!*"

"The tide's starting out," she reminded him.

"It does that," he admitted, "twice a day."

She deferred to male insouciance, posted the winners of the canoe event, and had herself one of Moscotti's free hamburgers.

But when she went back to the boat club shack, she surprised Willy Norton on the phone. With his commodore's hat on the back of his head, he was calling Shinnecock for the coast guard forecast. He hung up.

"Well . . . It's iffy." He moved to the window. "They say if the temperature goes down, we'll have fog. If the sun heats things up, we're home free."

"Remarkable," Ellen said dryly. "Are you going to recall them?"

"They're halfway across. We'd have to send the committee boat, and I don't know how much gas he's got. They'd never hear the cannon now, and we've only got one round left, for the winner."

"If you recall them," she pointed out, "you won't need one for a winner."

He nodded profoundly. "That's true . . ."

"So what are you going to do?"

He looked at his watch. "We'll give it another half hour," he announced triumphantly.

"Willy," said Ellen, "you should run for Congress."

She went out to look at the tide.

It was starting to ebb, gurgling under the pilings in swirls.

She hoped Mike, and the Moscotti kid with Sean, and the rest of them, remembered what full-ebb did to the Cape North tide-race and the mouth of Amity Sound.

Well, she wasn't going to squawk like a worried hen. She could still see tiny white sails halfway to Cape North. They'd be all right.

3

Brody hung up the phone on his desk. Unable to find the sergeant on the beach, he had become more and more concerned. Finally, he had called in everything on Jepps but federal troops.

He'd heard the cannon shot that signaled the start of the sailboat race, and he was angry at life for keeping him from seeing it.

Len Hendricks was exultant. "Solves our problem, right, chief? I mean, if he took off? Fugitive, federal warrant! Maybe he left the state!"

"Suppose he got wasted," remarked Brody, "as you war heroes put it."

"Solves it even better!"

"Does it, Len?" Brody asked heavily. "Does it really?" He heard a loud thrumming, suddenly, outside. A shadow passed over the window. He threw it open and saw a navy chopper suspended over Town Square.

Son of a bitch! He moved swiftly to Car #1, hopped into it and drove three blocks. The chopper had already landed, destroying three out of five of Minnie's remaining azaleas. The engine was cut. Out of the door dropped Tom Andrews, still in a wetsuit from the day before. Brody confronted him.

"How's Andy?"

Andrews gave him the news, not all bad, but bad enough. And he wanted to dive as soon as possible:

nobody could tell how the navy's ball would wander on the bottom, and the family could use the thousand bucks. Chaffey emerged from the hatch behind him, apologizing again for landing in Town Square.

Brody regarded the huge craft. It was gathering a crowd of tourists. Even spectators from the boat club dock were wandering up Scotch Road to look.

Well, it was in a good cause. The commander was looking past him, eagerly. Brody turned. His wife was moving through the gathering throng. Even in the silly cub scout uniform, she moved wonderfully.

"I thought you were counting sailboats," Brody said briefly.

She told him that the fog was coming in, you couldn't see the sails anymore, and the committee boat wouldn't start. Could he send Dick Angelo in the department motor boat?

"He's waiting in New London to bring Andy's folks home."

She seemed genuinely worried, and now he was too. He glanced seaward. The view out of Amity Harbor was clear, but in the far distance he could hear the murmur of the Cape North horn.

The soup would be coming in, all right, and they ought to be recalled. How? The coast guard? Maybe. If he could get them to do it. Or . . .

He turned to Chaffey. "You got a PA system?"

"I'll recall them," Chaffey nodded, then turned to Andrews. "Can you dive it alone?"

"I'll follow his bubbles," said Brody. "I've done it before."

Chaffey climbed into his craft. The chopper started with a cough, cleared its throat, and burst into whirling life. In a few moments it was aloft, in its own private whirlwind.

So much for the last of Minnie's azaleas, Brody reflected, driving Andrews to the *Aqua Queen.*

He stopped off to check on the search for Jepps. Nothing.

Flushing Missing Persons was on its way, and the County would be here by four.

Mike Brody trimmed his sail and brought the boat more tightly on the wind. Jackie moved her bare feet—most beautiful in the world—under the hiking-strap which ran along the length of the cockpit. She leaned far to windward, helping him stiffen the boat against the wet rising breeze. She caught a dash of spray in her face and shook it off.

Her trim tanned belly, with just the right curve, strained outward. She was strong, he reflected, for a girl, and had all the right moves on a boat. Her weight to windward compensated for the loss in speed he was enduring for having her aboard. Anyway, his dad was always saying, it wasn't whether you won or lost, but how you played the game. He had a game in mind, but he didn't see how he could play it without capsizing the boat.

At least, he had got rid of Sean, always restless and erratic, scrambling port and starboard. Sean was somewhere in the crowd of sails behind him.

And somewhere ahead, hidden by the belly of his own sail, was Larry Vaughan. Mike dropped his head to peer under the boom. He spotted Larry in the hazy sunlight. He tried to gauge whether they were gaining. He thought so. And with Jackie helping him stiffen the boat, stretching her body over the racing whitecaps, he had a better chance than Larry of pointing high enough to round the racing buoy anchored off the tide-race at Cape North.

Maybe Larry, with only his own weight to windward, would be swept to sea and never show up again.

Jackie turned aft, grinning, her bands forgotten in

the joy of freedom. She clutched his hand. "Mike-doll, this is it!"

"I'd rather be back on the sand."

Her eyes clouded. "Poor Andy."

A cloud obscured the sun. "If I'd kept him in sight . . ."

"Mike, don't blame yourself! Why do you do that?"

"I'm a mash . . . masho . . . You know."

"Masochist," she said. She reached over and ran her finger down his bare leg.

God, she was torturing him. The boat wandered to windward, luffed, and he lost fifty feet on Vaughan.

The Cape North horn groaned mournfully, two miles ahead.

Fog? Turn back? No, never. Not the famous Spitzer of Amity Beach.

He had no fears for themselves. Only for Sean, with the Moscotti kid somewhere behind. He didn't think they could find their butts with both hands in clear weather; what they'd do if the fog rolled in he hadn't the slightest idea.

"It's socking in at the Cape," he murmured to Jackie.

She didn't seem to care.

Shuffles Moscotti awakened in the driver's seat of his Ferrari. A low-flying helicopter passed above. He had dozed and missed the start.

He glanced at his nephew. The boy was sitting in stolid silence, dark eyes peaceful and half-lowered. No ulcers, there, no strokes or heart attack. The kid would live forever.

The race would take two hours. Moscotti decided to find out what the local druggist wanted. He checked for Brody's squad car, made a fast U turn in the middle of the block, and parked in front of the pharmacy. He motioned his nephew to follow him and shuffled in.

Yak-Yak Hyman wandered back from the crowd around the boat club shack. He looked at the lonely length of Town Dock with distaste. His bait shop was deserted. The regatta had taken away the fishermen he might have expected this morning. Damn fool kids, and their parents . . . a Sunday should bring him more business than the other days of the week combined.

He saw Brody and the diving guy—Tom Something—skimming out past the breakwater in the *Aqua Queen*. He moved to the end of the pier, checking to make sure that Dick Angelo was not back from across the Sound. The son-of-a-bitch was just as likely to ticket him as not if he found his crabnet.

Furtively, he pulled up the trap.

The half-cod he had placed in it for bait was suitably rotten, but no crabs had crawled in to investigate. He lowered it again, spitting in the water for luck.

He suddenly noticed, bumping the pilings, a submerged but solid shape. It was, perhaps, three or four feet under the oily water. At first he thought it was a waterlogged bale of engine-room rags, lost overboard from a passing freighter. Or one of the green plastic bags, carefully stuffed with garbage, that the damn fool yachtsmen used in the name of keeping the coastline clean, never thinking what happened to the bags themselves.

It was no garbage bag. Wrong color, and too solid. Curiously, he half-descended the wooden rungs in the pilings. In the hazy sunlight, the water, under its sheen of oil, shimmered just enough in the ebbing tide to fill it with dancing colors, obscuring his view of the object.

He climbed down three more rungs to get a better view.

Shuffles Moscotti leaned on the pharmacy counter. Starbuck's lean horseface twisted into a smile. "No, Mr. Moscotti. It ain't got to do with narcotics. I'm a reputable, licensed pharmacist."

Meaning, thought Moscotti, that he hadn't figured a way to pad his invoices for the bureau inspectors.

"So why am I here?" Moscotti asked, pleasantly enough. In Queens, he would have walked out. But he would make friends with these people or die trying. "This is a guessing game?"

Starbuck seemed to come to a conclusion. "They tell me you got a piece of the Casino."

Moscotti simply stared at him.

The druggist licked his lips. "I heard, it's a fair big piece?"

No answer. Moscotti watched him carefully. The man's face, as he had known it would, turned red. Moscotti used silence as a club and anger as a stiletto. It was hard to change your style, even in Amity.

"So anything hurts tourism," said the druggist, "will hurt you too. Me, Larry Vaughan, even Brody. He owns land. Catsoulis, Willy Norton's service station—now you. We're all in the same boat."

Enough of this, Moscotti decided abruptly. "You told my old lady you had something to say. What is it?"

Starbuck rubbed his hands across the keys of the oldest typewriter Moscotti had ever seen, squatting near the prescription window. The druggist said: "I'm giving you a chance to get off the boat first. It's going to sink. The guys that run this town, Vaughan and Brody and Catsoulis, they don't talk much."

"That's nice. You trying to make up for it?"

Starbuck looked pained. "Manner of speaking, yes. You remember The Trouble?"

"You had a *shark*. Say 'shark.' What's this 'Trouble' bull?"

"Suppose it was back?"

Moscotti hoped it was. A *pack* of sharks might be a good thing, to keep the sheep at the tables, where they belonged. "If your shark don't shoot craps, what do I care?"

Starbuck was crazy, small-town crazy, too many cousins got married, or something, he'd seen it in the mountain villages near Taormina.

Starbuck looked shocked. "You got a *hotel* there, too; people going to swim, kids want to play in the water. Only they ain't. Shark never left!"

"It was killed. I read it."

"*Brody* said it was killed. He owned property. Sold it to the Casino. *You* got it now."

The bottom line, thought Moscotti. He wondered what the idiot expected to get, for a rumor he didn't believe.

Starbuck went on: "I ain't told anybody else. Prices are up, now. If I tell Harry Meadows, at the *Leader* . . ." He flicked a skinny thumb downward. "Property . . . Wham!"

"*I* don't believe your shark. Why would the newspaper?"

Starbuck's mouth worked nervously. For a moment he looked like a horse chewing hay. "*I got a picture.*"

"Let's see it," Moscotti suggested, mildly interested.

Starbuck began to sweat. "It's worth money."

Moscotti grinned. He reached across the counter, took a bottle, glanced at its label. "What's this?"

Starbuck looked surprised. "Ellen Brody's thyroid."

"You take it yourself?"

Starbuck shook his head dumbly.

"You want to try?" Moscotti looked at him. He had got the message. "A bottle at a time?"

Starbuck backed up. Moscotti turned, hurled the bottle across the drugstore at his giant nephew's back. The boy was instantly at his side, eyes fastened to his lips. Moscotti swept his hand at a row of patent medicine bottles. The boy kicked the shelf under them. They crashed satisfyingly. Starbuck yelped as if in pain. Moscotti nodded again at his nephew. The kid overturned a perfume case. The scent of a thousand roses filled the drugstore. Moscotti held up his hand, turned back to Starbuck. "Picture worth *that*?"

Starbuck gulped like a landed fish. "Lena? *Lena*!"

Moscotti rounded the counter, faced the locked glass cases of prescription drugs, picked up the ancient typewriter, and hurled it through the glass. His nephew smiled happily, grabbed Starbuck by the front of his white jacket, lifted him from the floor, and pinned him against the wall. He cocked a fist.

"The picture?" Moscotti proposed pleasantly.

Mrs. Starbuck appeared at the back doorway. She was a skinny old bag, and terrified.

"The *picture*," Moscotti urged Starbuck.

Starbuck's lips pursed. "No!"

Moscotti flicked his eyes at his nephew. A stubby .38, holstered under the boy's left arm, appeared by magic in his hand. The boy leveled it at Starbuck's groin.

"The safe," Starbuck croaked. "We got to open the safe."

Yak-Yak Hyman, suspended over water, stepped down another rung on the piling. Whatever was in the water floated upward. He swung away from the piling, reached out a rubber boot, and prodded it. It broke surface. He almost let go. He heard someone screaming, and realized that it was himself.

Below, breaking the surface, was the headless torso of a man. Bits of flesh streamed from what had been the jaw and upper neck. A huge whitened cavity gaped where the chest had been. The right leg hung from a band of flesh as if suspended from a rubber band, and from it, streaming seaward, hung a striped pajama leg.

Still shouting, he scrambled up the piling, looked around wildly. Dick Angelo was rounding Amity light, a good half mile away. He yelled at him. Too far.

Chattering incoherently, he sprinted for Starbuck's Pharmacy at the corner of Water and Main.

Moscotti waited as Starbuck fumbled with the combination to the safe. The druggist was too nervous to open it, or to remember the combination, or both. Moscotti shoved him away.

He had worked for a locksmith. The only prison time he had ever served had been for cracking a supermarket vault. This one here was an old Sentry, with triples, and tumbled in 30 seconds.

Moscotti stepped politely back and motioned Starbuck. The druggist shambled over, dropped to his hands and knees, and groped inside. He pulled out a long envelope. From that he pulled a strip of film. Moscotti took it to the light. It had two pictures at the end. He gaped, felt for the glasses he almost never wore, put them on, and inspected it more closely.

His heart began to pound.

He had not really understood. He had seen sharks in the waters off Messina, as a boy. He had seen them on TV. He had seen them when he took his son to Sea World, tearing at hunks of meat for the tourists. They bore no relation to the monster on the film.

"Jesus . . ." he gasped.

Above a cowering scuba-diver loomed an enormous shadow, blending into a mammoth mouth studded with grey-white teeth. It looked like the garage door to his mansion on the Knolls. In the murky background he sensed the sweep of a tail as tall as his nephew.

A chill began in his gut, spread to his legs and arms, weakening him. He lurched to a stool behind the counter. Starbuck cowered on his knees, cringing.

Johnny was on the ocean, and the shark could still be there.

"When?" breathed Moscotti. Suddenly, viciously, he kicked Starbuck in the groin. The tall man hugged his knees, whimpering like a hurt dog. "When? When was it here? Who took this?"

"Divers . . . Last week," moaned Starbuck.

Moscotti felt a rage take hold of him greater than any anger he had known. And fear, more fear than he had ever felt, because it was not for himself, but for Johnny.

The monster on the film could smash a boat like his son's to powder, razor his boy in half with a flick of the tail, guillotine him with a fin, grind his flesh to pulp and his brain to water.

The divers had never been found . . .

There was a ski-boat, too . . . .

And yesterday, the kid diving . . .

He looked down at Starbuck. He did not see him groveling on the floor, he saw him lying in a deserted quarry he knew near Queens, a wire trussed from his neck in a way he knew, to backward-bent legs, feet upturned, head thrown rearward, writhing as he tried to ease the pressure, legs straining, for slack, hour after hour . . .

Starbuck might last the night, while they drank grappa and watched. If anything happened to Johnny they might let him last for days . . .

And the old lady, she'd known, too, she would be watching him die and wondering if she was next . . .

"*Shark!*" someone screamed from the entrance. "Goddamn shark's back! There's a *man-eater* out there, somewhere."

Moscotti swung around. It was the fish-guy, from the pier. "Where?"

"There's a body in the harbor," the man chattered. "Body by Town Dock! I looked down . . . Floating by Town Dock . . . Telephone! Brody . . . I looked down there, and—"

Johnny?

"*Whose* body?"

"Nothing hardly left," the man chattered. "Don't know!" The man, gabbling hysterically, was trying to dial the phone. "Bad. Nothing left. It's *back!*"

"A *kid's* body?"

The man was dialing. "No head. All chewed up—" He got through. "Brody? Len?"

Moscotti was filled with sudden calm. It *couldn't* be Johnny. There hadn't been time. Hell, it was probably Jepps, that was fine, sure, Jepps, no head, who else? But what now? The shark and Johnny were still out there, somewhere . . .

The fear returned, tenfold, and a rage that he turned to ice. He'll kill them all on the spot, the witness too; hole up in Queens, and let Brody try to prove it. He carried no gun, or he'd do it himself.

He turned to the druggist. "A week?" he murmured. "You said a week?"

Starbuck didn't answer. Moscotti turned to his

nephew. Slowly, ceremoniously, he put his thumbnail into his teeth, jerked it away.

"No!" the woman screamed, lunging toward her husband. Moscotti caught her in a steely arm.

And the gun was blasting, again and again and again, and with each shot the gaunt scarecrow on the floor jerked and slid further behind the prescription counter, while Moscotti watched, out of it, deep in a prayer that his son was safe, the shark was far away . . .

"Drop it!" someone screamed from the door. Moscotti whirled. The Italian cop . . . Angelo? Angelo fumbled with his gun as he stared wide-eyed at the shambles. "I said drop the gun!" he yelled again, uncertainly. Moscotti's nephew did not turn, only fired again at Starbuck.

"He can't hear!" yelled Moscotti scrambling for the boy.

Angelo's gun sounded like a cannon in the little shop. His nephew's knees buckled, he swung his great head around, looked at his uncle in astonishment, and dropped to his knees. A great red stain spread across the clean white shirt. But the gun was still in his hand, and he glimpsed his assailant and leveled it . . .

"No!" howled Moscotti. He dove for his nephew. There was a roar behind him. His nephew rose, spun, jerked in slow motion toward the wall, slammed into it, and lay like a huge bleeding scarecrow yanked from its vineyard post.

The man at the phone had dropped the instrument and was babbling again. The old lady drew in a breath and began to scream, far, far away.

At the door the cop was being sick. Moscotti clasped his nephew's head, closed the staring eyes, and wept.

4

Brody leaned on the rail of the *Aqua Queen*. They had moored on chain, using Andrews' immense storm anchor because he'd sacrificed his other yesterday to get to Andy quickly.

This time Brody had remembered to check his watch when Andrews slid into the water, and to ask him how long his tanks could last.

"Double tanks, 30 feet, about an hour."

Fifteen minutes gone.

The surface was becoming choppy as the sea breeze arose, and there was a long threatening swell which felt its way along the shoaling bottom until it found the rising shelf of Amity Beach, then, astonished, reared back to make a short, steep surf.

He looked into the dark green water. Andy might have tried to say "ball" to Andrews, but he had certainly tried to say "shark," or something like *that*, to Brody.

But when he had reported this to the diver, Andrews had simply shrugged. "I think he saw the ball. Maybe he saw a sandshark, too. They're all over."

Brody slipped into the little cuddy forward, found a can of warm beer, and cracked it. Sipping at it, he returned topside.

The shoreline was clear, Amity was perfectly visible, but he could not see the lighthouse on Cape North, and the horizon to seaward had disappeared.

The Amity horn blew. He could hear the clang of the number one buoy off Amity Harbor.

He shivered. He could hear the Cape north horn, too.

Hell of a day for a race.

He was glad Chaffey was leading it home.

Mike Brody handed Jackie the tiller, scrambled forward and braced himself by the mast. He peered ahead.

He had gained on Larry, and better yet, was easing to windward. They were knifing along at a good five knots. Jackie was good on the tiller. He looked at her. Braced with her feet on the leeward cockpit edge, black hair streaming aft, she looked as if she ought to be on the cover of *Yachting Magazine.*

Christ, he was lucky. When those bands came off, she'd probably marry Robert Redford or somebody, and he'd never see her again.

But until then she was his girl . . . She was falling off before the wind too much.

"Come right," he called back.

Amity was lost under fog astern. When they rounded the buoy, they'd have to steer home by the setting sun.

Lt. Cmdr. Chip Chaffey, cruising at 50 feet above the fogbank and making 100 knots, dipped into the rolling clouds, straining for a look at the ocean.

Twenty minutes ago he had caught up with the stragglers, three little dinghies, strung out and pounding away, already far to the rear of the invisible armada ahead.

He had announced on his PA system that the race was over, they must return, feeling as always like the voice of God when he saw the startled faces flip skyward.

He had had to intone it three times before they admitted they heard him. Then they waved resignedly. He hovered nearby to make sure they obeyed.

Finally they had. Presumably they were halfway home now, racing the incoming scud.

The problem of the main body of the fleet was something else. It was below him somewhere now, under the white blanket which, teasing him, opened now and then to show him dark patches of ocean, but never a single sail.

He had flicked on his radar long ago, but the boats were wooden or plastic and he got no reflection at all on his scope.

He cursed silently. He was suddenly in thick fog, and there was no up, down, or sideways. Automatically, he shifted to instruments, climbed out of the damp white mist, and got his bearings above the pink-tipped clouds, tinged by the dying sun.

If he didn't spot them soon they might be in more trouble than anyone thought.

He hoped the tide was coming in, not ebbing.

Tom Andrews, skimming the muddy bottom at 5 fathoms, checked his wrist compass. He was swimming each side of an expanding imaginary square, compensating for the tidal current sweeping him seaward.

When he had counted 30 flipper strokes, he turned north. He swam 40 strokes there, then turned southwest.

Stuffed under his weighted belt was a balloon and a long light line, carefully coiled. If he found the sphere, which weighed too much to lift, he would buoy it, blowing some of his regulator air into the balloon and letting it float to the surface.

Then he would rise, re-anchor the boat nearby with Brody, and hoist the ball aboard.

He was snaking along on the bottom, approaching

the end of the southerly leg, unable to penetrate the cloudiness more than 8 or 10 feet, when he glimpsed the black sphere ahead.

His heart soared. All would be well . . . Their luck had changed.

In a moment he was inspecting it. It was half-crushed. It rested in the mud on its flattened bottom. As he watched, it teetered in the muck, feeling the tug of tidal current sweeping from out of Amity Harbor. He could not understand what had flattened it.

He peered closer, rubbing at the yellow decal which claimed it as U.S. Navy property. He grew suddenly alert, bringing his face mask within inches of its thick steel case.

There were scrapes and dents along the top, as if it had been battered by the tines of some giant rake.

Studying the strange serrations, he fumbled with his balloon-buoy, shivered. He was feeling oddly.

He had never feared the bottom. He had endured the agony of anoxia, the bliss of nitrogen narcosis, and the spring-steel jaws of a moray eel, which had nearly cost him a thumb.

He had been trapped in wreckage under the Mississippi, and in 20-fathom kelp off Catalina.

He had stared into a Japanese pilot's bottomless eyesockets in the cockpit of a bomber at fifteen fathoms off Guam. He had watched his last partner writhing in the scuppers of an abalone boat racing, too slowly, for the California coast.

Until his student's accident yesterday, he had not considered another way of life. Until *this* moment, he had never felt real apprehension below. And now he could not explain it, only overcome it as best he could, and go on with his job.

So he shook off the nameless dread. He tied the

buoy-line to the cable projecting from the ball, which had somehow been snipped as cleanly as if by wire-cutters. Strange . . .

He removed the mouthpiece of his regulator and blew the balloon half-full. It would fully inflate on the way up, as the outside pressure eased: if he had filled it here, as Andy had filled his lungs, it would burst during its ascent.

He let the balloon go, watched it dance happily into the soup above, tugging its line behind it.

Again, he inspected the ball. He looked for evidence that it had snapped on projecting rocks, or that it had jammed in the superstructure of the *Orca*, or some anonymous boat submerged off Amity Beach.

But it was nothing like that. The marks were more like teeth marks than anything else . . .

Teeth marks?

For a moment the ghost of the Amity shark hovered closely.

Bull. No Great White he had seen, in movies or in books, could have encompassed the navy's ball, much less have torn it loose.

Slowly, he began to rise with his bubbles. He slanted his ascent in the direction of the *Aqua Queen*, and when he surfaced he was only 100 yards from his boat.

Through his water-smeared mask he could see Brody lounging on the taffrail, drinking a beer and gazing toward Cape North. A good man, even if timid of the water. God only knew if he'd ever let his son dive again after the Nicholas thing, but you couldn't blame him for that.

He began to swim toward his boat, still bothered by the odd discomfort he had known below.

Sharks were territorial. If the Amity shark had lived, it might never have left . . .

That was stupid. If Brody reported it dead, then the Amity shark was dead.

"Brody," he called. His voice was high, almost tremulous in his own ears. "Over here!"

Brody jumped as if goosed and began to search the water to starboard.

"Found it!" called Andrews. "Start hauling up the—"

Brody leaped suddenly, as if galvanized, pointing somewhere behind him. Andrews whirled in the water.

A bolt of terror ripped him. A hundred yards away, not far from the bright red balloon bobbing over the navy's ball, an enormous fin waved langorously.

His instinct was to jettison his gear and sprint for the boat, but he had watched makos and white-tips, and though this was three times the size of either, he had read of the Great White's speed.

He could never make the boat.

On the surface, he was vulnerable from below, would have no chance at all.

Below, in swirling clouds of mud, at least his belly was safe from attack, and he could try to hide.

He swished his fins silently, hurtled his bulk from the water, jack-knifed, and dove for the bottom.

He left hardly a ripple behind.

Brody hauled wildly at the *Aqua Queen*'s anchor chain. If the boat had been moored 100 yards closer to the balloon, Andrews would have been safely aboard.

Brody had spent the first few seconds rushing from side to side, peering into the water. He was in a state of shock. He had the nightmarish feeling that he was back on the *Orca* two years before, with the Amity shark slinking nearby, ready to charge.

Had he dreamed *that*, or was he dreaming *this*? *Another* shark?

He had tried to turn on Andrews' radio for help, fiddled with the "squelch" knob, heard only a high-pitched blast of static. Different from Car #1. No time to dope it out now.

What good would the coast guard do anyhow? The shark was here, with Andrews, and so was he. His place was as near to the diver as possible.

So he had abandoned the radio, jumped to the forepeak, and hauled fathom after fathom of barnacled chain aboard, leaving it jumbled on the foc'sle because he had no time to feed it through the forepeak chain-chute.

The fin had soared for an instant after Andrews dived, then slid below the surface, leaving a huge blister of upwelling water.

The Amity shark was dead. It *was* another shark. Bigger. Much bigger . . .

He found himself sobbing with frustration, or exertion, or fear.

Why in the hell had Andrews dived?

Suicidal. On the surface, he was at least half in his own element. What was going on below?

Now, by sheer strength, he had pulled the boat directly over the anchor, and there was no more slack in the chain. With each wave-trough, the links grew limp in his hands. As the boat rose to a surge, they grew bar-taut, skinning his fingers.

Andrews might have brought it up, but not he. It was fouled somehow below, or imbedded so deeply in mud that no normal man could move it.

He gave a final mighty heave, timing it to the slope of an oncoming wave. His back exploded in a jolt of pain. The anchor gave way, he lurched aft, crashed into the windshield, but hung on. All at once he could pull it up easily.

He brought it to the surface. Its flukes dripped mud. He got it over the gunwale, dropped it onto the nest of chain, and limped aft to try to start the engine.

He had no idea how to do it. There was no ignition key, just a row of corroded switches, buttons, and knobs. Helplessly, he looked to port. Nothing but the silly red balloon dancing on the water, a rising sea, and snowy banks of incoming fog.

The race!

The kids had no right to be in the same ocean with the monster whose tail he had seen. If the Amity shark had sunk the *Orca*, what would this beast do to a cockle-shell Laser?

He calmed himself. He glanced at his watch. Chaffey had found the sailboats long ago, turned them around. The kids had hauled out their boats and were safe ashore, stuffing themselves with hot dogs and bitching at the recall. No matter what carnage went on below, they were already safe.

The danger was here, not in Amity Sound.

If Andrews still lived, his life depended on Brody's being near the balloon when he surfaced. The boat, once free, had already drifted past it, heading seaward. He should have tried to start the engine first, *then* pulled up the anchor. Now, if he dropped it again, he'd never have the strength to get it up.

He pushed a promising button in the dash. It was the horn. He pulled a knob. The bilge-pump started. His fingers were trembling, his heart pounding.

He squatted and studied the panel. *Hang on*, he begged Andrews silently. *I'll figure it out and be back.*

* * *

Tom Andrews moved silently along the bottom, keeping his breathing slow so that the rasping of his regulator would not attract the fish. He finally found, growing from a barnacle-covered rock, a 6-inch tuft of eel-grass.

He grasped it and rested, conserving air and balancing his bulk against the tidal currents swirling past him. He had 40 minutes left if he could keep his nerves in check. If the shark did not smell him or hear him or sense him by whatever other means it hunted, he would wait until his air was exhausted and slip quietly for the surface. Perhaps by then the shark would have left.

He held his breath for a moment, listening. He heard nothing. Maybe the beast was gone already.

He was still awed by the size of the tail he had seen. His mind drifted to campfire shark lore, told in the evenings over wine and abalone at Santa Cruz and Anacapa and Todos Santos Island off the coast of Mexico.

An icthyologist from Cal Tech: "A Great White's got a nose you can't believe."

A marine biologist from Scripp's: "Lost a leg the first pass and his arm halfway up the humerus the next, and you say they don't like human flesh?"

"If they really liked you for dinner, you couldn't go wading on Malibu Beach!"

"Don't wear anything bright . . ."

"Never wear anything white . . ."

"Shark-chaser attracts sharks . . ."

"Swim toward them."

"Swim away from them."

"Bang them on the nose."

"Don't antagonize them."

"Don't dive at dusk . . ."

"Don't dive."

"You got a shipwreck, man, keep the choppers out! Sharks think it's jumping tuna."

"Sharks don't think at all . . ."

He waited, breathing quietly. He had plenty of air.

Brody had flicked every toggle switch, pulled every knob, pushed every lever on the dash. Nothing had happened. He peered under the panel.

There was a red button hiding there. He pushed it. The starter whined, groaned, faltered. Weak batteries.

He released the button. Christ, if he couldn't start the engine by the time Andrews surfaced, the *Aqua Queen* would be out of sight and halfway to England.

"*Start*, damn you . . ."

He tried again. The starter faltered and strained. Suddenly the engine roared, then almost died. He jammed the throttle forward. It came to life.

He began a wide turn back to the spot where the bearded giant had dived.

Tom Andrews heard a noise and stiffened. He could hear the faint, familiar whine in the starter above, then nothing, then all at once the throb of his big Chrysler mill. Brody had started the engine.

Getting ready to pick him up when he surfaced?

Or bailing out? Panicked! Bolting?

No way. Too solid a man for that . . .

But afraid of the ocean. Afraid to let his son dive . . .

He suddenly remembered the sailboat race. *Both* Brody's boys were in it.

The race was recalled, damn it! The kids were OK! The shark was here, not there!

But suppose Brody had broken under the strain? Thought he'd been killed already?

He listened with ears, skin, nerves, trying to decide whether the beat of his screw was growing stronger or weaker.

Weaker, he thought. But impossible, under water, to pinpoint the source.

He could not risk it. He let go the eel grass and floated toward the surface, silent as a rising bubble.

Fifteen feet toward sunlight, with 15 feet to go, he knew he had guessed wrong. Brody was not leaving. The boat was very near, and closing. For a moment he thought of descending again, giving the shark another half hour.

But the *Aqua Queen* whined closer. It would be stupid not to try for it.

He looked up. Already the world was growing lighter. A good decision: 10 feet to go, no more. Immobile, he drifted higher.

And then he saw it, blocking his ascent, drifting as he was, tail disappearing into the jungle-green murk, moving idly. A remora swung from its lower jaw.

The shark's black staring eyes seemed careless of his presence. For a moment he had hope. Then he saw that it was turning its body from right to left, slowly, doggedly, as if sparring for an opening.

A hard-hat Mexican diver, last of an ancient breed: "Hey, man, once he shake his head at you, ees muerta! *You be'r be somewhere else!"*

The swings were more swift now, like an elephant stamping its feet, a bull pawing, a rhino swaying. The beast was gathering momentum for the charge; he could feel it in his gut.

No escape, no way . . .

In a swift motion he doubled, drew the knife from the holster at his left calf. *Come on, you bastard,* he screamed silently. Still the beast kept its distance, moving obliquely, uninterestedly, but always with one vacant eye fixed blankly on his own.

"Swim toward them . . ." Icthyologist, diver, a partner, a book? He didn't remember, or care.

Andrews charged, knife thrust out like a lance. The shark met him head on, half rolled, flinched.

The knife flashed, plunged briefly into a staring ebony orb.

And then Andrews, crushed between enormous jaws, was rising, rising, rising into sunlight.

Tossed aloft, he glimpsed the boat, 10 feet away. Brody, his mouth a screaming void, was drawing his gun. Then Andrews was torn downward into oblivion, clasped in the jaws again.

But he never knew of that.

5

Brody leaned trembling against the coaming by the wheel. The *Aqua Queen* wallowed helplessly in the swell, sending him lurching against the instrument panel, then slamming him back to the cockpit rail.

He discovered that he was still holding his gun. He had fired one round, uselessly, at the sinking tail. He had hit it, but it had not even quivered.

For a long while, he circled the pitiful red balloon, searching the rising swells for a trace, any trace, that would show him that he had not dreamed it all.

He had found nothing, but the reddened water told him it was not a dream.

He tried the radio again. He heard the same squawk, but now, faintly, he could hear Shinnecock Bay Coast Guard, apparently talking to one of its cutters.

"Navy chopper is looking for them . . . Reports he is circling above the fogbank . . . Cape North . . . He has sent three sailboats home so far . . . find the others due to fog."

Brody chilled. Hadn't Chaffey found them *yet*?

He fought down his terror. Cape North was a long way off. His job was to report the attack, to call coast guard cutters to the spot, to search for Andrews' body before the fog closed in on Amity Beach. He pressed the mike button and called. No answer, only bits and pieces of the faint cold voice:

"Pilot reports . . . ceiling less than 30 feet . . . trying to find the racing buoy they were heading for . . ."

Brody hung up the mike, cursing. Staying here was stupid. Andrews was gone forever; he had seen the blood streaming from the massive jaws, reddening the water.

His place was at Cape North, if he could find it, looking for the living, not the dead.

He took the wheel, headed northwest, and gave the boat full throttle. It howled as it leaped from swell to swell like a coursing coon-dog with no master.

Mike Brody had lost sight of the Cape North racing buoy ten minutes ago. He was trying now to keep the hazy sun on precisely the same bearing from his bow. Jackie, standing braced at the mast where she could see best, was shivering with cold already and, probably, fear. "Hey, you suppose we missed the buoy?"

"We'll run her up on Cape North," said Mike, trying to sound as if he knew where they were, "and spend the night ashore."

"You may have to marry me."

She turned back to search. Mike ran his eyes along the curve of her hips and the gentle sweep of her waist. It wouldn't be a bad idea at that. How old did you have to be?

Somewhere above the clouds, a helicopter was thrumming. He was comforted by the beat.

They were lost, but not the only people in the world.

The shark swept northward. Now she had a purpose. She was within hours of birthing. The flashes of her hunger peaked less frequently. She had ingested nothing of the diver, simply worried him along the bottom and left his torn carcass bouncing seaward in the ebbing tide.

She passed through a school of cod. They sensed her indifference and did not deviate from their passage east. Her young were more active by the minute. It was their constant squirming that had killed her hunger. She was hunting now, not for food, but for a peaceful place to bear them.

Once born, they would be, as always, safe from all but their own species. But programmed into her slender brain was a mindless knowledge that others of her kind could destroy them.

Until they were safely launched, she would eliminate anything threatening that ventured into range.

Along the strip of coast she had annexed last week, she had been dangerous only when hungry.

Now she was simply dangerous.

Cruising hurriedly at five fathoms, she angled herself into the ebbing tide. She sensed a minute difference in salinity. She processed the input and banked toward the water spilling from Amity Sound, her destination.

As she turned, her ears, *ampullae*, and lateral lines picked up a rising crescendo of information.

The strange thumping she had followed before was somewhere ahead.

Before, she had tailed it from hunger. Now, it was a predator intruding on her world.

It was over the spot she had chosen to birth.

Mike Brody luffed into the breeze to slow his progress. He was trying to home on the sound of the Cape North horn, but it reverberated from all directions at the same time, like the thumping of the chopper circling somewhere above.

Over the drumming of the sail he thought he

heard a yell. He tightened the mainsheet to quiet the dacron.

The Cape North horn boomed again. When the echoes died, he himself yelled: "Ahoyyy . . ."

"Brody?" he heard faintly. "That you?"

It was Larry, from somewhere ahead in the whiteness.

He put the helm to weather, slacked the sheet, and glided into a curtain of mist.

"You find the buoy?" he shouted.

"Hanging on it!" called Larry. He sounded frightened, wherever he was.

Suddenly he was in sight, 100 feet ahead. His sail was unfurled and lying in a mess in the cockpit. He was kneeling on his foc'sle, clinging to the float, with the orange pennant slapping him in the face in the gusty wind.

The buoy lay flat, tugged by the seaward rush. All the water in Amity Sound was trying to get through the Neck to Cape North tide-race at the same time.

Mike rounded into the wind, intending to raft alongside Larry.

"No!" yelled Vaughan. "You'll pull me loose."

"Shut up and grab," Mike ordered. He dropped his sail, unsheaved the mainsheet, and tossed the end of the line to Larry. Fumbling from cold or fright, Larry tied a knot on the buoy, took a turn around his mast, and got the rest back to Mike.

The mayor's son sank back. "Man! That tide!"

Mike Brody couldn't answer. He was afraid his voice would break in front of Jackie. They had made it, they were safe, but what about Sean?

Why had he forced his brother to join Moscotti? Between the two of them, they couldn't sail a toy boat across a bathtub.

He scrambled to the stern, sat disconsolately. His

hand fell on the tiller. Rough, a really crummy paint job, but the kid had worked on it for a week. For what? To be swept to sea on another boat.

He was close to tears. Jackie sensed it. "I'm *sorry* I came, but he'll be all right."

"Not your fault . . ." he mumbled. He took a deep breath, got it all together, and made Larry and Jackie join him in yelling.

They began to scream in unison after the sound of each blast from the Cape North horn.

Sean Brody huddled miserably over the tiller of Johnny Moscotti's Laser. He was cold and scared. Johnny had already abandoned his captaincy and was scrunched in the shallow cockpit, trembling, seasick, and close to tears.

Ape Catsoulis, who was over 16, was intermittantly in sight ahead, and it was on Ape's dinghy that Sean placed his trust. Ape was not the sailor that his brother was, or even as good as Larry Vaughan, but at least he was someone to follow.

Whenever Ape's dinghy dissolved into the fog ahead, Sean's throat would tighten in terror. When he reappeared, it was as if the whole day brightened.

Sean half stood, peering wildly forward. Ape had disappeared again, was lost somewhere. They would float out to sea as the tin cans and egg cartons did twice a day from Amity Sound, and he would never see Mike or his mother or his father again.

"Ape!" he piped.

Moscotti looked up at him reproachfully. "I coulda kept up, alone."

The heck with him. Crummy city jerk. He was not about to let him see the tears in his eyes. "Shut up! Hey, *Ape!*"

Nothing. Only the slap of water against the flimsy

hull, and somewhere far ahead, a helicopter pounding above the clouds. He wondered if it was looking for him.

"Ape!" he yelled again. Couldn't he slow down, just a little, give a guy a break?

Ape didn't answer, or slow down, but the fog lifted and Sean could see the ghostly outline of his sail.

He hung on to its shadow like grim death.

Ellen Brody could no longer stand the strain in the boat club shack. She left Willy Norton on the telephone, and plodded through the weeds by the dock to clear her head with a walk along the flats of Amity Sound.

She glanced at the foggy waters. She had no real fears for Mike, only Sean. It was full ebbtide now. Without a landmark, God only knew if Sean and Johnny Moscotti would remember to claw against the current.

Where was Brody?

The last half hour had been unmitigated hell. Len Hendricks, chief pro-tem with Brody gone, had raced to the boat club, a babbling idiot at the instant of his greatest opportunity.

Nate Starbuck was dead. Lena was hysterical. The young deaf-mute Sicilian's body lay next to Nate's and the Flushing sergeant's lacerated remains in Carl Santos' "coroner's lab"—Amity Funeral Home.

Dick Angelo had held himself together long enough to get Moscotti in custody, and to contact Suffolk County Homicide. Then he had collapsed into a black depression, and would speak to no one.

And all the time Len Hendricks was at her, like a confused yellowjacket.

Where was Brody? Why had he gone diving? When would he be back?

"Damn it, Len," she had finally flared, "you get that police boat out looking for those kids!"

"With Angelo? He can't remember his *name*!"

"Drive it yourself!"

"And who handles *this*?" He'd jerked a thumb toward town. "You're out of your mind!"

The committee boat had left, faltered, and returned with a faulty carburetor. Chip Chaffey, presumably, was still out there somewhere, looking. The coast guard had promised, when their cutter returned from the scene of some foggy collision off Block Island, to send it. They promised nothing until dark.

Where the hell *was* Brody?

Now she had wandered as far as home. She looked up at her clapboard house. It seemed suddenly shabby, weatherbeaten, and very empty in the fog.

She heard a muffled bark and looked down. Sammy regarded her with moist reproachful eyes. She rubbed his head.

"OK, stay," she muttered, "until he comes back."

He shook himself, showering her with gray tidal mud, tossed his head disdainfully, and flopped into the water.

She watched him swim away.

Then she returned to the boat club dock.

6

Martin Brody hated the ocean. He had hated it all his life, often searching for some reason, perhaps in childhood experience, for his fear and dislike.

Now, creeping through the gray waters toward the mournful Cape North horn, he had no need to wonder why.

Any sane man would hate it. It was a cold surging hell, and all of its creatures were demons, and the devil had an ebony, blinded eye.

Twilight was creeping in. He wondered if he would be able to see, through the fog, the 1,300,000-candle-power Cape North light, before he ran Andrews' boat onto some hidden rock.

He throttled back and put the engine in neutral, listening for the beat of waves on the shoal which streamed outward from the Cape.

He thought he could hear surf ahead, but he was not sure. And always there was the chomping of the helicopter above. He tried again to call: "Navy helicopter, navy chopper, this is Brody, on the *Aqua Queen*. Do you hear me?"

This time, at least, he got an answer, from the coast guard. "Station calling chopper on Channel 16 . . . Say again?"

He tried it once more, and again, and when he got no answer, hung up the mike.

He put the Cape North horn on his starboard

beam, as nearly as he could judge, and began cautiously to grope west, against the current.

He hoped he had enough gas. But the tank was built in, he could see no gauge, and he knew of no way to find out.

The boats had drifted toward them out of the fog, one by one.

Mike Brody counted the craft which had tied to each other, rafting against the pull of the current, and all hanging on to the straining buoy. Nine. Too many for the little mushroom anchor on the bottom, dropped from Tony Catsoulis' committee boat at dawn to secure the buoy for the race.

The thing was bound to drag, might be dragging now, there was no way to tell, with no landmarks, and they'd soon be past the shelter of Amity Sound, through the tide-race, and if they survived that, in open ocean, lost in a sea of fog.

Nobody in the whole fleet had as much as a dinghy anchor to help. Everybody had lightened up for speed.

There had been fourteen in the race. Five were still missing. Sean was one of them. If he hadn't turned back at the first sign of fog, he was in trouble.

The horn blasted, everyone yelled for the umpteenth time, and the invisible chopper circled again. It ought to be looking further back, for Sean.

From the fogbank, another dinghy took shape. It was Ape Catsoulis. Mike could recognize his stocky figure, half standing in the cockpit, tense with the strain of his passage. "You see Sean?" Mike called.

Across fifty feet of water he could see Ape shake his head. "Not for half an hour. Boy, am I glad to—"

Ape suddenly straightened, staring back into the

mists from which he'd emerged. For an instant he was rigid. All at once he screamed in terror.

Mike found himself on his feet. He had the impression of a towering fin, a gray belly rolling, a jagged white mouth spread wide, and all at once Ape's dinghy hurtled end over end.

Ape, tumbled aloft, hit the water swimming.

And then he was gone, as if he had fallen into a hole in the surface of the sea. Fog drifted over the spot.

For a long moment there was silence.

The Cape North horn shattered it.

When it stopped he could hear a rising howl of fear behind him.

Jackie, he found, was in his arms.

"Mike, Mike, *Mike*!"

He fought down the hysteria plucking at his throat.

On Amity Sound, two years ago, the man on the rubber raft had died near him, shouting, and all had gone mercifully black. He felt himself slipping away now.

He must not let himself go.

Somehow, as he clung to the girl, he calmed himself and her.

The daylight was waning fast. When Brody tried the radio again, he could hardly find the microphone under the dash. And still he got no answer, although he could hear intermittently the coast guard talking to the helicopter above.

In less energy-conscious days, the Lighthouse Service had advertised that the mighty Cape North light drew more power in one day than the whole Township of Amity did in a week. Now, with luminescent flashes through the fog, it was lighting the whole sky to the north. It seemed to be penetrating the fog more thoroughly with every sweep of its giant glass orb.

He estimated that he was rumbling along at perhaps five knots, although it was already too dark to read the speed indicator on the dashboard and he had not been able to find the dashboard light.

But the fog was lifting. He eased the throttle forward. Every four seconds, now, he was lit by the sweep of the searchlight.

The thumping of the chopper above the clouds grew louder. He could not see it. It passed above him, still hidden, and drew ahead.

The radio, peppered by static, crackled into life. The coast guard sounded excited: "Navy chopper 45312 . . . Shinnecock coast guard . . . a report from Amity police . . ."

Brody stiffened and turned up the volume.

". . . a body . . . floating near Amity Dock . . . apparently shark attack . . ."

Thank God they knew . . .

But *whose* body? Andrews? No, too far from Amity Beach, too soon . . .

". . . draw your attention to danger of helicopter rescues in shark-infested waters . . . evidence blade-vibration drawing sharks to marine disasters . . . Suggest you terminate search and return to base . . ."

Brody froze. It was a nightmare. "Drawing sharks to marine disasters?" What the hell did that mean? *Get out,* he begged the chopper. *Get away from here . . .*

For a long moment he sweated. Wherever Chaffey went, he seemed to trail trouble behind him. *Holy Mary, Mother of God, suppose he'd brought it here?*

All at once he heard the chopper's blades increase their beat. The thing was climbing, thank God—Chaffey had heard, and heeded. In a few moments the sound had changed to a faint far drumming and then it was gone.

He eased the throttle forward another notch. The *Aqua Queen*'s bow rose, her tail squatted, and, at last, he was jolting through the water at a decent rate, into the clearing fog.

The chopper had given up, apparently, and left them to die.

Mike Brody found himself staring wildly into the night, squeezing Jackie's hand, and waiting. He noted that the fog was lifting.

The first two attacks had been on the outside boats. Mike had seen the fin, dimly in the dusk, weaving from right to left, seen it disappear and screamed a warning to those on the perimeter. They scrambled across the hulls. Bob Burnside tumbled into their laser, knocking Jackie flat into the shallow cockpit.

It was Burnside's catboat that the shark hit. It went skyward in a froth of foam, came down capsized, and lay with a broken painter, drifting swiftly out to sea.

"Oh, Jesus," Burnside breathed. Mike glimpsed him in the sudden glare of the Cape North light. His eyes were wide with fear and his wispy blond moustache, the only one in the class, ran sweat.

They were forgetting to yell. "Hey!" bellowed Mike. "Hey, Sean!"

Not a sound from anyone else, except someone sniveling in the dark rafted mess, and Larry cursing steadily.

"Brody, the buoy's dragging."

Mike disengaged his hand from Jackie's and crawled into Larry's boat. He snaked forward to the foc'sle, where Larry was hanging over the bow, feeling the line. The stem dipped under their weight, and they almost went over.

Mike tasted salt water, and the chill entered his bones, though he had dressed for the race in his wetsuit. He touched the line, could feel the tremors, and visualized the mushroom anchor below dragging clouds of silt along the bottom.

"When's slack?" he asked, glancing at a full moon haloed by the mist. "Half hour, you think?"

"Here it comes!" Jerry Norton yelled. The J.P.'s son was braced in his dinghy, immobile with fright.

"Move!" yelled Mike. "Come here!"

But Jerry simply cowered, and the great snout appeared, and the belly flashed in the moonlight. The astonishing jaws encased the stern of the dinghy, jamming Jerry into the debris like a giant wine-press. Mike glimpsed a slate-black eye, oozing blood itself, and utterly unconcerned. Jerry and dinghy were yanked below.

Marcie Evans, in Bugeye Richard's Flying Dutchman, began to scream.

Larry Vaughan, Jr. got up, braced at his mast, and stared down at Mike in the moonlight. His face was twisted and his eyes were wide with hate.

"Your old man said he'd killed him!"

Mike did not believe his ears. "It's *another one*!"

"Bull!"

Mike gathered himself for the charge. "You're going *in*, Vaughan."

"Try it, Spitzer!" Larry lifted a foot, clinging to the mast. "Try it."

"We're loose!" cried Tommy Carroll, pointing at the Cape North light. "We're moving out to sea!"

"Later," Mike promised Larry. He was ready to jump to his own boat to cast off from the rest when he saw the dark shadow easing in from seaward. He yanked Jackie into Larry's boat, shielded her with his body, and waited.

The snout rose again, so close he could have jammed an oar into the black oozing eye.

The shark crushed his Laser, tore it loose from the rest, and tugged it below.

Its rudder, torn loose, floated away, with Sean's painted tiller pointing straight up, white in the moonlight. When the yelling had died down, Mike could hear the surf crashing on the Cape North rocks. The rip was running full force, and from the sound of it less than a quarter mile away.

Sucked into its vortex, they would be dead ducks, shark or not.

The moon was high in the east, teasing Brody from behind the rear-guard wisps of fog.

He throttled back, turning shoreward toward Cape North light. So far as he knew, he was near the spot where each year they planted the racing buoy. He could not understand why it wasn't in sight. He put the boat in neutral and idled.

The tide was it its peak: he was sliding down the coastline toward Cape North light almost as fast as if he had been powering. Perhaps the buoy had been swept to sea, and the racers, unable to find it, had tried to take shelter on the granite shore.

He slipped the boat into forward and moved in closely, searching the little sand coves behind the swirling rocks. He saw nothing, except the sign under Cape North light: CABLE CROSSING: DO NOT ANCHOR.

So he headed away from the shore, cutting toward the Cape North tide-race.

He was very jumpy. When a wave slapped aboard, stinging his cheek, he recoiled as if someone had struck him. The great light towered above, sweeping its beam 30 miles to sea, tracing a path of whiteness that approached, fingering him, and retreated, bathing him and all ahead in a blinding glow, then diminishing as it returned ashore.

In the old days, there had been a lighthouse

keeper, who might have known whether the boats had passed below.

But now it was all automated.

He was getting too close to the rocks, now, so he turned away, fighting the current, half sick from the jolting maelstrom. The gleam approached, caught him, traveled off, touching, he thought, a whitened mass to starboard.

He found himself on the gunwale, craning. A wave slashed his face. He tasted salt.

There was something there, for sure. A raft? No, boats, many boats, undulating on the ebb as they swept toward the Cape North rip.

He jammed the throttle forward, felt the *Aqua Queen* squat, and went leaping from crest to crest.

When he was 100 yards away, he could hear the yells. He had found them, then, they were safe. It was not until he was within 25 yards that he saw that everyone was huddled on the seaward three boats.

The Cape North light swept past again, catching the monster like a flashbulb as it tore at a bright green catboat.

Brody sheared away, in shock. A bright white belly shone in the glare, and the shark was gone.

He circled the mass of boats until he reached the kids.

Mike Brody worked fast. He recognized the *Aqua Queen*, was puzzled that it was his father at the wheel, not Andrews, but there was no time to ask about that. He was more at home on the sea than his father, and Brody seemed to realize it.

His father tossed him a hawser. The line looped toward him. He lunged and almost went in. The line slithered from his grip. He made a last quick clutch and grabbed it. Quickly, he took a turn around a mast.

The surf was booming louder on the rocks ahead. "Anchor!" he yelled.

His father didn't seem to understand.

"Drop your *anchor*, damn it!" he yelled again.

This time, his dad got it. He leaped to the bow, tossed over Andrews' big storm anchor. Mike heard its chain clatter through the hawsepipe. He saw Brody trying to stop it on the forward bitts, finally succeed, move aft, flipping a hand in agony.

The anchor dragged, then held. The crazy hodgepodge strung out a hundred yards: taut anchor chain, the *Aqua Queen*, 100 feet of hawser, rafted boats at the end of the tether, behind them all, the Cape North rip.

The kids began to haul on the hawser. Imperceptibly, they tugged the floating mess to the stern of the *Aqua Queen*, sickened by the chop of the riptide and the exhaust from her idling engine.

When they had the mass snugged tightly, they scrambled aboard the boat in seconds. Mike was last over the stern. His father yelled: "Cast off that mess!"

Every boat in the Amity Boat Club would be swept to sea. Mike felt no regret.

His father moved through the milling kids. The searchlight passed, etching the lines on his face in black and whitening his skin.

"Sean?" he murmured. "Where's Sean, Mike?"

Mike felt like crying. "It got Ape, and Jerry. Not Sean."

"Where is he?"

Mike nodded across the Sound. "Out there, somewhere."

His father moved faster than Mike had ever seen him. He was on the foc'sle, had the anchor chain in his bleeding hands, was tugging at it against the tide. Mike moved forward to help him. Larry took the throttle, powered ahead to ease the strain.

A tiny white sail grew from the moonlight. Mike grabbed his father's arm and pointed.

"Sean?" bellowed Brody. "*Sean!*"

Sean's faint voice came back: "I'm trying!"

The searchlight swept past, and they could see Moscotti's Laser, 100 yards away. Two figures huddled in the stern.

If the anchor chain had been rope, they could have cut it and been free to pick them up. Chain was another matter.

For Mike knew instantly that there was no way his brother could angle the tide to make the *Aqua Queen.*

Brody, still heaving on the chain, sensed that the Laser clawing against the tide would fall far short of their stern.

"Line, dad!" Mike yelled in his ear. "Heaving line?"

Brody, afraid to lose the progress they had made, continued to haul on the chain. "Don't know where . . . he'd stow it . . . in this tub . . . Too far to heave it . . . anyway."

Mike shook his head. Out of the corner of his eye Brody saw him scrabbling in the cockpit, tossing life-vests, pillows, airtanks, aside. Brody's grip was failing on the slimy links of chain. He managed to snub it on the bow-bitts, holding what they had. What the hell had snagged it below? But snagged it was . . .

He whirled and dropped into the cockpit just in time to see Mike, with a fluid, sidearm grace, send a yellow polypropolene line looping into the moonlit night.

It snaked through the air and dropped across the bow of the Laser.

Johnny Moscotti sat dully by the mast and let it slither away. Everyone yelled, too late.

Mike jumped to the rail. Instinctively, Brody grabbed his leg. He gripped only the rubbery slickness of his wetsuit and lost him.

Mike split the water in a silent, arrow-dive. Brody heard Jackie scream in protest. And then he had dropped his gunbelt, was on the rail himself, had belly-flopped into the water, and was tracking his son in the strange, jerky style that he had never improved, nor until this moment wanted to.

He kicked off his shoes, feeling nothing; not the frigid water, nor the sting of salt on his bleeding knuckles. He simply swam, his clothes growing heavier with every stroke.

Ten yards short of the Laser he bumped blindly into his son. Mike had stopped, wildly searching for the line he had thrown, floating somewhere in the chop.

"Get back on that boat!" Brody gasped. "Now!"

"No!" Their eyes met. No way, thought Brody. No way at all . . .

Suddenly he felt something. It was rough and coarse, twining around his body in the tide race. It was the line. He glanced ahead. He could never get it to the Laser; not in time. He handed it to Mike.

"OK. Try."

His son churned off in a froth of foam. Brody turned and began to struggle back to the *Aqua Queen*.

He heard Jackie scream, and then the others. The rising crescendo told him that the kids had sighted the shark again.

And so, finally, a shark would get Mike, as one had got the swimmer close to him that day. Fate had simply put off the moment for four years, and it would all end the same after all.

But the monster need not get them both.

He began to beat the water, begging for the beast's attention, not even close to fear.

The screams from the *Aqua Queen* rose in pitch. He sensed that he had done it, baited the monster away from his sons, and struck out again for the stern of the motorboat.

But now the fear came in a rush that almost paralyzed him. Some grinding instinct told him that he had succeeded too well, that from somewhere below the White was rushing him, and very, very close.

He twisted in panic, knotting himself into a cringing ball. He felt a crushing blow on his hip, found himself half rolled above the surface, tossed toward the *Aqua Queen*. He felt the sandpaper rasp of the mammoth snout, glimpsed the gleam of a black eye, and heard Larry's voice, screaming into his very ear. He looked up.

A half dozen slender arms reached down for him from the stern. He found himself yanked from the water as it erupted again. He felt the sandpaper scrape of sharkskin again on his bare toes, and crashed into the cockpit on his shoulder. He fought himself to his feet and looked back.

Mike had made the Laser. He had carried the line, too; he was out of the water, pulling frantically to the *Aqua Queen*. But the great black fin was weaving back to the tiny boat. Brody groped on the cockpit deck for his gunbelt, drew his .38, leaned over the transom aft, and thudded three quick shots point-blank at the water close to the stern, almost hitting the *Queen*'s own diving step.

The triangular black blade, seemingly as high as the Laser's mast, waved angrily. It seemed to hesitate indecisively.

"Oh, Christ," moaned Brody. "Send it *here*!"

The white belly glistened in the moonlight and the shark reversed.

"Get clear!" he screamed, leading the rush forward.

There was a moment of silence.

And then it hit, somewhere astern, with a shuddering crash that knocked half the kids on the foc'sle, sprung planks enough to start a hissing leak, and must have bent the propeller shaft.

A girl left in the cockpit was crying. He heard someone yell: "We're sinking!"

He went back to the anchor chain. He heaved, and heaved again, breath rasping and blood from his lacerated toes splattering the deck, showing red with each sweep of the Cape North light. Larry and three others joined him. The anchor was snagged on a rock below, or something: they were trying to lift half the ocean-bed; nothing would move it.

"Pull!" he groaned. "Goddamn it, pull!"

Imperceptibly, it gave. It was straight up and down now, coming a little, coming a little more.

The shark hit again. This time they did not see it, only felt it, as it launched itself from somewhere in the depths, tossing the stern high from the sea, spilling everyone in the cockpit and nearly jolting Brody back into the water from the foc'sle.

Incredible . . . Not a living creature . . . A force of nature . . .

He was overcome by the futility of it. The shark would simply sink them where they were, as the other had the *Orca*, and destroy Mike and Sean and everyone else afterward. Nothing could kill it.

He had the nightmarish thought that The Trouble . . . the shark off Amity Township . . . had never died at all. He had imagined it, not really seen it slipping dead into the shadows, it was immortal, invulnerable, would be here when all that he knew had left.

"It's coming," Jackie said behind him. Her voice was without hope, factual, cool. "It's coming up again."

The shark struck, this time to starboard, and Brody heard Mike yell from the cockpit: "Bail! *Bail.* Hands, hats anything!"

So Mike had got his brother and the Moscotti boy back, just in time to sink with the rest. And so even that had been in vain.

The anchor appeared as they pulled, glowing phosphorescent in the moonlight, fouled in something from below. The Cape North light impaled them all briefly, Brody snubbed the chain on the bitts, bent over the bow to see what the anchor had snagged.

It looked like a giant sea serpent, entangled in the anchor flutes. It was black, shiny, and as thick as his upper leg. How he and a few teenage kids had got it from the bottom, he had no idea.

But he had no time to think of that. The shark had circled for a run on their bow, and was rising from the depths in a comet-swirl of fluorescence, speeding up at them from a storm of phosphorescent meteorites growing and growing and growing, and the great wide jaws were studded with curved and angry teeth. He caught a glimpse of the flat black eye, and shrank back, knowing that the beast had won, that the first shark had been avenged, and wishing that Ellen could know how hard he had tried.

He glimpsed the huge white belly upthrown in an arc, had a nightmarish vision of a smaller replica squirming from its thorax, screamed as the jaws opened on the bow, encompassing rails, anchor, and the strange serpent line.

The jaws ground shut in a rending crash.

There was an instant of silence. Then the bow lit in a blue electric glow.

He smelled ozone, burning insulation, and a raw acrid odor he could not place.

Then he knew.

The teeth had cut the power-line to the lighthouse on the point.

The Cape North light went out.

The great fish, as long as the boat, seemed to grow before his eyes. It snapped suddenly bone-rigid, danced across the water on its tail, emitting a pale blue luminescence, weightless and graceful as a vision in a dream.

By moonlight, he saw the shark, belly up, slithering into the depths.

He crawled back to the cockpit, sloshed aft, and sat down in water 6 inches deep beside Sean, who was weeping. He squeezed his shoulders, looked up into Mike's sky-blue eyes. He gripped the boy's hand, not allowing himself to hug him too.

"OK," he told Mike. "You take the wheel, and let's go home."

7

Martin Brody stood up at his desk. His office was crowded with Flushing and Suffolk County homicide men, and he intended to leave Moscotti to them.

He had called New London. Andy Nicholas had survived the operation, and the bubble of air had been relieved.

Brody waited until Swede Johansson had signed her report on Jepps, and took her to her car.

"Very succinct evaluation," he remarked, opening the door. "I just hope you're not *assuming* that shark couldn't have mutilated his head the same way."

"I'm not assuming anything. A 12-gauge shotgun did it, and *then* the shark got him."

"What makes you so damn sure?" Brody asked. He was exhausted, ached in every joint, and needed a drink.

"Because I'm a lieutenant," she said. "And sharp, right? How could a black girl get to be a lieutenant unless she was sharp?"

He looked into her lively brown eyes. "By turning over ballistics reports to politicians? Handing them over to the defense before the investigator even sees them?"

Her eyes fell. "Do you think I did that?"

"I *know* it, Swede."

She climbed into the car. "You're quite a guy, Brody. From what I hear, you're a hero."

"My kid is."

"You didn't do bad. And you're chief for life here, if you want it. I can tell you that. And I will."

He shut the door, opened it again. "What do you mean by that?"

She grinned. "There's a guy down there wants your job. Name of Sgt. Pappas. Next time you want a *private* report, bring the evidence to me. Direct. Don't stop at the desk. OK?"

"I'll be damned," he breathed. He grasped her hand. "Okay."

He watched her drive down Main and turn onto County Road 5. He felt five years younger, suddenly. Tired blood, coming to life.

Hell, he had a woman as sexy as that at home. He climbed into Car #1.

The lights at home were out. He felt suddenly let down. He noticed Ellen in the solarium, gazing out at the moonlit water. He poured a drink for both of them, and joined her.

"Andy's going to be OK," he reported.

"Did you tell Chip Chaffey?"

He stiffened. "No. Why?"

"I'll call him, tomorrow."

"*I'll* call him," Brody said tensely.

"I thought you would," she giggled. She moved closer and took his hand. "There's nothing there, Brody. It's just that . . ."

"It's just that nobody looks at you that way, anymore. Right?"

"How did you know?" she murmured.

"I've been watching."

"I noticed."

He leered at her, putting everything he had into the longing in his eyes, and when she had enough of that, he pursed his lips like a bar-room Lothario and kissed the air. "I'm looking at you. That way. OK?"

"You nut," she said. "You know, it works?"

They went upstairs to bed.

Epilog

The seal had cruised Amity Sound for hours, seeking its mother. He had not heard or sensed her off the tideflats for days, but when he had flounced into the water, some thinking memory had been triggered which gave him hope.

Now he had lost it. He skirted the breakwater, surprised a school of haddock, took one and missed another before he had to surface.

The Amity bell-buoy clanged. There were harbor seals riding it, like him, but adult, and he was too small to lift himself out beside them.

So he swam slowly along the breakwater, lolling in the moonlight. He longed for his kind.

He became suddenly nervous. There were emanations around him, like those his mother had feared, and deep down, they made him uncomfortable.

He dove.

The vibrations were even stronger there. He surfaced quickly. He headed for the breakwater. Not knowing why, he swam very swiftly. He increased the beat of his flippers, using his tail to steer. Finding surface swimming too slow, he dove again.

He twisted his neck, searching to the rear. A flash of white, a perfect little replica of the white death his mother had dodged, sent him into a blind, panicky dash for the rocks. He sensed danger overtaking him, descended, doubled, caught a flash of white grinning teeth and black saucer eyes already the size of scallops.

The shark nearly missed him, grazing his soft belly with its thrashing tail, slashing fur, and tearing flesh from his right flipper.

The seal found a surge of vital energy. He spurted for the rocks and floundered out, cutting himself on the barnacles.

For a long while he lay panting on the seawall. He heard a furtive bark and inched higher.

The seal was female, bigger than his mother, and quite old. She was not his mother at all, but he felt comfort in her presence.

After a while he slept.

DON'T MISS

THESE CURRENT

Bantam Bestsellers

☐	11001	**DR. ATKINS DIET REVOLUTION**	$2.25
☐	11580	**THE CASTLE MADE FOR LOVE** Barbara Cartland	$1.50
☐	10970	**HOW TO SPEAK SOUTHERN** Mitchell & Rawls	$1.25
☐	10077	**TRINITY** Leon Uris	$2.75
☐	10759	**ALL CREATURES GREAT AND SMALL** James Herriot	$2.25
☐	11770	**ONCE IS NOT ENOUGH** Jacqueline Susann	$2.25
☐	11699	**THE LAST CHANCE DIET** Dr. Robert Linn	$2.25
☐	10422	**THE DEEP** Peter Benchley	$2.25
☐	10306	**PASSAGES** Gail Sheehy	$2.50
☐	11255	**THE GUINNESS BOOK OF WORLD RECORDS 16th Ed.** McWhirters	$2.25
☐	10080	**LIFE AFTER LIFE** Raymond Moody, Jr.	$1.95
☐	11917	**LINDA GOODMAN'S SUN SIGNS**	$2.25
☐	2600	**RAGTIME** E. L. Doctorow	$2.25
☐	10888	**RAISE THE TITANIC!** Clive Cussler	$2.25
☐	2491	**ASPEN** Burt Hirschfeld	$1.95
☐	2300	**THE MONEYCHANGERS** Arthur Hailey	$1.95
☐	2222	**HELTER SKELTER** Vincent Bugliosi	$1.95

Buy them at your local bookstore or use this handy coupon for ordering:

Bantam Books Inc., Dept. FB, 414 East Golf Road, Des Plaines, Ill. 60016

Please send me the books I have checked above. I am enclosing $________ (please add 50¢ to cover postage and handling). Send check or money order—no cash or C.O.D.'s please.

Mr/Mrs/Miss ________________________________

Address ________________________________

City ____________________ State/Zip ____________

FB-3/78

Please allow four weeks for delivery. This offer expires 9/78.